Frances Ferguson originally trained as a nurse, but gave it up to get married and produce three children in quick succession. She started writing as a way of earning without leaving her infants; now that they are all grown up she is still writing, but for her own benefit.

Her grandfather was a judge in India who eventually retired to New Zealand, and most of her paternal relations still live there or in Australia. However, she herself has been settled in East Kent for the last twenty years, and says it is a good place to put down roots.

This is her third novel featuring Jane Perry. The others, *Missing Person* and *No Fixed Abode*, are both available from Headline.

Also by Frances Ferguson

**Missing Person
No Fixed Abode**

Identity Unknown

Frances Ferguson

HEADLINE

Copyright © 1995 Barbara-Serene Perkins

The right of Frances Ferguson to be identified as the Author of
the Work has been asserted by her in accordance with the
Copyright, Designs and Patents Act 1988.

First published in 1995
by HEADLINE BOOK PUBLISHING

First published in paperback in 1996
by HEADLINE BOOK PUBLISHING

10 9 8 7 6 5 4 3 2 1

All rights reserved. No part of this publication may be
reproduced, stored in a retrieval system, or transmitted,
in any form or by any means without the prior written
permission of the publisher, nor be otherwise circulated
in any form of binding or cover other than that in which
it is published and without a similar condition being
imposed on the subsequent purchaser.

All characters in this publication are fictitious
and any resemblance to real persons, living or dead,
is purely coincidental.

ISBN 0 7472 4914 8

Typeset by CBS, Felixstowe, Suffolk

Printed and bound in Great Britain by
Cox & Wyman Ltd, Reading, Berks

HEADLINE BOOK PUBLISHING
A division of Hodder Headline PLC
338 Euston Road,
LONDON NW1 3BH

To Andrew and Alex, with thanks.

Chapter 1

The funeral was at noon. Jane Perry, taking her place towards the back of the small country church which was filled almost to overflowing, noted the glint of several chains of office in the pews ahead of her, and a preponderance of dark suits and respectable hats on carefully coiffured heads. This was a formal, well-attended affair, filled with councillors and local worthies. It might be out here in the village of Tissingham rather than in the solemn grandeur of the city cathedral, but it had drawn the city's officialdom just the same, to come and make a point of paying their respects.

Richard Musthill had, after all, once been Mayor of the city, albeit some years ago. Besides, his position as a prominent local builder deserved a good turn-out. He had plainly been well-liked, from the expressions Jane could see on various faces. A good number of people had made a particular point of going up to murmur their condolences to Heather Benbridge, the daughter who sat pale and grieving with her family in the front pew. There was a certain awkwardness in some of the body language, but that was natural enough. The burial of a man who had died by his own hand is a difficult subject.

Everyone knew why, and it had come out clearly at the inquest: the slow creep of depression following the long drawn out final illness of his wife. Still, what did you say to the family of such a man if you were to avoid the crassness of 'I'm sorry, I wish I'd noticed'?

As official police representative and here to attend the obsequies as such, Jane might have come in uniform but she had decided on plain clothes out of the feeling that it would be more tactful. Mrs Benbridge and her family must have seen enough of police uniforms during the time following Richard Musthill's death and could do without a wincing reminder. However, as she rose to her feet for a hymn into which the organist launched with what seemed a slightly unseemly bounciness, Jane caught herself reflecting wryly that she probably ought to have come in full dress – wasn't that what showing the flag meant? – and that her sensitivity might have had something to do with the fact that she was not used to her new position yet. To being 'Inspector, Community Liaison' rather than an ordinary and much more anonymous sergeant in CID.

Was she regretting it already? Surely not. Well, apart from the odd pang. Promotion was promotion. And she had been promised that 'community liaison' was an umbrella term, the post intended to widen to include general liaison with her EU counterparts. That had made it worth considering, and worth accepting even though she had always visualised her career as staying in CID, had always said she would not go back to the uniformed side or into anything administrative, let alone public relations.

But she had done it now. As of two weeks ago, she was

IDENTITY UNKNOWN

Inspector Jane Perry. 'Ma'am' instead of 'Sarge'. No longer a villain catcher, or not primarily; more a kind of – roving public face?

The thought made her feel almost inclined to pull a face of her own, but the hymn was ending, a prayer beginning, with a general shuffle from standing to kneeling. As Jane sank to her knees she watched the lozenges of coloured light from a stained-glass window as they sent splashes across the polished wood of the coffin on its stand at the front, turning the wreath of white flowers on its top into a sudden blaze of crimson and cobalt and yellow. The job would be all right, she thought; she could always weigh the advantages. And there was no real need to wonder ruefully how often it would turn out to consist of attending the funerals of local dignitaries.

The service wound its way on. The vicar, young but apparently High Church enough to follow the old traditional forms of service if his congregation so wished, gave the rolling words a suitable gravity. When he stepped forward to deliver a short eulogy, it was couched with careful tact. He mentioned Richard Musthill's deep sadness after the death of his beloved wife Sheila but went on quickly to say how well-respected he had been in the community, and how sorely he would be missed as father, grandfather, colleague and friend. The phrase, 'a life grievously cut short at the age of sixty-four' brought a muffled sob from the front pew, but there was a diplomatic avoidance of anything to do with the way Mr Musthill had died. The modern church was kinder than the old to suicides.

Jane let her gaze wander among the congregation, aware

that it was worth her while to make a mental note of faces. She would be expected to know exactly who was who in the community in the future. The Lord Mayor was a recognisable figure, particularly when identifiable by his heavy gilded chain; the lady in the lesser chain next to him was probably his Lady Mayoress. What were the others? A sheriff? A deputy mayor? There were one or two faces to whom Jane had certainly been introduced at some time . . . She was drawn back to the service as the vicar summoned them to pray again.

Then another hymn. At its end, bearers stepped forward to lift the coffin off its stand. A solemn hefting of the weight on to one shoulder per man (was Jane the only person present to wonder irreverently what would happen if one of them muddled the neat movement and ended up facing in the wrong direction?) and then the beginning of a slow pacing down the aisle. The family followed, the vicar behind them, while the congregation waited to file out in their wake for the interment in the churchyard.

It had been a fine if blowy April day when Jane arrived and there was still a gusting wind to catch at the brim of a hat or seize on any long strand of hair hopefully plastered across a bald patch. Spots of rain were beginning too as the congregation emerged from the grey stone porch to follow the bier along a path between ranks of weathered, lichened gravestones separated by close-cropped grass. Tissingham churchyard had a peaceful prettiness, surrounded by high hedges to shield it, and with no overlooking windows. The village itself, it seemed, had spread away from the church rather than around it. Only one pair of grey slate cottage roofs could be seen peeping above the hedge. The cortege was making for the far corner where a tarpaulin was being rapidly stripped away from a newly dug grave. This part of the churchyard held none of the older headstones but looked rather as if it had been recently turfed.

The vicar's white surplice ballooned out as a whip of wind caught it. Then it was as abruptly damped by rain which gulched out of the sky, the opening spit rapidly developing into a heavy shower. Umbrellas mushroomed, some a suitable black, others floral, one or two showing the vivid stripes of golf accessories, to add an unexpected and unsuitable gaiety. As the procession drew to a halt its followers fanned out into a surrounding circle, a tactful distance back from the family's pre-eminent position at the graveside.

Jane found herself standing close behind two people she knew by sight – Tina and Gavin Levitt, she remembered, reaching for the names. She had seen them at some charity affair and could remember Mrs Levitt acting as judge for a fancy-dress competition. Unusually for a married couple, both held seats on the city council. Edged almost up against them as she was in an attempt to gain some benefit from Gavin Levitt's umbrella rather than receiving drips from its edge, Jane could scarcely help noticing how deliberately he was holding it so that it failed to cover his wife. And that Councillor Mrs Levitt, after one angry glance at him, was making a point of getting wet rather than moving any closer to him. There was a distinct sense of ice between them; a private war apparently being waged behind the veneer of official togetherness. Jane was in the unavoidable position of overhearing, too, as Gavin Levitt murmured in the direction of his wife and with an audible sneer in his voice, 'I see *he* hasn't come!'

It sounded like a deliberate needle. Tina Levitt's response, however, was no more than an icy look and a turn of her shoulder.

'You'd think he would. After all—'

Mrs Levitt's reaction this time was a sharp 'Ssh!' as the vicar's voice began to intone the traditional burial prayer. The old words rose in measured dignity.

'Man that is born of woman hath but a short time to live, and is full of misery. He cometh up, and is cut down like a flower . . .' Jane could see through a gap that the coffin had begun its steady descent into the grave, the bearers slowly and solemnly paying out the straps. 'He fleeth as it were a shadow—'

'Stop!'

The command, loud and a little breathless, cut sharply through the air. Heather Benbridge jumped and turned her head towards the sound. The bearers hesitated, their hands braced, strain visible in their bunched forearms. The vicar paused, startled.

'Stop this funeral *at once*!' the same voice uttered. On the words, a woman came bursting through the crowd. She was wearing a light-coloured trouser suit in a safari style, with a rucksack slung over one shoulder. Ignoring the rest of the assembled company, she glared at Heather Benbridge with an anger which looked as if its spark might even ignite the rain which draggled her short brown hair. 'How *dare* you?' she flung. 'How dare you shuffle Dad off into the ground and without me being here? Without my even being *told*?'

'Anna—'

'Take the coffin out. Out! I'm Anna Musthill,' the newcomer informed the vicar as he stood disconcerted with his mouth still open, 'the daughter of – of the deceased. His *elder* daughter. And I forbid this burial to go ahead, so you can stop it right now!'

'Anna, we did try to get hold of you—'

'Miss Musthill—'

'Yes, I got your message – eventually – telling me Dad was dead. And how. He'd no more commit suicide than he'd fly! I want it properly investigated. I want— I said, take the coffin out of the grave! I've the right to forbid you to continue this ceremony, and I do, until such time as I find out what really happened!'

There was a likeness between this woman and the one in heavy mourning. It was the same face, though thinner and more angular. And this one clearly had no time for tact. No careful avoidance for her of the sad cause of death. A distinct indrawing of breath could be heard all round the gathered crowd. There was also an involuntary movement, a sense that everyone was craning forward, like an audience to a play which had suddenly produced unexpected drama.

The bearers, with their burden awkwardly poised, looked to the vicar. The vicar looked at Anna Musthill. He must have seen something inflexible in her gaze. A rapid sign brought a careful haul upwards, the polished wooden coffin with its brass handles slowly rising again. For a moment it looked as if Heather Benbridge might give vent to an angry countermanding in her turn but the vicar got in first with a swift and, he must have hoped, soothing suggestion.

'Miss Musthill, this must be most distressing for you. I do understand. Perhaps if you could take your place with the rest of the family, and we could start the prayers again in your presence—'

'No! I've told you, I'm stopping this whole thing until I get to the bottom of it. I'm not in the least satisfied, and I don't intend to see my father buried until I am!'

'I'll never forgive you for this, Anna, never!'

'Ladies, please . . .'

His plea plainly falling on deaf ears, the vicar did what was probably the only thing he could do. He gave a further sign to the bearers who, expressionlessly, lifted the coffin back on to their shoulders in a shuffling movement and made for the shelter of the church porch. Heather Benbridge, her husband, Anna Musthill, and the vicar rapidly followed – after the vicar had cast a slightly helpless look round at the assembled mourners, with the appeal, 'Please wait, if you would.'

The murmur which immediately arose held both excitement and several clearly audible comments.

'Of all things to happen!'

'*Did* the police look into it properly?'

'Well, I suppose they did, and after all poor old Dick—'

'Yes, but she wouldn't come and butt in like that, surely, if—'

Jane knew she would have to go and join the family conference. It was visibly taking place in the shelter of the porch, though the coffin had been taken right inside the church and out of view: the bearers had presumably needed somewhere where they could put it down. Jane moved quickly through the crowd, now breaking up into clumps under their sheltering umbrellas, and reached the arguing group in the porch with rapid steps.

She was the only person here who could tell Anna Musthill that her father's suicide had been properly looked into and that there had been nothing doubtful about it at all. As an official police representative, her reassurances might even be believed.

'Please excuse me, but I might be able to be some help. I'm Inspector Perry of the City Police. I'm here to represent my superintendent, in response to the notice you put in the paper, Mrs Benbridge, saying that all official bodies who wished to would be welcome to attend your father's funeral and pay their respects.'

Her polite words had gained their attention. Heather Benbridge turned to her with an immediate look of relief; the vicar seemed equally glad of her presence. Heather Benbridge's husband broke off from an attempted argument with Anna Musthill, and that lady swung her fierce gaze onto Jane. Fierce, yes, but there were tears on her face as well as rain, though she dashed them away with impatient fingers.

'I do have the right to stop the funeral, don't I? I know Dad wouldn't—'

'How can you possibly know when you weren't even here? And we did try to get hold of you! It's hardly my fault if you decide to drop out and go exploring the Andes where nobody can find you.'

'Mrs Benbridge, please,' the vicar began, but Jane put in her word, smoothly.

'Since there seems to be some misunderstanding about it, I thought I might be able to reassure Miss Musthill that there was a proper investigation into Mr Musthill's death. I'm sorry,' Jane said directly but gently to Anna, 'but there really was no doubt it was suicide. Everything was properly checked. That included an autopsy. And he did, also, leave a note.'

'But he wouldn't—'

'He was profoundly depressed, I'm afraid. I don't know if you've been told, but he took sleeping pills as well as . . . He would have been asleep by the time the car exhaust finished things for him. And he'd written down very clearly what he intended to do. I'm so sorry,' Jane went on quickly, because Heather Benbridge was opening her mouth. It looked all too likely from her scathing expression that she was intending to fling another, '*You* weren't even here!' at her sister. 'I'm afraid there's no doubt,' Jane reiterated.

'You really know all that, do you? I mean you haven't just *heard* it?'

'No, I actually know it. I was working in CID at the time, and I saw the reports from the officer who was covering the case.'

Anna Musthill let out a sigh. It looked very much as if the fight was going out of her. Jane opened her mouth to suggest, gently again, that the funeral perhaps could be allowed to go ahead. Before she could do so there was a further interruption. Sudden and shocking, and coming from the graveside, a terrified scream rang out.

'Mum! Oh Mum! Oh Daddy, Daddy, it's awful, there's a – there's a—'

A bedraggled, white-faced, hysterical figure came flying towards them. It was Heather Benbridge's teenage daughter who had remained standing at the graveside during the parental arguments. Evading the hands which tried to catch at her, she ran pell-mell towards her parents. Her father moved to reach for her and she wrapped herself in his arms, sobbing. Her words could still be heard, however, as she babbled them against her father's chest.

'There's a body in Grandpa's grave! Down at the bottom! There is, there is – the rain's washed the earth away and you can see it!'

'There can't be, Sarah. You must be mistaken. It's all right, darling, you've just seen a twig or something and thought it was a skeleton—'

'No, it's *not*! There's a foot down there – it's not bones, it's a *foot*. With toenails! Sticking up out of the earth! It's there, it really is, in the bottom of Grandpa's grave!'

A shocked murmur was already spreading out in the graveyard, the sound of exclamations and cries as people moved to look down into the grave. It seemed Sarah was not alone in being able to see something. The vicar was already moving swiftly out into the churchyard. Richard Musthill's family was standing immobile in a clump round the sobbing girl. Jane, with a feeling of increasing unreality, followed the vicar. It was hardly police business if he ran his burial system so badly that one body ended up stacked on top of another, but she could at least perhaps be helpful in crowd control, or in calming what seemed to be a general excitable panic around the graveside now.

She had to elbow her way through, as politely as possible. One person remained standing, stiff and still, at the side of the grave, looking down in shocked and frozen disbelief. It was Gavin Levitt, she saw, as he turned abruptly and almost mowed her down in a jerky, unseeing move away. He was as pale as a ghost, his features standing out sharply in a white face, a greenish tinge suggesting he might be sick.

There certainly was something in the grave. Its outline could be seen in the wet ground. A torso, arms and legs . . . Could it be some nasty joke played by local teenagers? Had someone put a bundled-up shape down there in the hope that it would be noticed when the tarpaulin was taken away from the grave and give everyone a fright?

But that was definitely a foot. It was sticking up out of a puddle of rain, almost washed clean. A human foot, with skin and sinews and flesh and, as Sarah had said, the clear and visible presence of toenails.

'But it's not possible! I inspected the grave myself after the sexton had dug it and there was nothing there then. It was quite properly empty!'

That was the vicar, looking at Jane with a plea in his eyes. Before she could answer him he went on, 'This plot couldn't possibly have been used before. It's part of the clearance we made where there used to be a couple of old trees. That's why I was able to oblige Mrs Benbridge who wanted her father to have a traditional burial here. We don't usually have room – I mean we didn't, but one or two of the older villagers do often ask. There couldn't have been a previous burial here! And particularly with no coffin!'

IDENTITY UNKNOWN

No coffin, but a body. A recently deceased body, at that: the whole sole of the foot was visible now, and clearly had flesh on it.

Jane made up her mind abruptly, aware of the battery of curious eyes surrounding her. 'I suggest you put the tarpaulin back over the grave,' she told the vicar, 'and I'll get someone to see what really is down there. In the meantime, could everyone please step back? That's right – yes, thank you, just put the tarpaulin in place and weight it down with stones. And could we clear the area? Yes, I'm going to send for my colleagues in the police right now – because even if it's just a prank on someone's part, it's a silly and distressing one.'

People were obediently moving back. It was remarkable what an air of command could do, though the Lord Mayor could be seen to be hovering as if wondering whether he ought to show a willingness to help. He made for the Musthill family instead, his rotund retreating figure speaking volumes of shocked sympathy. The vicar, despite looking pale and shattered, complied with Jane's request for the re-covering of the grave. He could presumably be trusted to put some kind of guard on the spot too, while she made for the mobile communicator she had left in her car. And she had better ask him to keep the funeral congregation here in case they were needed as witnesses.

To what, though? The presence of a corpse in a graveyard?

Chapter 2

'It's a body all right.'

The constable who had climbed down into the grave straightened up from his crouch with a peculiar expression on his face. 'Better send for backup, ma'am. It's – well, it's most of a body. Wearing a suit, though it's got no shoes or socks. But it doesn't seem to have a head.' He swallowed hard, glanced down, looked up again. 'I – I haven't found any hands, either.'

'All right, come out and put the cover back on. Have you got tapes in your car? Good, get the immediate area cordoned off then.'

It was better to give him something to do than to show sympathy for his sick expression. Practicalities had to come first. As Jane put in a rapid call, she was glad the mourners had been ushered away – back into the church, though what the vicar was doing to keep them occupied she could not imagine. He could hardly be rerunning the funeral.

He had sent for the sexton and a verger was hovering under cover of the church porch with the air of a look-out posted to pass messages back within. The sexton, a middle-aged man with a country face, broad weatherbeaten palms, and a distinct attitude of being ready to take offence if his skills were criticised, had already reiterated that there was nothing there when he finished the hole. 'And a right bugger it was with bits of tree root to be got out on the way. But you ask Vicar, it was all properly squared up like it should be. If there's something there now, it's someone else's dug it in there overnight. Desecration, that is!'

Concealment of a body, certainly. The corpse of a murder victim, almost as certainly. A body without head and hands could scarcely be an accidental death.

It was very nearly a successful concealment, too. If Anna Musthill had not arrived to stop her father's burial at the last moment, if it had not been raining, if the sudden shower had not been heavy enough to wash away the top layer of earth in the extra corpse's improvised resting place – had all these things not occurred, the coffin would have been lowered into its appointed place and someone would have got away with hiding a semi-dismembered body safely and permanently.

The rain had thankfully swept on now, departing as suddenly as it had arrived. There was probably more to come from the high, blowing clouds, but for the present the churchyard was left sparkling with crystal drops. Muddy smears showed where the constable had climbed into and then out of the grave, and the damp turf around was thoroughly trampled. No use looking for relevant footprints after the crowd that had been here.

The two constables who had answered Jane's original call were taping off the immediate area now, as instructed. A canvas tent would have to be put up over the grave.

IDENTITY UNKNOWN

Somewhere would have to be found to conduct interviews. A local incident room would need to be set up . . . Jane's mind was flying over things to be done. The DI would take charge of this himself, but he would expect her to organise—

No, he wouldn't. She was abruptly reminded of that by the three figures which appeared at the churchyard lych-gate and began to make their way across to her. The man in the lead, with his sharp hollow-cheeked face under curly black hair and his air of practical efficiency, was her recent replacement. DS Phelps, transferring to the city from Faversham, was senior CID sergeant now, not her.

'What have we got, ma'am?' he greeted her with brisk politeness as he arrived beside her. 'The guv'nor's on his way, but if you could give me a quick rundown? Where's the body – under there? Right, I'll have a quick look, though we'd better not disturb anything until the pathologist gets here.'

Murder investigations no longer fell within her remit. Discovering how much of a pang that gave her, Jane had to remind herself quickly that she had chosen to move out and up. Or out in order to move up. With a DI who was very little older than she was and only six months into the job, she would have had little chance to be anything but stuck at sergeant level indefinitely otherwise. Unless she moved locations, which she did not now want to do, and anyway . . .

She abandoned the involuntary wistfulness which was suddenly catching her and decided to make a point of showing DS Phelps that she had no intention of trying to take over from him.

It was odd just the same to know that DC Kenny Barnes,

standing by with WDC Jennie Cullen, who was the newest recruit to the enlarged Criminal Investigation Department, would no longer be looking to her for orders. Jane spared a passing thought for the pleasing knowledge that CID had taken on two females as DCs lately – even if both its sergeants were now male – and pulled herself back into the present. She would have no official position in this inquiry – not unless she was specifically asked to help.

'You'll want me as a witness as to how the body was found, I suppose,' she addressed DS Phelps as he came back from a quick frowning glance under the tarpaulin. 'Other than that, it's over to you now. Constable Gore got down into the grave to check that it really was a body because my first thought was that it might be someone playing a joke with something from one of those horror shops. Aside from that, nobody's touched anything. I've been told the grave was definitely empty when the sexton finished digging it yesterday. He's over there, waiting for you to interview him.' The sexton's views on the desecration of graveyards did not seem to include sitting on someone's headstone and smoking a roll-up, and he was still wearing his sulky, injured air. 'The grave was covered with a tarpaulin, as now, until it was opened up for the burial but there was a hitch due to a family quarrel. So the hole was left open, and what's there now became visible when the rain got in. It must have been quite shallowly buried. As far as Constable Gore could see, it's headless and handless. Oh, and,' she gave him a grin of apology, 'I'm afraid there's an entire funeral party in the church, waiting to see what you want them to do next.'

'Who was the first one to spot the body?'

IDENTITY UNKNOWN

'A teenage girl. She's fairly distressed.'

DI Hollings, a familiar tall, broad-shouldered figure, arrived at that moment, and Jane ran through it all again for him. There was nothing in his expression to suggest that he was wondering what Jane had got herself into now. 'Thanks, Jane,' he said pleasantly as she finished. 'Can you provide me with some names? The teenage girl, for instance – who is she, exactly?'

'Sarah Benbridge. She's the granddaughter of the man whose funeral this is – or was – Richard Musthill.' Jane added the names of Heather Benbridge and her husband, and Anna Musthill, and explained Miss Musthill's sudden arrival, apparently from somewhere abroad. And her objections to the funeral. 'We'd just sorted that one out when Sarah Benbridge came running up in tears because she'd seen the body. Everyone's back in the church now,' she finished, and added, to give him fair warning, 'You'll find half the city council there, they were funeral guests.'

'Thanks.' He managed not to say that drily, though his eyebrows went up. He turned to DS Phelps. 'Doug, I'll leave you here to wait for the pathologist. And get a SOCO and a photographer, will you? Gore and his partner can stay with you, on guard. Keep that sexton here until I've got time to talk to him. Right, DCs Barnes and Cullen, you can come with me while we go and see what we can sort out with the funeral party.' His attention swung back briefly to Jane. 'Was it the local vicar who was taking the service? The one with his name on the board outside? Or have I got to look for someone other than the Reverend Michael Mather?'

'No, that's the man.' It was typical that he had already

taken care to note it. Jane was glad she could answer him, though she was aware she could only give the confirmation because she had absently observed the name printed at the top of the service sheet. 'Would you like me to come and help with the funeral party? There's a fair number of them.'

'It's all right, thanks, we'll manage. There's no need for you to stay. I can get anything else from you later if I need to.'

He delivered that with a smile, but it was still a polite dismissal. He wanted her to go. Jane tried not to feel a sense of exclusion.

She fielded the swift backward grin Kenny Barnes cast at her as he set off after his chief, a nice mixture of respect and mischief which said as clearly as if he had spoken, 'Missing it, ma'am?'

Yes, she was. A murder with all sorts of interesting sidelines to consider, and her not there to help solve it? It felt downright unnatural.

All the same, there was nothing else for her to do but give DS Phelps a nod and then take herself off.

'It's not the usual sort of thing. It could even be a gangland killing. A body with no head or hands sounds like execution style.' Jane broke off to regard what she was supposed to be doing, and drew in a rueful breath. 'Damn, I was supposed to put the carrots on ten minutes ago and I haven't. Oh well, I suppose if I turn the oven down the meat won't end up overdone.'

'I don't know why I bother to teach you to cook if you won't concentrate,' Adrian said amiably and moved up behind her in the tiny kitchen to slide his arms round her and give her a hug. 'And do you have to choose the most gruesome of subjects to go along with food?'

'Sorry, sorry. It's on my mind, that's all. Besides, you're quite capable of discussing swine fever while we're eating sausages.'

That brought a chuckle. Now that they were living together, arguments never held quite the same edge. For one thing, Jane thought, no one could storm out when there was nowhere to storm to; and, besides, Adrian had wanted a commitment from her, and she had given him one. She had informed her superiors that she intended co-habiting with someone outside the force (as she had to) and had offered the necessary details. After the first small buzz of gossip – fortunately drowned out, at the time, by other subjects to occupy wagging tongues – the fact that she was now living with a local veterinary surgeon had gone into the annals of non-news, a fact simply to be accepted.

'I thought you'd got away from the violent side of things with your promotion,' he said now, still hugging her. The words were a tiny source of irritation, though she took care not to stiffen. Yes, public relations was the less dangerous end of police work but she would rather his pleasure in that was less obvious. 'You don't really want to be around if someone's chopping people's heads off, do you? Let someone else do it for once, and good riddance!'

'Got no choice, have I?' She went on quickly to hide the slight grouch in her voice. 'Anyway I doubt if we're – they're – looking for a fullscale axe murderer. Removing the head and hands is the ideal way to prevent identification, that's all.

But Tissingham? It seems a hell of an odd place to dump that sort of body. And in an out-of-the-way churchyard where there just happens to be a convenient grave dug? Sorry,' she added, turning her head to see Adrian's patient expression, 'but the damned thing did turn up right under my feet!'

'Mm. Tissingham . . . I can't immediately place it.'

'About ten miles out, on the Petham side.'

'Oh yes. It's all arable round there.' A typical vet's remark; classification by lack of animals. 'I think I've driven past it on my way to somewhere else, or even through it. Small village, pretty, narrow streets, a few posh houses round the edge?'

'That's the one. They had to organise a special field for the guests to park in because so many cars would have clogged the place up otherwise. As it is, they must have had a problem getting the hearse through the lane to the church. So why someone should go all the way out there—' Jane stopped, and gave Adrian a wry grin. 'All right, you want me to let it be. You have to admit, though, it's a little bit more interesting than chairing community meetings.'

'And old habits die hard. You're going to have to stop sounding plaintive because it isn't your case, though. Think of the advantages you've got now instead. No DCI Morland sniping at you and eager to reduce you to the ranks.'

'Yes, I'd certainly have to say life's easier working to Chief Inspector Lowell and the Super.' The chief inspector who was now her immediate boss seemed only too glad that an extra person had been put in to share his workload; and relieved rather than resentful that she was specially appointed to take over any EU liaison which might occur because he lacked the necessary foreign language skills. He also seemed happy to let Jane organise most of her own time, and she had an office to herself, small but pleasant, the trappings of her new rank.

It wasn't CID, with a suddenly interesting case to follow up, that was all.

'It's all right, you can stop being patient,' she told Adrian with rueful resignation. 'It's just a bit soon to remember to get my feet out from under. I'll drop it. Tell me what else I haven't done. Though if you want gravy you're going to have to make it yourself because I haven't mastered that yet.'

He gave her one of his amused, placid looks, and took over. She hoped he appreciated the fact that she was at least trying to develop some culinary skills. If only, as she had told him, out of a sense of fairness.

She was managing to be tidier too – at least some of the time. Luckily, when she forgot, he just moved things without comment.

'How are things at the practice?' she asked now, dragging her mind firmly away from speculations on stray corpses and reaching for a handful of cutlery to lay the table. 'Any more applications for the partnership? I suppose Trevor hasn't decided he wants to stay after all?'

'No, he's still keen to go back up north. I was waiting for the chance to tell you. As of today, I'm rather less sorry Trevor doesn't want to carry on. Someone's come up who may be ideal – I hope.'

'Yeah? A good prospect and with the capital to buy in?'

'Yes. And it's someone I already know. We were students

together. If she's still as good as she always promised to be, I'll take her on like a shot.'

'She?'

'A woman can do the job, if it's the right sort of woman.' Adrian cast Jane a quizzical look as if waiting for a few feminist comments, but when she merely raised an eyebrow he went on, 'Strong enough. I need someone who can deal with horses and cattle as well, not just the small animal side. The latter's what Fliss has been lumbered with, apparently, and she's dying to get back to more general practice.'

'Keen to wrestle the odd cow?'

'As I remember, she could do that with the best of us. There was a Hereford bull once while we were in training which was bad-tempered enough to frighten me . . .' He broke off with a reminiscent grin and turned his attention back to doing efficient things with pots and pans. 'Anyway, she's free right now. Something to do with her father dying, I gathered; at least she said she'd left her previous practice for personal reasons. And she's keen to move to a new area. Her father's death gives her capital. So when she saw my ad, she gave me a bell.'

'Sounds promising, then. What did you say her name was?'

'Felicity Rathbone. We always used to call her Fliss. Come to think of it,' Adrian said over his shoulder as he opened the oven, 'I'd better see what she wants to be called now in case she's grown out of student nicknames.'

A jolly cow-wrestling Amazon called Felicity? She would probably be no worse than Trevor, the gloomy locum. At least Jane had always found him gloomy. 'Sounds like a piece of luck,' she said agreeably, 'and she can take over the flat as well, can't she? Unless she's got a husband and family. No? Let's hope she'll realise her good fortune, then, and grab the chance of joining you and having accommodation thrown in.'

Adrian could do with a new permanent partner rather than a locum who had spent months trying to decide whether he could really bear to live south of Manchester and with southerners. Jane glanced at Adrian affectionately, aware that it had required a lot of quiet tenacity to make sure the practice continued to run smoothly. She would keep her fingers crossed that Felicity Rathbone turned out to be both compatible and useful – even if it meant he had to spend a lot of time all over again settling a new person in, and just when she was getting used to not having any regular weekend duty, and the bonus of not being expected to work in the evenings either, except by prearrangement.

If she had been part of the team for this new murder—

She forced her mind swiftly away from that as they sat down to eat. She was just raising the first forkful to her mouth when Adrian clapped a hand to his brow.

'Oh, your postcard! Did you find it? I put it on the side somewhere, I think.'

'Getting as bad as me about where you've put things? It's supposed to work the other way round. Who's it from, did you notice?'

'Someone with scrawly writing. Hang on, there it is. You put your bag down on top of it.' He reached an arm to the bookshelf to extract the pasteboard rectangle. 'The Tower of

London, photographed in garish colour for the tourists. Does that give you any clue?'

'Not unless my parents have suddenly decided to fly in from New Zealand for a home visit, but arriving without warning isn't exactly their style. Oh, it's from Matty! Honestly, doctors. Her writing really doesn't improve.' Jane inspected the brief message, and gave a snort of exasperation. 'She doesn't say why she's suddenly sending me postcards either. Just two sentences – "Expect a surprise! I'll phone you!"'

'Maybe she and Steve are going to come down. I'd like to meet them.'

Somehow there had been no chance so far to introduce Adrian to her closest friend, with all of them busy about their careers. Jane looked across at Adrian and gave him a smile. 'Yes, I'd like you to meet them. But when you do, remember not to let your jaw drop – I warned you she's stunningly beautiful. I wonder why she's making such a mystery? A consultant surgeon job at last, and she wants to tell me in person so she can hear me crow for her? Or . . . God, you don't suppose she's pregnant? Or they're going to get married? Or even both?'

'You'll just have to wait and see.'

'Yes, I will. I've tried to phone her a couple of times and never managed to catch either of them.' Jane let out a chuckle. 'And that means I've got a surprise for her, too: I haven't managed to pass it on yet that I've made promotion.' And accepted the compromise to her ambitions in so doing. Steve would certainly put an edge of teasing on his congratulations having worked with her down here before he went back to his DS job in London.

No, she had made a firm resolution when she took the job that she would not think in those terms. It was only today that had thrown her back into it. Today, and the Tissingham murder.

Not her business. Still, she would keep her ear to the ground and make sure she heard how they were getting on with it.

Chapter 3

'No, we're no further on about who he is. They've dug all round without finding the rest of him. Someone took the trouble to cut the labels out of his suit too.'

'Shirt? Underwear?'

'The shirt's a standard size sixteen, expensive silk but no labels again, and the underpants came from Marks. You can buy them almost anywhere, but since they're marked St Michael with the washing instructions in English, I suppose that might suggest nationality, or at least that he shops for his smalls here. No socks or shoes so maybe those were something fancy. Handmade shoes might have given us something. Whoever decided to dispose of him seems to have been careful.'

'Head and hands cut off after death, you said?'

'That's right, and by someone who knew what they were doing, according to the pathologist. A tidy professional job.'

'So what you've got is an Identity Unknown who's been professionally dealt with. Any suggested MO for the killing?'

Kenny Barnes shook his head. He seemed quite happy for Jane to pump him. She had run into him in the canteen. 'No wounds in the body, so the supposition is he was cracked over the head, or shot in the head, or smothered, though probably not since there aren't any unusual dust particles in the lungs, or in some way disposed of via the skull, up to which time he was healthy and well-fed. He wasn't strangled, because there's a nicely cut trachea with no marks on it. All we actually know is that he was middle-aged, forty-five or so, and he hadn't been dead long. Twenty-four hours at most, probably more like twelve. That's all the path report could give us. Oh, and that he was moved from wherever he died and dumped in the grave. No bloodstains in the earth besides a small bit of leakage, so it has to have been done somewhere else.' Kenny paused from his practical catalogue of the facts, then resumed, 'And burial wouldn't have taken long, with a hole ready dug and a pile of earth beside it. Even a spade handily there. The sexton had left it out since he reckoned no one in the village was going to nip into the churchyard and nick it.'

'But no unexpected prints on the spade handle, I suppose?'

Kenny shook his head; if there had been prints he would have mentioned them.

'And you say you haven't found anyone at all who saw anything?' Jane persisted.

'Not so far. It seems to be the kind of village where people keep themselves to themselves. There's a back gate to the churchyard, too, a small one going out into a lane with no houses that end of it. You could even drive there and park beside it.' He gave a sigh and put up a stubby hand with forefinger and thumb held barely apart. 'Someone came this close to being clever, didn't they? If their luck hadn't run out . . .'

'Mm. You'd need to be lucky or know the area to find a handy grave just when you wanted one, though.'

'True enough. So we've got endless house-to-house inquiries, though they're not producing any results so far.' He pulled a face. 'The villagers don't like any of it, either. You know the kind of thing – "We're respectable folk here, can't you go and ask questions somewhere else?"'

'Oh dear, one of those, is it?'

'Yes. You're well out of it, ma'am,' he added with a grin, and then began to stack up his empty lunch plates, casting her the apologetic look of one who ought to be going. 'We've got to go out and do another search of the ground this afternoon, though the last one didn't turn up anything.'

'I wish you luck. Hope you get a break soon.'

His wry expression suggested he found that unlikely. He sketched her a friendly salute, then left. He was one of the people she had been aware she would miss most by changing departments – steady, reliable, even fatherly towards her occasionally, within the bounds of rank, and she had known he would satisfy her curiosity. Jane mulled over what he had told her. It didn't sound as if they had got far towards a solution in the last four days.

But then it was a hard one. No identity for the victim, therefore no easy leads. So it had to be down to the small change of any investigation: house-to-house inquiries, interviews in case anyone just might have seen something, searches for anything, however small, which might constitute a clue. And all of it to be logged, put down on paper, entered into the computer, put on the file cards.

Kenny was probably right and she was well out of it.

Anyway she was out, period. Chris Hollings had asked her for a written report on the events in the churchyard and she had given him one. Aside from that, he was plainly more in need of troops on the ground than stray community inspectors. Even Geoff Madox, the disabled sergeant who now ran the collator's office from his wheelchair, was more use to this inquiry than she was. He could make a search for any locally-based villains who might have gangland connections, since the condition of the body did suggest an execution. He could see if any of the Tissingham names being so meticulously collected came up with a computer cross-reference, make a sweep of any missing person reports . . . That was what the DI would be asking him for.

It was possible, just, that the conveniently empty grave had been a random find by someone who just happened to be searching for a place to dump a body. The funeral had been widely publicised, with that advertisement in the paper. A paper which was distributed all over Kent. That was a thought . . .

She knew it was crazy to let her mind nag on over the possibilities. Unnecessary, too. Chris Hollings was no slouch and anything she might think of would certainly be somewhere on his list. Nobody had even suggested she might be useful with soothing the Musthill family's feelings. The task had probably been delegated to one of the WDCs. Jane allowed herself a small sigh and followed it with a wry grin at her own inability to accept not being involved. Like it or lump it, she was out, so she had better turn her thoughts in some more suitable direction. Such as finishing her lunch and returning to her office with its burden of community affairs.

It was three days later when she found herself involved after all, if only on the margins. Chief Inspector Lowell popped his carefully-combed grey head round her door and gave her a look which was distinctly harried.

'Jane, how are you with the doyennes of the WI? I've had Mrs Parrot bending my ear for a full twenty minutes. From Tissingham. When are we going to finish using their village hall, and isn't it rather inconsiderate of us when they need it for meetings, let alone the annual cake competition. Then apparently the cubs have got nowhere else to meet. It was a thoroughgoing complaint. She's not happy, and according to her the rest of the village isn't either.'

'What do you want done about it, sir? If CID's using the hall as their incident room, they won't want to move out until they've covered everything.'

'I know. Mrs Parrot obviously considers murder inconsiderate too. And definitely our fault. She told me so at some length. What we need,' he added, regarding her hopefully, 'is someone to go out there and make placating noises. Today. Talk to her. Talk to several of the other villagers as well, since she seemed to suggest a fairly general anti-police feeling, and appeal to their patience and understanding. You know the kind of smoothing-down it needs.'

'You don't want to leave it to CID, sir? Since they're there, on the ground? I'll go of course if you think it's the best idea. We ought to clear it with DI Hollings first, though. I wouldn't want to tread on his toes.'

'That's all right, I've already had a word with him and he agrees. He says they've got quite enough else to do and they'd be grateful for the input.'

'Right, then, I'll go this afternoon. I've got that meeting with the probation service this morning, but I should be through by twelve thirty.' Jane flipped the page of her desk diary back from where she had been checking her future activities and wrote 'Tissingham – Mrs Parrot' across the afternoon. 'I'll see what I can do to calm her down, sir.'

Tissingham, at first sight, looked as pretty and peaceful as it had a week ago; a jumble of cottage roofs tucked into a valley, with the pointed spire of the church aimed heavenward like a prayer behind some trees and just visible at the village edge. A slate roof on some tall building offered a silvery gleam at the opposite end. There were gated entrances to a couple of drives to be passed on the way in, and the solid brick of a modern detached house visible behind one large garden. This time, however, as Jane took the winding lane downwards at a decorous pace, she was not following a queue of cars converging on the village for a funeral, and there was no dark-suited marshal to pop up from the gateway of a smartly converted oast house to direct the drivers up the nearest turning to park. Instead, as she went on into the small main street, there were two squad cars parked just ahead, and the yellow jacket of someone apparently on police point-duty fifty yards further up. If Jane's memory served her right, the village had not boasted so much as a local bobby on a bicycle until now.

She edged her way past the squad cars, noticing as she did so that the one small general store which the village street contained was displaying a new-looking notice in its window announcing 'We Sell Sandwiches!' It looked as if one resident of Tissingham at least had decided to take advantage of the influx of strangers.

The WPC on point-duty saw Jane's uniform and snapped a rapid salute, then leaned down to the car window. 'If you want the incident room, ma'am, turn off at the next right and then turn right again.'

'Thanks, I'll probably look in there later. At the moment I'm looking for something called The Street. Is that this? And do you know a Wistaria Cottage?'

'The Street's the sharp turn back on your left, you've just passed it. This is the High Street. They've also got a New Street and an Old Street. They're not very imaginative with their names,' the girl added with a grin, then returned to helpfulness. 'You'll have to go on and turn to come back, ma'am, and the easiest place to do that is to follow this road, and then where it curves round to the left you'll find it widens out a bit and there are some wrought-iron gates set in a wall on your right. There's space to turn in front of those.'

'Thanks. I can see why they need you!' Jane gave her a smile and moved on down the narrow twisting street.

White-painted cottages crowded in along each side, here and there with an exposed beam acting as a support for the upper storey. Doors opened directly on to the pavement; windows were masked with thick lace curtains. Once or twice a larger double-fronted cottage boasted a pedimented front door. The varied roofline was broken here and there by the slip of an alley. Finally she reached a left curve with a sudden outbreak of flint-faced houses, low and huddled with tiny windows, followed by a group of cottages fronted by the typical Kentish weatherboarding. One was bright and pretty with a hanging flower basket outside its door; the others were distinctly shabbier.

The village street seemed to run out here, with an earth bank topped by a hedge on the left, a high, smooth stone wall set back a little on the right. It was pierced by the promised wrought-iron gates. They were tall, black and ornate, a gravelled drive visible behind them, then some masking greenery and the brief glimpse of a large house. A manor belonging to some local squire? Jane swung her car into the convenient curve in front of the entrance, and as she did so saw that a lettered wooden board had been fixed to the wall beside the gates. Peering, she saw that it announced in small but neat letters, THE SPIRITUAL LIGHT COMMUNITY.

A retreat centre, perhaps. In this part of Kent with its long religious history such things were apt to be set up. And that might well be another part of the village which was disconcerted to find itself in the middle of a murder inquiry, Jane thought as she completed her turn to retrace her course. Not what they would have come here for at all. Though presumably they would be more charitable about it than the likes of Mrs Parrot. She was caught by a sudden wicked vision of the house-to-house teams trying to pursue their inquiries in the face of a community of silent monks. Oh dear, Chris Hollings really did have his hands full with this one.

The sharp turn which she had been directed to find for The Street appeared, and proved to lead to a whole new section of Tissingham which had obviously grown sideways from its main street into a rather smarter area of detached cottages, each with its own surrounding garden. Most of them, Jane judged, had probably been bought by incomers and then done up, though a few might have been built within the last twenty years but designed to fit the concept of village life. Mrs Parrot's was one of the former, a small and highly decorative brick affair with an oak-beamed front. The name 'Wistaria Cottage' was helpfully displayed on an ornamental pottery plaque on the door.

An hour later, Jane had done her best with the soothing tactics she had come to apply and had been instructed as to which other members of the village she should call on to hear a confirmation of Mrs Parrot's opinions. That lady – of advancing middle years, with pendulous wattles which made her resemble a turkey rather than any other bird, and the possessor of an extremely commanding upper-class voice as well as a selection of apparently vicious-tempered Jack Russells – was, Jane thought, rather less of a power in the village than she would like to be. It had transpired that she actually had no official post in the local WI but was merely 'an active member'. It also finally became apparent what she really wanted to say.

It was couched in sentences which began, 'One wouldn't wish to be prejudiced, of course, but . . .' and, 'As our dear vicar so often tells us, there's room for all sorts in the world, but all the same . . .' The real source of her objections turned out to be none other than the Spiritual Light Community.

'They're not even Christians, my dear, they're one of those dreadful sects dressed up in pale green robes. One wouldn't wish to be prejudiced, of course, but nothing untoward ever happened in Tissingham before their arrival. Who knows what practices they get up to. The police should be looking no further. It's quite ridiculous that— Down, Hector, the inspector doesn't want her ankles examined. He's just a little bit inclined to nip, I'm afraid. Do help yourself to another biscuit, and then you can give him a piece to distract him. Where was I?'

'Have you had any reason to complain about the Spiritual Light Community, Mrs Parrot? Do they cause disturbances in the village, or beg, or anything like that?'

'It's disturbance enough to know that they're there, even if they do keep themselves to themselves!' This was delivered on a snap. 'Ever since they arrived just after the New Year... It's a disgrace that they should be allowed to take over a manor house in a respectable village in any case. The house may be something of a Victorian monstrosity, but it's perfectly sound and could have been put to use to house several homeless families!'

Jane could imagine the objections Mrs Parrot would have made if several of the city's homeless families had been rehoused in Tissingham. Particularly some of the more recalcitrant ones. She looked carefully blank. It was interesting that a sect should have established itself out here, a fact which had certainly gone unnoticed in official circles. That probably meant that they had been behaving perfectly inoffensively and keeping their heads down. 'I'm just trying to establish whether there have been any actual causes for complaint,' she said politely.

'Martha Latimer has heard them chanting. I told you that you should go and call on her. And old Mr Baines in the same row of cottages – the ones almost opposite the manor entrance – is quite apprehensive about having all those young people on his doorstep. And now, of course – surely murder's enough of a cause for complaint!'

'If there's any connection at all between the community and the recent events, I'm sure our team will find it. We can't just leap to the supposition, though, can we, without cause? As I was saying earlier, the reason the police are spending so much time in Tissingham is because we have to be thorough. It's unfortunate, and naturally we regret any inconvenience which is being caused. Once our local inquiries are concluded—'

'As they never will be if you keep inquiring in the wrong place! I'm not alone in believing this, even if most people prefer not to say anything openly. Particularly since the vicar chooses to preach sermons on tolerance.' Mrs Parrot, a trifle flushed, completed this sidelight with, 'Dear Mr Mather, he's such an idealist. And so young, of course. But one can scarcely feel comfortable living alone any more. At least one wouldn't, without the boys!' The adoring look she gave her pack of nasty little dogs indicated to whom she was referring. Jane forbore to suggest that the police presence in the village must be reassuring, then, rather than otherwise. They would after all eventually withdraw, and it would be unwise to give Mrs Parrot a new subject for complaint. She sought to bring the conversation back to reasonable grounds.

'As I've said, I do apologise for the inconvenience you've had to put up with, and we really are most grateful for your patience. I'm very glad to have had the chance to talk things through with you. Naturally I shall follow up anything you've told me. And in the meantime, I do hope you'll find you can put up with a police presence for a little longer. We have to do our job, you know, but we'll try to be as unobtrusive as possible.'

Escaping eventually, though not without further urging to call on some of the villagers Mrs Parrot had listed, Jane drew in a deep breath, glad of the fresh air and feeling awash with cups of tea. She would probably be offered more at her other ports of call too. It might be a good thing to look in at the incident room next, if only to make her presence known. It would be as well to check in with whoever was there so that they knew she was about in the village, and why, and to make sure she was not getting in the way of any further house-to-house inquiries.

The village hall was tucked away behind various cottages but did at least have an open space next to it which could accommodate the various cars parked there. It was a square building of unprepossessing modern design, obviously built for practicality rather than beauty, and had wire mesh set into the glass of its windows to discourage vandalism. Inside, it was surprisingly spacious and had a carpeted floor and a small curtained stage at one end. It had been transformed into an efficient police working area, with a VDU screen plugged in against one wall, piles of paperwork on tables and a couple of mobile telephones. Chris Hollings was in the middle of all this consulting some papers a collator was showing him, and looked round as Jane came up to him.

'Oh yes, CI Lowell told me you were coming over. Thanks for your help. Have you been to see the complainant yet, or are you on your way?'

'I've just spent an hour with her but she wants me to visit one or two others. Is that all right with you? I thought I'd better come and ask.'

'Be my guest. Smooth as many ruffled feelings as you can. They're not the most helpful bunch – entrenched insularity tucked away behind thick walls. I always thought nothing could go on in a village without everybody knowing about it. If anybody knows anything here, they're certainly not saying. Unless it's just that they don't like strangers, and that includes us.'

'I've just had my ear bent about one set of strangers. The Spiritual Light Community at the edge of the village, in the manor. I expect it's come up – they're outsiders, so if there's been a murder here, it must be them.'

'I don't think anyone else has actually said that outright, but it's been inferred here and there. According to the vicar it's a guru with a teenage following, and they've never been any trouble. House-to-house tried knocking on the door but got a pretty unfriendly reception – some lad in robes saying "This is private property, please leave". I sent someone back to try again but that time the door wasn't answered.' He gave an impatient shrug. 'I can't force them to talk to us or it'll look like harassment. Anyway, they're at the opposite end of the village from the churchyard, so there's no reason to suppose anyone might have seen anything.'

'I could see if I could get in, wearing my community liaison hat. If you like.'

She saw him consider her offer with his usual care. 'I doubt if they're relevant,' he decided after a moment. 'We're not looking for amateurs on this one. All we're doing here is checking and double-checking in case anybody saw anything. Strangers – genuine strangers – asking casual questions. Or a car coming through at an odd time. If you and your CI want to follow up this community for your own benefit, do that, and if you manage to ask a few questions at the same time, let me know the answers.'

'Will do. They probably won't let me in either, but since it's always as well to know who's on our patch, I might just try a visit in a couple of days. Out of uniform. All right if I go off and do a bit more local calming, then? By the way, I suppose you can't say how much longer you'll be here, in case I'm asked?'

'Don't be specific, but I'll probably pack this end up pretty soon. Staying close in doesn't seem to be getting us anywhere.' She could see the frustration this was causing him. Then to her surprise he gave her a genuine smile. 'Oh, while you're here, and on a completely different subject, would you and Adrian like to come to dinner with Elizabeth and me some time? Say, one evening at the end of next week, given that this case seems to be going into limbo and I should be able to take a normal evening off?'

'I'm sure we would. As long as Adrian isn't on call – I'll have to check that one.'

'Fine, I'll get Elizabeth to give you a ring and confirm it.'

Now that they were both inspectors, she was on the socialising list. Interesting. Now that she was on level rank *and* part of a couple, Jane corrected herself. It was wryly amusing to know how much difference such things made. She had met Elizabeth Hollings a couple of times briefly, and had liked her. It might be a pleasant evening.

Meantime, she had to go and see a Mrs Martha Latimer and a Mrs Cross and a Miss Haley, and discover if all of them agreed with Mrs Parrot that the Spiritual Light Community must be a nest of murderers. Then she would have to try to persuade them diplomatically that wearing robes and chanting had no necessary connection with a predilection for crime while at the same time assuring them how grateful the police were for their co-operation and patience during this difficult time.

That, for today, was her allotted task, and what community work was about.

Chapter 4

The projected date for dinner with the Hollingses was before Felicity Rathbone was due to arrive to take up her share of the partnership. That meant Trevor would still be there and could take any calls. Felicity had made a flying visit and had apparently approved of all she saw, and had shaken hands on an agreement. Jane had not met her during her brief presence, but Adrian was obviously extremely satisfied with the situation. Felicity – to whom he still referred absently as Fliss – was going to be an asset. She had all the right qualifications and was a good organiser too. She had changed very little. He thought they could work well together. Jane had only to make agreeing noises.

Presumably she would find Felicity reasonably likeable. The main point was that Adrian should be pleased with her. And it had to be a good thing that she had stated the intention of settling here permanently.

Mulling it over idly as she drove to work, Jane let her thoughts drift to the fact that there had been no sign yet of the promised phone call from Matty. If it was just some idea for her and Steve to come down on a visit, she hoped it wouldn't collide with new practice partners and sociability with her former boss. It would have been easier if she had managed to get hold of Matty; she had tried ringing her again but without success. Why that maddeningly mysterious postcard? What was Matty up to?

Jane drove into the police station yard and flipped her parking pass onto the windscreen. She let herself in at the back of the station and decided that this would be as good a time as any to make a call at the collator's office, on her way up to her own. Sergeant Madox would undoubtedly be functioning with his usual efficiency by now.

'Morning, Geoff. Have you got a moment to look something up for me?' She gave him a smile as he turned his wheelchair round from a filing cabinet. He operated it neatly in the small space, making it seem an asset rather than a disadvantage. His reassignment here after a spinal injury on active duty had lost him the use of his legs had necessitated a widening of the door, the room's contents rearranged at lower levels, and the presence of various ramps about the station, but he had made it quietly and pleasantly plain from the first day that he neither wanted nor expected any other special treatment. He was proving to be a good, and good-tempered, collator, with a rapid assimilation of local knowledge and the advantage of an apparently prodigious memory.

'Sure, ma'am, what are you after?'

'You've probably been asked already. Have we got anything on file about the Spiritual Light Community at Tissingham?'

'Yes, the DI did ask me for that one. There's nothing in our files. I haven't found anything with that specific name on a cross-check either.'

'We've never had any official complaint about them from anyone in the village, then? I only ask,' Jane told him, 'because I had my ear bent thoroughly with unofficial complaints yesterday, though nothing specific. Only the fact that they're there.'

'I haven't found any note that anyone's rung us to object to them. They're at Tissingham Manor, aren't they? I did find an earlier complaint about the manor, but that turned out to be eighteen months ago, well before their arrival.' He made a swift circling movement to reach another filing cabinet. 'Yes, here it is: Someone wanted to buy the property and turn it into a prep school, and a Mr and Mrs Liston rang to object that it would cause traffic problems in the village. They were told to take it up with the local planning authority rather than us. The school never happened anyway, and the house went to another buyer, a firm called A1 Data Commerce. They got permission to run a small business from there. Still listed as owners.'

'You have been thorough. A1 Data Commerce must have folded, I suppose, and sublet. The Spiritual Light Community's been there for around four months, I'm told. They appear to be harmless and causing no trouble, aside from the odd bit of village prejudice. And even then they've got the vicar on their side, because he told me so.'

The Reverend Michael Mather, to whom Jane had also talked yesterday, had been mildly informative. He had been able to tell her that the Spiritual Light Community was a group of young people in their teens and twenties who had chosen to live their lives dedicated to peace, under a guru who went by the name of Senander Baba. 'I've met him,' the

Reverend Mather had assured Jane, 'and he's an extremely gentle man. Very dedicated to the care of the young people who follow him. I'm sorry if you've been hearing any intolerant remarks, Inspector. I have tried to explain to my parishioners often enough that God should be seen as equally available to different faiths.'

Geoff Madox was still waiting to see if Jane wanted anything else. She pulled herself out of her thoughts and smiled at him. 'Okay, thanks. It's a blank, but I suppose even that's constructive. At least they don't sound like Waco extremists.' She gave him a nod and then left him. The Reverend Michael Mather had also been able to tell her that Richard Musthill had by now had another, quiet, funeral elsewhere. Anna Musthill must have accepted the fact of her father's suicide. There had been nothing to query, anyway, as Jane had told her.

In her office, Jane looked at her diary and pencilled in a time on the following morning to visit the Spiritual Light Community. Today she had an estate meeting with a group of young mothers who wanted to complain about persistent vandalism (and a persistent lack of police interest) and then a visit to another group which wanted to talk about their Neighbourhood Watch scheme. The afternoon was a lot more promising. She had to attend a meeting of a committee set up to look into any problems of jurisdiction now that the Channel Tunnel was operating – whose law took precedence exactly where, and how such things were functioning on the ground. It was no more than a low-level forum for discussion and reporting back, since any decisions would be taken a lot higher up; but it would be the first Jane had attended and would give her the chance to talk face-to-face with her European counterparts. That would mainly be the French, but she understood Belgium and the Netherlands had asked to be represented too.

She came back from the meeting satisfied that she had been able to keep her end up in various multilingual discussions, and pleased to find that the next committee was due to be held in France – a good excuse for a swan to the other side of the Channel. She was scarcely aware that she was passing the CID room door without any wistful pang for once when it opened to let Kenny Barnes out of it. Mike Lockley was behind him, WDC Rachel Welsh following him. The younger two both gave Jane a smile before moving away, but Kenny paused to speak to her.

'You're looking cheerful, ma'am.'

'Am I? Have you lot returned to base or are you just in to catch up on paperwork?'

'Finished for the day, but they're closing down out there tomorrow anyway and transferring everything over.'

That should please Mrs Parrot. Except that the police were not removing the Spiritual Light Community along with themselves. 'Still no leads?' Jane asked. 'Nobody who saw anything anywhere?'

'Not really. We did finally get a statement from an old woman who told us she heard someone shouting in the churchyard the night before the funeral – two men, she says, and it sounded as if they were having a fight. At about half past ten, she thinks, though she can't be sure because she didn't notice the time.' Kenny gave a shrug to indicate the vagueness to which witness statements were prone. 'She thought it was drunks and she certainly didn't go out in the dark to see. Wouldn't have been able to see anyway unless she'd gone right out and peered through the hedge. You can't blame her for not bothering, she's quite frail. It's hard to know whether to believe what she says since she didn't tell us that story the first time she was asked.'

'It can't have been the victim and an attacker, since he was dismembered elsewhere. I suppose you could just about imagine it as two villains falling out over dumping the body, but—'

'But they'd hardly be yelling their heads off about it.' Kenny gave a gusty sigh. 'What seems the most likely is that Mrs Emmett got her days wrong, or she's suddenly come out with the story to get a bit of attention. She lives opposite the churchyard and the only other cottage there is an empty one which used to belong to an old man who died a month ago. So she's got nobody to deny what she says, and it makes her important, doesn't it?'

'The SOCOs didn't manage to come up with anything?'

'Not so's you'd notice. The grave was thoroughly mucked about where the coffin was lowered. There was too much mud all over the body to find any fibres from anyone else's clothes. The churchyard was a mess of prints from any number of different kinds of shoes. Oh, by the way, ma'am, I suppose there wasn't anybody at the funeral wearing trainers, was there?'

'Not with the kind of gear they had on! Why, did a trainer print come up?'

'There was a clear one in some mud by the hedge. As if someone had been standing still just there. It's a standard make and looks as if it could have been almost new. It's far enough away from the grave to be probably irrelevant in any case. It only showed up because it was so far away, practically under the hedge, like I said. Probably comes from some kid bird's-nesting. They all wear trainers nowadays. Just thought I'd ask,' he said with a weary grin, 'so we could rule it out.'

'Sorry, I can't recall seeing anybody lurking under the hedge with evil intent. And there certainly wasn't anyone among the guests wearing trainers.' Anna Musthill, the only person informally dressed, might have had trainers on. But she had come from the other direction. 'No, can't help you on it.'

'We haven't found anyone in Tissingham with known criminal connections. It must be the most law-abiding village in the district, not a record between the lot of them.'

Jane gave him a parting grin and let him go on his way, home to wife and children. She went to file her notes of the committee meeting, then went home herself.

Elizabeth Hollings phoned to confirm a dinner date (oh dear, they would have to invite them back; Adrian would certainly have to do the cooking) but otherwise it was a quiet evening. Adrian was busy organising a new partnership agreement to be signed and notarised when Felicity arrived, and Jane made herself settle down with a 'Learn Spanish' tape. At least nowadays she had the prospect of finding a use for any extra language skills she could develop.

She tried a different route to Tissingham next morning, and found it was actually quite easy to approach the village from the manor end providing she kept her eyes peeled for the right turnings. It was a day to lift the heart, one of those fresh, fair, early May mornings when the Kent countryside was at its prettiest, all burgeoning trees arching to turn lanes into bosky green tunnels, then opening out to show the soft roll of fields or neat ranks of fruit orchards. Old and mellow-looking farmhouses in rosy brick could be glimpsed amid the more modern clutter of aluminium barns. If it was necessary to slow to a crawl behind a chugging tractor sometimes before it turned off sharply into a field, or to pull into a passing-space in a narrow lane while some other piece of farm machinery swayed by, that seemed a small price to pay for the fact that this part of the Garden of England, away from the motorways, was indeed still a garden, green and leafy and flourishing.

Jane was half amused to find herself thinking so. Whatever had happened to her old urban self? Well, it was at least partially still alive, since when it came actually to living, she would certainly choose the city. All the same, this, right on the doorstep – there was a lot to be said for it. A rest to the spirit.

She could even forget the nagging ache in her shoulder which had come back to plague her this morning, a reminder that bruising inside a joint could be annoyingly slow to heal. A reminder, too, that that had been practically her last piece of work with CID – a carefully set up surveillance resulting in a satisfactory arrest, despite the fact that she had been barged to the ground by one of the villains while he was trying to escape.

She pulled up outside the wrought-iron gates of Tissingham Manor. Presumably she could park here, since there was just enough room next to the wall for her to be off the actual road. It would be less intrusive than pushing the gates wide – they appeared not to be locked – and driving right up to the house. A curtain twitched in the cottages opposite as she locked her car and she resisted the impulse to turn round and wave. It was old Mr Baines's cottage; Jane had called there as part of her sweep a couple of days ago. Mr Baines was practically senile and would undoubtedly be alarmed to receive a wave from someone he probably would not recognise out of uniform. He had complained in a quavering voice and with a gesture out to the manor gates, 'People go in and out all the time!' which was directly the opposite of his neighbour Martha Latimer's assertion that although she had heard them, 'They keep theirselves to theirselves and don't never come out of there'. They could scarcely both be right.

Approaching the manor on foot up the crunch of the gravel drive, Jane could see little of it until she rounded a bend among the overgrown trees which screened it. The house that Mrs Parrot had described as a Victorian monstrosity was certainly large and remarkably tall, but it seemed to have no clearly defined shape. Every part of it showed corners and angles and excrescences. There was even a small turret which bulged out halfway up one wall and was crowned with a round, pointed roof, looking for all the world as if Rapunzel might appear at one of its windows and offer to let down her hair. Elsewhere, one piece of wall was topped high up with small square battlements, though the chimneyed section of roof which sloped steeply up behind them was plain grey slate. A paved area below disappeared into a shrubbery. Windows in the multi-cornered walls looked out in a remarkable variety of directions. Some of them were plain in shape, others had carved Gothic tops in another outbreak of mock-medievalism.

One corner of the house looked as if it might be out of use; the ground floor windows there were masked by tightly sealed external shutters covered in peeling green paint. The rest of the edifice, tower included, was faced with plaster and painted cream, slightly stained in places, and crisscrossed with what seemed to be an enormous number of drainpipes.

The house had a certain mad charm, Jane decided, gazing up at this jumble of styles made solid. Whoever built it had certainly gone about things with zest, if with little sense of proportion. Nobody could have described it as dull.

A pair of small carved stone lions, one of them with a chipped nose, flanked steps up to a tiled porch. To add to the air of random decoration, the wide front door had a top half which suddenly blossomed into colour, its upper section made of thick stained glass in dark reds and blues with a white lily in the middle of each panel. Reaching for a heavy lion's-head knocker which graced the wooden centre between the panels, Jane gave it a sharp rap. She wondered if her arrival had been observed from one of the many windows. She had caught no glimpse of anyone, but there were certainly plenty of places from which her approach could have been seen.

It was several moments after her knock, and she was looking round to see if there was also a bell, when the door abruptly swung open. A stocky youth with very blond hair and bright blue eyes, with a pale green robe wrapped round him over a T-shirt, inquired, 'Yes, please?' with what looked more like bewilderment than hostility, and a definite breathlessness as if he had come rapidly from somewhere else.

'I've come to see Senander Baba. Will he grant me an audience, do you think? The Reverend Mather suggested I call.'

Jane offered this pleasantly, well aware that it was against official policy for her not to introduce herself as a police officer but having decided she would risk it unless specifically asked. She would inform Senander Baba himself of her status if she was allowed to meet him. This particular acolyte showed no inclination to ask, but gave her another confused look and stepped back, saying, 'Please to wait?' in what was definitely a foreign accent. He turned and limped away, leaving the door open. Then he seemed to remember something and came rapidly back with his awkward gait – it looked as if he had a twisted leg under the robes – and cast her a look of apology, then closed the door in her face. At least he was going away to ask.

The wait was short and it was the same young man who returned. 'The Baba will see you,' he said with great solemnity, and stood back to let her enter. He led the way across the black-and-white tiles of a hallway, empty of furniture but with several closed doors each side, and along a narrow corridor with a worn drugget of carpet along it. He opened a door at the far end and pointed for her to go into what appeared to be a medium-sized, fairly sparsely furnished but otherwise perfectly ordinary sitting-room. A roll-topped desk stood against one wall, and a vase of white flowers decorated a table by the window.

The room was, at the moment, empty. Left alone by the departing acolyte, Jane was still glancing round when a second door in the corner opened and a tall man in a long white robe stepped in.

He had fair skin, a shaven head, and a pair of alert grey eyes in a lean face. Late thirties, Jane thought, not one of the youthful followers. Some senior member? His voice when he spoke had the faintest twang of an Australian accent.

'Good morning. You've caught us at a busy moment, I'm afraid, there are various classes going on. Michael Mather sent you? Is there something he wants us to do for him?'

'The Reverend Mather suggested I called on Senander Baba.' There was no use supposing it would be advisable to con her way past the highly intelligent eyes regarding her. 'My name's Jane Perry and I work in community liaison for the City Police. This is basically a social call. Do you think Senander Baba will see me?'

'That's me,' he replied, and to her surprise the thoughtful look he had been giving her broke into an extremely charming smile. 'I'm glad you didn't mention the word police at the door. It might have panicked Erik and given you quite the wrong impression. Do we rate a social call for a reason? No, if you've come from Michael Mather he would have warned me. So, sit down, Miss Perry – take the armchair, it's the only thing in here that's comfortable – and ask me whatever it is you want to ask me.'

Chapter 5

Senander Baba possessed a great deal of charisma, Jane thought. And – tranquillity? He certainly seemed in no particular hurry as he reached a long arm for the upright chair which stood before the desk, settled himself down on it, and regarded her with a steady, pleasant, and apparently friendly air.

'As I said, I'm really just making a social call,' Jane began. 'It's part of my job to know who's where. And whether we can offer anything in the way of help or advice.'

'I don't think so, thanks.' Was that a gleam of humour in the eyes thoughtfully regarding her? Yes, it certainly was. 'Why don't you just ask me what we're doing here, and why, and get it out of the way? The village can't claim we're any kind of nuisance, I'm glad to say – that's not the reason for your visit, is it? Because I can promise you, it's unjustified.'

'I've been told you keep yourselves to yourselves. Aside from – some chanting?' Martha Latimer's description of that had actually sounded more like imagination than reality, but Jane produced it in response to the smile he was giving her. 'Not, of course, that people aren't allowed to chant on their own property if they want to.'

'We don't, so that one's an illusion. We study, meditate, work around the house and grounds, but we don't chant.' He offered that patiently and with a look of rueful amusement. 'We wear "funny clothes" because that gives us a sense of identity. And have "funny beliefs" as well, I suppose – like peace, and discipline, and care for each other. And no hassle from other people, in exchange for offering none to them. Is that really an awful lot to ask?'

'I really didn't come here to criticise—'

'No, I'm sure you didn't. Sorry if I seemed to be sounding off.' Again that warm smile, with a lot of charm in it. It was the kind of smile which made you want to respond to it, and Jane had to bite back her surprise that he seemed so human. And definitely more practical than mystical. The friendly voice continued, 'If you want to know about us, that's basically it. We choose to live as we do because we find it preferable to the world outside. And yes, I'm its leader. It's a job which falls somewhere between being a spiritual guide and a social worker – if you don't find that description too banal.'

He said that cheerfully, and still with that underlying humour in his eyes. There was a faint reproach in them, however, as he went on, 'We had the police knocking at the door the other day too. In uniform that time. Do you think you could be kind enough to assure your people that we're harmless?'

'There was no inference intended. It was only a matter of general house-to-house inquiries, looking for witnesses to a crime which was discovered at the other end of the village.

That's one of the reasons I thought I'd call, to make sure you knew it wasn't just your community, and that you weren't being hounded.' Jane offered that quickly, a polite excuse for her arrival. 'It did seem as if there might have been a misunderstanding.'

'What was the crime?'

It sounded as if he genuinely didn't know. 'A murder. The body was found in the churchyard,' Jane told him. And was startled to see the very briefest flash of relief in his eyes. It was gone as she looked, but she was sure it had been there, as if murder could be dismissed as anything to worry him. 'Everyone in the village was being asked if they'd seen anything. You hadn't heard?' she asked, raising a polite eyebrow.

'No. What was it, something domestic?' He caught himself up on that and gave her another smile, this time with apology in it, and sympathy, and a return to the tranquillity touched with amusement which seemed to characterise him. 'No, don't tell me. You probably can't discuss it, and to be honest I don't really want to either. The kids here certainly don't want to be reminded how violent the world can be outside.' At the look of query she gave him, he went on with a touch of wryness, 'Not escapism, Miss Perry, just the experiences they've had before they came here. Oh, by the way, would you mind very much if I asked to see your warrant card?'

'Of course.' Jane took it out and handed it to him. He inspected it with careful thoughtfulness, then handed it back. 'There's a reason? I'm sorry, you're perfectly entitled to ask for it, of course, but I just wondered—'

'It suddenly seemed a good idea to make sure you weren't a journalist.' He said that amiably, then added with a smile, 'Your official photograph doesn't do you justice. You're probably mulling over why I said a police uniform might have panicked the lad who answered the door, so perhaps I'd better explain. Most of the kids here would react the same way. Not, I can assure you, because they're criminals. More because they're . . . how can I describe it so that you'll understand? Social rejects? The unwanted ones who've been pushed around too often.'

He paused, but before Jane could say anything he was speaking again, and with a sincerity which made her feel as if he had leaned forward, though in fact he had made no movement, remaining in his easy stillness. The planes of his face had a calm gravity. 'That's the reason they're here. Because I offer them rescue, and a structure to live by. They're the products of dysfunctional families whose care for them was so lacking or so oppressive that they had to opt out, live on the streets, sell themselves, take drugs, become the victims of violence. Before you ask, none of them take drugs now. And those who had no homes now have one. In some cases the first real home of their lives. Sometimes the first real care of their lives. No, they don't like the police – why should they? It's a word which as far as they're concerned usually spells trouble. Can you understand that?'

Runaways. Jane had barely framed the thought when he took it from her and gave her a sudden flashing smile. 'No, they aren't kids you'd be looking for. They're all over eighteen, I promise you. I make sure not to enrol anyone under-age. And they've joined me voluntarily. They're also perfectly free to leave if they so choose. Does that answer the question you were about to ask?'

'How many of them are there?' Jane inquired, framing it that way rather than 'How many followers have you got?' which somehow sounded crass. He had offered his explanation with an impressive sincerity and a charm which made it possible to see why anyone might be drawn to him.

'Here? Eighteen at the last count. So we're not overcrowded.' He said that with an extremely human grin and a glance round which seemed to encompass the building. 'Extraordinary place, isn't it? And a lucky find for us. We only have to pay a tiny rent, too. I think the idea is that our presence will keep squatters out.' It was a return to complete practicality, so that she felt slightly confused again, faced with the difficulty of assessing him as a person. An idealist? A charlatan? No, it was difficult to think of him as the latter, in spite of the charismatic appeal which was practically palpable. And if his followers were those who would otherwise be street kids . . . But in exchange for what? That was the thorny problem, however genuine and sincere he might be.

He was watching her face, waiting for her attention with apparently no haste, and he asked amiably, 'Would you like a guided tour?'

'Is that allowed? Sorry.' For a moment she had forgotten that if he was the holy man, the Baba, he must be the one who made the rules. 'Yes, I'd be interested, if you don't mind showing me.'

'Not at all.' He got up in a smooth fluid movement which set his white robe flowing around him. He wore thonged sandals on his feet, she saw – amused suddenly to find herself noticing that they were perfectly ordinary large male feet. 'You'll find us quite shabby and not very thoroughly furnished by most people's reckoning, but then how much furniture does one really need? Besides, what we've got is what other people have thrown out. We collected most of it from dumps.'

'Is poverty part of your rule?'

'No. Minimum necessity is, though. And what's given. To have no more than a roof overhead can be luxury, after all.' He was opening the door through which he had originally appeared, and ushered Jane through into another room which was octagonal in shape and bare but for a few cushions on a scuffed parquet floor. 'This is one of the meditation rooms, though it's just big enough to use for exercises as well. I think whoever designed the house must have liked rabbit warrens. Most of the rooms seem to lead out of each other. Or out of and then back into pieces of corridor.'

'Have you had – other headquarters before?'

'You mean, are we part of a wider group? Not exactly, though other people are doing the same kind of work. There are lost young people floating about all over Europe.' He opened another door which took them out into a passage. Everywhere, Jane noticed, was carefully swept, even if bare. 'Our last house was in Holland. Mind this step, it can catch you unawares.'

'What does the community live on? You said what's given.'

'Donations, yes. We don't beg.' He added that as if she had asked. 'One or two of the kids have money of their own.

Allowances from parents which,' there was a trace of grimness in his voice all of a sudden, 'could actually be called Go Away money. We all share what we have. And we also earn. We have a craft workshop. I'll show you that, too, when you've seen the house.'

He seemed determined to demonstrate that everything was open and above board. Or perhaps determined was the wrong word; happy about it? They had reached a staircase and he led her upwards into more wide, bare corridors with strips of dark red carpeting running along their centres, possibly left behind by a previous owner. An open door showed a large room with no beds but sleeping bags laid out neatly in lines along the floor. A large shabby chest of drawers stood in one corner, a giant mahogany wardrobe in another, looking as if it might have been left there because it was too big to move. A couple of boxes turned on their sides made lockers beside sleeping bags. Round a corner, another room, more sleeping bags . . . A notice pinned on the door said 'Girls Only!' which suggested the sexes were firmly segregated.

There was nobody about. A narrow staircase went even higher but, Jane was told, led only to unused attics. Senander opened a door briefly on a small room with more cushions and what appeared to be a makeshift but carefully arranged shrine – to some Indian god? Although he glanced at Jane he offered no comment and she solicited none. It would have been difficult to ask, 'What do you actually believe in?' without sounding baldly intrusive.

They returned downstairs by a different route, another staircase, another empty corridor. The house was certainly a maze. A sharp turn to more stairs took them down to a basement and opened out directly into what was obviously a kitchen, large and Victorian in style, with a big wooden table in the middle of it. The table's scored top had been scrubbed to a pale creamy colour, very clean. There was also a built-in dresser showing quite a lot of mismatched crockery, and some bright modern mugs. An old-fashioned blackboard graced one wall as if expecting Mrs Bridges to chalk up menus on it; at the moment it showed a stickman with a smiling face, drawn in white chalk. Two battered but apparently functional gas cookers stood against the wall, and there was a deep old-fashioned white sink with scrubbed draining boards.

'That's about it, unless you want to see our walk-in larder. The house provides us with all we could want, and gives us room to spread out too. Oh, and we have a furnace which heats the water,' Senander Baba said with an air of placid pride. 'It even warms the radiators, which really is luxury. And luckily it burns wood, so we could keep it going through the winter on a lot of lumber which had been left unwanted in the outbuildings. You see, things are "given", if you look.' He gave Jane a smile, and added, 'Come this way and it will take us outside.'

As they passed an open door to a scullery with another white sink in it, Jane saw a large modern washing machine, looking remarkably new. Had someone thrown that out too? And the tumble drier which stood beside it? It was the one touch which seemed more than 'minimum necessity'. Though perhaps it was, for the pale green robes of the acolytes and the guru's white ones . . . She wondered where everyone was. He had said, when she arrived, that there were classes going on, but where?

As they came out of a back door which led up out of the basement into some gardens, she found some of the followers at last, their cotton robes hitched up to show jeans underneath, digging what looked as if it might become a vegetable patch. Two boys and a girl. They all ducked their heads respectfully at the sight of their guru but glanced at Jane out of the sides of their eyes. Senander returned their greeting with a small bow which held equal respect, his palms pressed briefly together, a clearly affectionate smile curving his mouth.

Shortly, the tour took them to an outbuilding with a low barn-like appearance. The opening door brought a smell of paint and newly-cut wood and the sound of soft chatter which stopped at once. Four more of the young people were in here, all of them busy. One girl was painting what looked like a distinctly New Age picture, swirls of mist round a rather misproportioned dragon. Another was rolling up what might have been posters and inserting them into cardboard tubes, while the boy next to her was carving a criss-cross pattern into the top of a small wooden box. Another boy was decorating a row of ugly-looking plaster statuettes, adding colour to them in series to give each blue hands and red feet. All of them stopped briefly to give Senander their respectful nod and receive his return bow with palms together, then returned to their tasks. They looked, Jane thought, quite healthy.

'We have a market abroad for what we make,' Senander said after they had emerged from the workshop. 'It gives us something constructive to do, as you saw.' His voice was mild, and as Jane glanced at him she met an innocent gaze under a lifted eyebrow.

She had the immediate feeling that they were carrying on a conversation in which she said disbelievingly, 'You've got a market for that?' and he answered drily, 'You'd be surprised what people will buy!' No, she was imagining that there had been a flash of amusement in his face. He was merely regarding her with pleasant politeness. He also seemed determined that she should have a full circular tour, since he was indicating a different way back to the house.

'We've been trying to tidy the gardens where we can, but they're still fairly overgrown. The vicar came up with a lawnmower for us recently, which was a help.' This comment came as they moved out of an overgrown path through a shrubbery to find a sunken lawn below a balustrade just ahead. 'So now we've cut the grass and the weather's better, this class can be held out in the open air.'

Jane had already seen to what he was referring. Figures – not in robes – were lined up on the lawn below, gesturing, twirling with one leg raised, lapsing into sudden immobility with hands crossed in front of faces. There was an intense concentration about it which was almost frightening. As Jane watched, the group copied the figure at the front with a sudden swift kick, sharp and somehow vicious even though aimed at an imaginary foe. The young man out at the front was the best at it. As he turned into another fighting stance with the class copying him, Jane found she had caught her breath, her eyes fixed on the instructor.

He had the most extraordinarily beautiful face, a classical balance of symmetry and proportion, arched brows, straight nose, full mouth, short chin, under a slightly curling but very short cap of hair. It was a face that could have posed for a Greek statue. The eyes in their concentration on what he was doing had almost the blankness of a statue, too. He wore jeans and a shirt and his feet were bare. His breadth was a little too much for his height, his hands too square on thick wrists, but his face . . .

As if he could feel her eyes on him, the boy – for he looked little more – turned his head abruptly to give her a level stare. There was something unsettling in it. It felt abruptly as if the movements he was now demonstrating to his class were aimed directly at her. Even when he turned away for a flying backward kick, Jane could still feel the searing sense of an inimical response to her presence. When Senander Baba touched her arm, she almost jumped.

'Martin is an example of what I was talking about earlier. He was born profoundly deaf. Both his parents rejected him. He grew up in a children's home – not a good one, either – and when he was fostered he made very sure nobody could cope with him. Then he lived on the streets. In the past two years he's changed a lot. He's learned to use the untapped talents he's always had locked up inside him. And he's learning that he is acceptable, and that it's all right to care for people.'

Jane's immediate instinct was to doubt that. If Senander radiated calm, this boy radiated hostility, and it came out in every move he made. He was training these others to copy his savagery too. Even while she was thinking this, a frail-looking girl with a cloud of dark hair suddenly slipped on the grass and fell in a crumpled heap, and Martin, with a sharp gesture which stopped the class, was beside her in a flash, bending over her with obvious concern. He helped her to her feet with such an air of gentleness that it might have been a different young man entirely. Even his face was suddenly that of someone softer, filled with kindness and anxiety.

Perhaps his guru had a point after all.

And perhaps it was also true that membership of a cult was better than being left uncared for on the streets. Jane had been wondering about that. It was a philosophical problem, because would that also apply whatever the cult's disciplines and beliefs? The rigour of the martial arts class bothered her, with its air of training for a private army. And yet Senander himself claimed a belief in peace.

'We'll go back indoors and I'll offer you some herb tea while you see if there are any other questions you want to ask.' His touch on her arm was moving her on again. As they went out of sight of the class, he said conversationally, 'You're right, of course, some people would find it a moot point whether dressing the young in robes and encouraging them to follow the disciplines of some weird religion is any healthier than letting them sleep in cardboard boxes. That was what you were wondering, wasn't it?'

There was a distinct gleam of humour in the intelligent grey eyes which met Jane's as she turned her head. It made her bite back a polite disclaimer, and say instead, 'Do you always read minds?'

'No, just body language.'

'Without wishing to be rude, it's a question anyone might ask, isn't it?'

'Sure. I could ask it myself. I'm not so interested in

theory, though, more in what works. If it weren't for the fact that this does, I could go and sit on a mountain somewhere and be a contemplative. It would definitely be easier.' He looked at her with that steady, direct gaze again, a half-smile on his mouth. 'Sometimes I'm not even sure why I took it on. Perhaps because . . . if you discover a belief system, it's only fair to share it. Or because I know an empty world is a very cold place, and holds too many wrong turnings you can take.'

They had come all the way round to the front door again, and he produced a key to let them in. As they started to cross the hall, Jane began, 'How did you—' She stopped speaking as one of the closed doors suddenly opened and a man came through it, in dark business trousers and shirtsleeves. He came to an abrupt halt, looking disconcerted and slightly annoyed. Beyond him, to her extreme surprise, Jane could see what appeared to be a thoroughly modern office and the grey metallic gleam of a bank of computers.

The sight of the two figures in the hall seemed to change his mind about wherever he had been going; he cast them one irritated look, then turned on his heel and went back into the office. The door closed behind him.

'Who was that?'

'Our landlord. He only needed a couple of rooms and the flat above, that's why he let us have the rest. We make a point of not getting in each other's way, but it does have the advantage that he pays the electricity bills,' Senander said with extreme tranquillity. He added, 'To some people I suppose a computer's another sort of god. Something to be served night and day, anyway. They have something to do with data processing, I believe.'

Jane might have said it was an odd co-existence – even if A1 Data Commerce, apparently still here after all, did pay the electricity bills – but they were interrupted once more, this time by one of the acolytes. It was the limping Erik again, as breathless as ever. He came to a stop directly in front of them with that same respectful bob of the head.

'Baba, I apologise for interrupt. Kelly feels sick again, very bad. She goes to lie down upstairs. May you come?'

'Poor child, does she? All right, go and tell her I'll come in a few moments.'

Erik went away. Jane looked up curiously at the tall man beside her and couldn't help asking with a touch of amusement, 'You're nurse as well?'

'If it's required of me. I'm sorry, I'm afraid I'll have to draw our meeting to a close. Please come again if you feel you'd like to. Just you, though – I explained how much psychological damage the sight of police uniforms might do. But if you'd ever like to go on discussing your version of youth care as against mine . . .'

He left the sentence unfinished, and with a quizzical look in his eyes. Almost like a tease. But also, Jane thought, as if he would quite welcome a philosophical discussion. Particularly with her. That was all part of the charisma, no doubt; the ability to make whoever he was talking to feel that he found them particularly interesting. She had to force herself to remember that piece of cynicism, all the same, like pinching herself to make sure she stayed awake.

'Thank you, and thank you for your time. It was good of you to give me so much of it.'

'You're welcome. You know,' he said with a suddenly abstracted look in his eyes, 'when I first saw you I thought you might have come for healing. How did you hurt your shoulder? If you'll just stand still a minute . . .'

He raised his hands and put one each side of her shoulder, without any kind of self-consciousness, just as if it was a perfectly natural thing to do. There was a sense of warmth, a sudden feeling of concentrated heat, then he took his hands away. 'See if that's better,' he said calmly, smiled at her, and walked back to open the front door for her. 'Goodbye for now, then.'

She had to have imagined it. It had to be imagination that her shoulder wasn't nagging any more too. Or maybe it was a kind of hypnotism. But he had admitted he read body language, and she had probably been carrying her shoulder with a slight unease . . . Now that the door had closed between them, she felt like shaking her head to cast off a spell. A guru with a box of magic tricks? And she, a trained police officer, taken in by them? That was thoroughly out of order.

On a personal level, she liked him. It would have been difficult not to. He was quite extraordinarily charismatic.

On a professional level she had found out what she wanted to know about the Spiritual Light Community, had been given answers to whatever she cared to ask with complete openness and could keep an eye on them. That was all that really mattered.

With that thought, Jane took herself back to her car and drove with deliberate steadiness back to the city. It was, actually, foolish of her to feel so unsettled by something he had done as naturally as breathing. There were people, so she had read, who could heal merely by touch. The idea simply made her uncomfortable, that was all. And inclined to a bout of self-mockery. She had been told her shoulder would feel better and that was why she couldn't feel it any more. There was no more to it than that. She was in no way taken in by what had probably been a deliberate demonstration.

She could pass the word to Chris Hollings that it seemed highly unlikely anyone at the Spiritual Light Community would have seen anything connected with the murder. Situated where they were, happenings at the far end of the village would be right out of their ken.

She swept into the police station forecourt and immediately forgot everything else. A very familiar, slender, dark-skinned figure was just emerging from the station's front entrance. Jane let out of crow of delight and slammed on her brakes.

Matty Ingle was beside her by the time she had wound her window down, and greeted her with a dancing smile.

'Well now, I've just left a message for you – Inspector!'

'Don't complain because I didn't tell you, I've been trying to make contact for yonks! What are you doing here? And,' Jane uttered accusingly, but with no attempt to stop a grin of her own spreading across her face, 'whatever happened to that phone call you gave advance notice of and then never made?'

Chapter 6

'I decided surprise in person was better after all. I came by to see if there was any chance you might be free to come out for lunch. I don't suppose you are?'

'Yes, I could be. What time is it now – half past twelve? Hold on a minute while I park, and then you can come back in with me while I check what time I need to be back.'

'I'll wait out here, or you'll have to attach one of your labels on me before you can let me in to your inner sanctums,' Matty said. 'Inspector Perry no less! Congratulations. Be quick, then you can tell me when you made it, and how, and all about it.'

'I will. Don't go away.'

Matty, turning up out of the blue. And how long was she here for? What was it, just a visit to her old stamping ground? Jane made haste, saw gladly that nothing had appeared in her in-tray which would prevent an extended lunch hour, and was soon back with her friend. Before long they had traversed the couple of corners which took them round to the Sea Rose and were ensconced in its back half where an added conservatory had been turned into a bistro with white wrought-iron tables and chairs and blue-checked tablecloths. It was pleasantly quiet with plenty of space between the tables. On the way, Matty had insisted on hearing about Jane's promotion before anything else could be talked about. Putting down the tomato juice she had collected from the pub bar on her way past, Jane completed the story.

'So I suppose you could say it kind of fell in my lap. I couldn't really turn it down when it was offered. Your turn! What's brought you? The sudden desire to visit?'

'A job. Temporary attachment, anyway, a kind of completion of training. It was here or Sheffield, so here was where I chose. I decided to switch fields. So, what I'm going into now is forensic pathology. Don't gape. It's actually no worse cutting up dead ones than trying to mend live ones. And you probably don't know but I did do a course in forensics at the end of my medical training before I decided to go into straight surgery, and then neurosurgery.'

'Sorry, did I look startled? It's just such a switch.'

'Not really. It seemed pretty logical to me. I seemed to be trapped in endless accident work, and there really wasn't any promotion going—' Matty broke off as a waitress appeared beside them, and the next few moments were taken up in choosing what they wanted to eat from a selection chalked up on a blackboard on the wall. Matty opted for vegetarian lasagne and Jane for something which called itself Chinese ribs with dim-sum. 'Well, anyway, there it is. I did a refresher course, and this attachment will render me full-blown. Here was just a piece of luck. You've got a Dr Ledyard who's taking maternity leave.'

'So you'll be working for her boss? He's a bit of a curmudgeon. At least I was always glad when it was Ruth

Ledyard I had to deal with rather than him!'

Matty had been delivering her news with a very good imitation of normality, and now she responded cheerfully that she'd worked for snappy bosses before. But something was wrong, and Jane had known it even before they sat down. They had been friends for too many years. It felt like something more than the decision to make a change of job, too. Once you really looked at her, there was a lack of glow in the clear dark skin, an extinguished look in the beautiful brown eyes. When Jane had seen her a few months ago she had looked so happy.

'We're both into a change of direction then,' Jane commented. She added with careful casualness, 'What do you plan to do while you're on this attachment? Whiz back up to London for weekends? How is Steve, anyway?'

'He's fine. And Adrian? I really am looking forward to meeting him.'

'He's fine too. Listen, while you're working down here, do you want to stay with us? Our spare room's not enormous, but you're very welcome to it.'

'I've already got digs, thanks. They were found for me, and I certainly wouldn't want to overcrowd you. When I'm due to be here for three months, that wouldn't be fair.' Matty gave a determined smile. 'Come on, tell me some more about Adrian, now I've broken my news to you. And some more about this community liaison job of yours. Are you liking it? Is it turning out well? I'm really pleased for you, and it's about time they gave you a boost up after missing the last one.'

It was no good. Matty might not want to be asked, but

Jane was going to do it anyway. 'Honey, what's wrong? It's no good telling me nothing is. This is me, remember? So what is it? Steve? You've had a fight? He doesn't like your coming away to do this job?'

The waitress had to arrive with their food at that moment and force a hiatus. There was silence for a moment after she had left. Matty picked up her fork, put it down again, then gave a small sigh. Words came out of her like a dam breaking.

'You know what? I didn't tell him I was doing the refresher course. Or that I was thinking of switching to pathology. I wanted to see if it looked possible first. I had some crazy notion that it would be a good idea for us to be involved in – in the same sort of area, police work, forensic pathology. I thought I'd be able to take more of a share in his life, you know? Instead of being in something completely different. It seemed,' her voice was suddenly bitter, 'like a good idea at the time!'

'And what? After you'd got as far as doing it, he didn't like the idea? Of what, you and stiffs? Anyway, if you find it interesting enough—'

'I did, as it happens. I do. And having to be away for a bit, that didn't seem insurmountable, we'd always said that if something came up for me, one or other of us could always commute.' She sighed again, and her mouth twisted. 'But what happened when I told him this was something different. Shall I tell you what the first thing he said was?'

'Go on.'

'It was, "You're going to be a police pathologist? Why? So you can keep an eye on me? Who's been telling tales?"'

'Christ. What— Did you find out what he meant?'

'Oh yes. He could hardly not tell me after that defensive reaction. Not difficult to guess, either, is it?'

'A girl?' Jane hazarded, carefully.

Matty gave a bitter nod. 'One of the WPCs at his station. We hadn't mixed with his crowd much. I'd met one or two of them briefly but our lives hadn't – hadn't really coincided. We were always too busy just finding time to be together. It never occurred to me that he was actually keeping me away.' Matty's mouth twisted again. 'Anyway, this girl. They'd had something going before . . . before I came along. This time was a kind of retake, I suppose.' Her beautiful brown eyes were bleak. 'You'd have thought I might have had some clue, mightn't you? Well, I didn't. Oh, I knew he had various ex-girlfriends, and that they were round and about. I didn't know any of them were current. Or that— Anyway. That's it.'

'What did he say about it?'

'He spent quite a lot of time trying to persuade me that she just wasn't important. That yes, he'd slept with her, but it was only casual. A quick fuck in passing for old time's sake, as you might say. It didn't make any difference to *us*, he was sorry, it wouldn't happen again.'

'And all that. Yeah. He probably means it, you know. Oh God, honey, I'm sorry, it must hurt like hell. But I'd thought, felt, seeing you together, that he did love you.'

'Sure. I'll even admit that he's had a lot to put up with. Yes, he has,' Matty said quickly to the denial in Jane's face. 'I didn't tell you, did I, that we had a visit from my mama? At her formidable best, playing the lady ambassadress to the hilt, and making it utterly if politely plain that she hoped he was a temporary aberration in my life.'

'Oh lord. And addressing you as Tiamat all the time, just so you'd know she was somewhat displeased with you?' Jane had met Matty's mother and knew what she could be like. Very much a scion of African nobility, very high-status, utterly charming if she chose but with the equal ability to freeze a polar bear. Even her English husband was apt to treat her with care, and there was little doubt that the United Nations department to which she was attached did likewise. 'But surely you got over that? I mean, Steve's a tough cookie, and—'

'Oh yes. We even had a good laugh about it afterwards. I suppose it might have been partly that which made me . . . Well, never mind.' Matty had been stubborn enough, and in love enough, to react by making a point of throwing her life in with police work, Jane thought, hearing what was unsaid. To show that what she had was permanent.

Only to get a kick in the teeth afterwards. *Damn* Steve Ryan! Couldn't he have been satisfied with what he had been lucky enough to win? Did he really have to fall to temptation just because there was an ex-girlfriend to hand and still willing?

'So where are you now?' she asked, looking at her friend with sympathetic eyes. 'I mean, here, at the moment, I know. But . . .'

'Is it mendable? Oh Jane, I don't know. I haven't told you the worst. *He* wouldn't have told me if he hadn't thought I'd heard something.' Matty paused, then came out with, 'This girl of Steve's is pregnant. He says she's going to have it terminated now he's told her he's not prepared to play. He says how does he know it's his anyway, even if it could be. He says mistakes happen and that I mustn't let it break us up. He says it doesn't matter!'

'Ouch.'

'We had a nonstop fight for two days. At least, nonstop every time we were both in.' Matty looked down at her plate, and at the congealing lasagne she had not so far touched, then up at Jane. 'Then we had a couple of days when we didn't speak to each other at all. I'm – I'm sorry if you were trying to ring me, I'm afraid I made a habit of unplugging the phone.'

'Honey, that's understandable. Then what?'

'After that it was time for me to come down here. Since I'd left telling him until it was all fixed.' Matty glanced up at Jane with a tiny bitter smile. 'When I sent you that card none of the – the *mess* had happened yet. So even though I got down here a couple of days ago . . . Well, today I thought I was feeling strong enough to let you know I was here. I wasn't going to tell you about—'

'Idiot!'

'It doesn't always help if people take sides. And I knew you would. Well, I've told you. But could we leave it to lie fallow?'

'Am I allowed to ask if – sorry, probably not, but I will anyway, and then shut up. Do you still love him?'

'God, how do I know? I do know you can't just switch it off. I just – don't know – if he's the person I thought I loved.'

There was a sudden film of tears across her eyes and Jane leaned forward swiftly to touch her hand. 'Okay, I'll leave it alone. I won't curse and swear and call him a rotten bastard and a ratbag.'

'Oh, you can do that! I did, to his face.' Matty was trying to smile. 'I'd like to – to leave him and the whole thing out of my thoughts for now, though. Just give me a few more days to pull myself thoroughly together and concentrate on settling in to the new job, will you? I'll feel like being more sociable then.'

'Yes, of course. As long as you remember I'm here, if ever you want me.'

'That's a promise. So, now, tell me about your life,' Matty said determinedly and with a heartbreaking air of putting everything else behind her. 'I've obviously got a lot of catching up to do. What does community liaison work cover? And do you like it? No, let's start with Adrian, because I haven't seen you since you started living together. You're all right, aren't you? You're happy?'

'Yeah. Getting used to each other. Not crashing into too many rough edges. It still feels a bit strange sometimes, and then other times it doesn't.' It wasn't the moment to say 'Come and meet him, come and see the man I love and am content with' when Matty's own love life was in such a bruised state. No wonder she had not wanted to come and stay. 'I'll tell you one thing,' Jane said with deliberate lightness and a look which invited Matty to laugh, 'if you live with a vet you become an expert on the weirdest things. Would you know how ticks feed? Or what causes bovine brucellosis? Well, there you are, you see, and I don't even have to listen to *The Archers* to be able to converse on all sorts of esoteric subjects!'

She went on to describe the multilingual committee meeting as an example of what she hoped would be an increasing part of her job; they talked a little about what Matty's digs were like, and where her pathology work was based; Jane told her about the Tissingham corpse and the difficulties it was presenting to police investigation. Then a drift into inquiring if either had heard anything of mutual friends. By the time they walked back to the police station, Steve Ryan's name had not been mentioned again. Jane looked at Matty as they paused to part on the station doorstep.

'Ring me when you feel like coming round for a meal.'

'Yes, I will. Give my love to Adrian even though I haven't met him yet.'

'It's good to see you, you know? And I've got your number, and you've got mine.'

Matty nodded and smiled. She had other people to get in touch with – friends from her time working at the hospital here – but to all of them she would have to make some smiling noncommittal answer when they inevitably asked after her London life, whether she was back here for good, what had made her decide to go in for forensic pathology after all instead of staying with neurosurgery. *Damn* Steve Ryan, Jane thought again with a burn of anger. How could he spoil what those two had had?

She went in and distracted herself by writing up a report on the Spiritual Light Community. She might just call there again some time, since she had been invited to do so. Or she might not. With their presence duly noted and their behaviour giving no apparent cause for complaint, a second visit was hardly necessary. She made a note of A1 Data Commerce's presence, though they were scarcely likely to have any relevance to any inquiries since they seemed to lead as unobtrusive a life as their spiritual neighbours. Presumably they carried on all their business by telephone or computer link. Jane's memory of the layout suggested theirs were the sealed ground-floor windows, perhaps because artificial light was better than daylight for working on VDU screens.

She reached for a telephone directory to look them up, just to complete her notes. Yes, there they were – A1 Data Commerce, Investment Brokers, Tissingham Manor, Tissingham. Two telephone numbers, the second listed slightly differently as A1 Data Commerce (D. Armistead). Senander had mentioned that they had a flat above their office, so perhaps the second number was that. Maybe D. Armistead was the man in shirtsleeves who had come out of his office and then gone back in again looking irritated. It was easy to imagine he might find it disconcerting to be reminded of his odd tenants.

It still amused Jane to think of the robed acolytes occupying one part of the house in spartan simplicity while the ultra-modern technology of the computer god, to quote Senander, hummed away to its own devotees in another small section under the same roof.

Jane flicked through to see if the Spiritual Light Community also had a telephone. She couldn't remember having seen one. Nothing was listed, and this directory was only a month old. Probably a telephone did count as more than minimum necessity. She could imagine Senander Baba saying so, calmly but with that practical and humorous glint in his eye.

She really must stop letting her thoughts drift to the man and his way of life. From the police point of view, his rescue of the young simply meant a few less to be picked up for vagrancy, so as long as they kept their noses clean, that was all that should concern her.

With that piece of firm self-instruction, she filed her notes, made out a brief memo to pass to Geoff Madox and another one to let Chris Hollings know that the Spiritual Light Community seemed as irrelevant to his inquiries as he had thought it was, and set herself to see which of the letters in her in-tray required an answer.

She had a planning meeting with Chief Inspector Lowell at four, so she would keep one eye on the clock while she composed suitable answers to be passed down to the civilian secretaries to type up for her.

And there was Matty to touch on in her thoughts. Poor love, it was a real bummer. In spite of that, it was good to have her closest friend near at hand again.

Chapter 7

'We thought we might have a lead with a report from Gillingham that they've had some kind of gang vendetta going on up there. The gangs concerned turned out to be Chinese, though, and Dr Kremer is quite sure our victim isn't of Asian origin.'

It was Rachel Welsh who was Jane's informant this time. The WDC had worked with Jane in the past and seemed unsurprised that she was taking an interest. 'Definitely a Caucasian corpse, according to him,' she went on. 'Forensics thought the suit was Italian, but that doesn't make a lot of difference when you can buy Italian suits over here. Then we hoped we had another lead when a woman in Leyford, one of the nearby villages, reported her husband missing and the time seemed about right – and he had previous, too, though it was fairly minor. But he turned up again, to fetch his clothes and tell her he was going off to live with another woman. So that was another possibility out.'

'You just don't seem to be winning. No doubt you've had the usual confessions?' There were always some when a case had received wide publicity, and Rachel's resigned nod showed that they were the usual, uninformed or attention-seeking or simply pathetic. 'It's still the DI's thinking that it's most likely to be someone with criminal connections?'

'Everything does seem to suggest it.' There was no need to state the reasons behind the supposition, one of which must be that removal of the hands indicated the victim's prints were likely to be on file somewhere. Rachel pulled a wry face. 'We can't know for sure, though we've put the word out via Central Records in case some other force happens to have noticed one of their villains is conspicuous by his absence. Our man had his appendix out twenty years or so ago – that's a great clue to identity, isn't it? – and he's got a mole on one knee. That's still all we know. And that nobody in Tissingham saw any strangers, of any sort, at any time. Well, aside from the old man in the cottages at the far end of the village, anyway, but he's fairly gaga and seems to see strangers everywhere.'

'I thought it was an old woman with a story about hearing people fighting.'

'That's a different one. We've got that one filed in case it turns out to be relevant. No, this was a very old man at the opposite end of the village, who whispered in my ear with great secrecy that he sees men in suits going in and out through the manor gates opposite his house. And since that's—'

'Yes, I know. You must mean old Mr Baines. He probably could have seen a man in a suit going in, actually. There's a small computer company running what seems to be a perfectly respectable business in one corner of the manor. So it could have been one of their clients, or even the guy who runs it.' Jane gave Rachel a grin. 'Yes, it does seem an odd mixture, doesn't it? The computer company bought the manor a couple of years ago and I suppose subletting seemed practical, since it's so big. And maybe nobody else came up with an offer.' She added, 'So it was you, was it, who was the pretty young lady Mr Baines kept asking me about, wanting to know when you were coming back?'

Rachel gave a rueful grin. 'He thought I was the health visitor most of the time I was there, even though I tried to explain to him several times that I wasn't. He kept wanting to take me up to his bedroom, too. No, it's unfair to laugh, he really could do with someone to look after him instead of being left there with his mind wandering. According to his neighbour, who's rather a scathing lady, he talks a lot of nonsense and spends all his time imagining things.'

'It must be frustrating that nobody in the village could offer anything helpful. It's not your average straightforward murder, is it?' Jane gave Rachel another smile and prepared to move on up the stairs on which they had met. 'And now you've got all the usual burglaries etcetera to catch up on, so I'd better not keep you. Which is top of the list this month, car break-ins or office premises?'

'Running neck and neck. But I'm still not sorry I got into CID, ma'am, rather than the DVU!' Rachel gave a cheerful grin as she went on her way.

Jane could remember a past occasion when the young WPC had shared her ambitions to get into the detective side, and Jane had encouraged her, telling her that she herself wouldn't want to do anything else, despite the difficulties. If she had got DI instead of being pipped at the post by Chris

Hollings . . . She closed her mind down on that. It was the past.

At dinner with the Hollingses a few nights ago, there had been no chance of a lapse into police shop-talk. Another couple had been invited too and five different professions had been represented among the six of them. Adrian's job had received more focus, in fact, because Elizabeth Hollings was the possessor of an endearingly lolloping Labrador which had recently come out of quarantine and the other two guests had a young child who was determined to own a mynah bird. This pair, a graphic designer married to a solicitor, were very pleasant. It had been a surprisingly enjoyable evening. They had come back feeling mellow, feeling like a couple. Jane had given Adrian a loving grin as they came into the house, saying, 'You were very patient about having your brains picked.'

'Goes with the territory. That was an enchanting blonde, anyway – and before you throw something at me, I mean the canine variety!'

'He was certainly a lot nicer than the last dog called Hector I met.' Jane gave him a serene look to prove that she had never had any intention of rising to the bait. 'I liked both the Moretons, didn't you? And Chris is really quite human when you're not working for him,' Jane added, half on a yawn and half on a chuckle. 'He's clearly less of a management freak when he's at home. I wonder if the new DS got picked for an ability to talk about psychological profiling in staffing. I'll bet he—'

'Do you have to start wondering what CID's up to even at this time of night? At least your ex-boss is better at leaving police work behind him when he gets home than you are.'

'Hey, wait a minute, that was supposed to be a joke!'

'Or a gripe? A touch of green-eyed envy because someone else is still there at the sharp end and you're not?'

'I didn't take him on one side and ask him how the murder case was going, did I? You know something, you get aggressive when you drink. Even when it's only a few glasses of wine.' It had been accepted that one out of each couple, in this case her, would stick to soft drinks in the interests of driving home. One thing about dining with the police, such things were taken as automatic. 'And I was *not* griping!'

'All right then. You just . . . Oh, come here and let's not start a quarrel. I thought you were getting one of your wistful fits, that's all,' he said, cuddling her. 'You and your awful addiction to crime. You've been like a cat on hot bricks ever since you discovered that body.'

'No I haven't. Adrian, don't you dare start tickling me!' But there seemed no point in protesting that he was being unfair, and that he was the one who had seemed inclined to start a sudden spat when he was making it plain he had quite another sort of body in mind . . . It was much easier to let herself be distracted. And definitely preferable.

It was a lot later when she found herself remembering Matty, and turned sleepily against his shoulder to ask, 'Would your mother approve of me, do you think?'

'Not in the least.'

'Why?'

'Because you're not shaped like a bolster, and you're not a nice quiet Methodist girl, and you don't walk two paces behind me saying "Yes Adrian, no Adrian". Or make cakes or cook Sunday roasts with all the trimmings and heavy enough to glue me to my chair.'

'Ah.'

'But I take after one of my uncles whose tastes are quite different.'

'Just as well.'

'Yes, isn't it?' She felt his ribs move on a drowsy chuckle, and the light touch of his lips on her forehead. 'Goodnight, love. If you've got any more gnomic questions, save them till morning.'

Two nights later Matty came round for a meal. Jane had primed Adrian not to ask after Steve, though she had shared no details, merely giving him the warning. Perhaps because of that it had turned into another evening where any discussion of police work was avoided. It was interesting and, Jane had to admit to herself, even slightly satisfying to find that Adrian showed no sign of reacting to Matty's undoubted beauty in the way most men did, with an instinctively fascinated attention. He had simply greeted her with one of the pleasant smiles which lit his serious face, and each of them had appeared to find the other likeable.

Things had broken up fairly early, but only because Matty had a 7 a.m. start the next morning. She added the wry comment that Dr Kremer seemed addicted to early hours, and yes, he was as curmudgeonly as Jane had warned. On the other hand she was learning a lot and finding the job absorbing.

And today Felicity Rathbone was arriving, Jane remembered, glancing at her calendar as she came into her office. Gloomy Trevor would be on his way, the new partner would take his place. That would keep Adrian thoroughly busy for a while. It should also cut down the risk of his noticing if she absent-mindedly let fall something to show she was still taking an interest in the Tissingham murder. He did seem to be thoroughly out of sympathy with the idea. Well, she would just have to hold her tongue and keep her own counsel. She could hardly think about nothing but the public relations side of policing, for goodness sake! Murder was murder, with its own intrigue, its own sinister puzzle to be solved. And she had been in at the start of this case.

Later that morning she found she was going to have to forget it in favour of a different kind of puzzle. There was a tenuous connection, but only because of the Musthill family.

Superintendent Annerley sent for her. He greeted her with great amiability and addressed her by her first name, and as she was ushered to one of the low chairs which encircled a coffee table in one corner of his office, she saw that this was a private meeting.

'Miss Anna Musthill has been to see me,' he began. 'She asked to see me personally. I believe you met her at the Musthill funeral.'

'Yes, sir. She was the one who stopped the burial continuing, and I assured her that her father's suicide had been properly looked into.'

'Yes, I remember, it was in your report. Her query now is about something else. A matter concerning her father's company, in fact. That's the builders, Musthills – or Musthill and Pemberton as they're officially called nowadays. You know of them?'

'Yes, sir. They do quite a lot of local contracts, don't they? I've seen their board up in several places.'

'Quite. Miss Musthill told me she's a trained accountant, though she's been working abroad. She's staying here at the moment for the settlement of her father's estate. Recently she decided to go into Musthills and have a look through the company's books to see how things stand before they call in the auditors for probate.'

'And there was a problem?' Jane inquired as he paused.

'She thought so.' He had the air of someone who was picking his words carefully as he went on. 'She seems to have felt it necessary to look for anything that might present an anomaly. Going through the general accounts, she noticed certain payouts which seemed to her to be insufficiently explained. They were variable, but amounted to something between five and ten thousand pounds a time. What struck her most – and please be clear that I'm saying this confidentially – was that each time, the payouts coincided with Musthills having been awarded a building contract by the council.'

Jane's lips formed a silent whistle. Someone at the council offices taking a kickback? It could certainly sound like it. 'Did she query it with the chief accountant? In case there was some other explanation?'

'The chief accountant happens to be away at present. She was called off in a hurry to nurse a sick relative, apparently. Neville Pemberton, the surviving partner, is also away, on a buying trip. Miss Musthill tells me that apart from making general and quite normal inquiries, she didn't raise the subject of what she had found with anybody. Instead she thought about it, and then came to me.'

Jane looked puzzled. Why was he telling her? It was surely a CID matter if there might be a case of corruption. She had, of course, been involved in a fraud investigation last year . . . The super was clearing his throat preparatory to going on.

'Miss Musthill is extremely unwilling to think that her father's name might be blackened by any unnecessary suspicion about the company. I quite agree with her on that. The man is dead after all and can't answer any accusations. It's not only Richard Musthill's reputation which is on the line either, so this is something which needs a high degree of confidentiality. That's why I felt you might be in a position to handle it. We need to use discretion. In your present post—'

'Excuse me, sir, but,' Jane found she was sitting up a little straighter, 'it's scarcely a community relations matter, is it?'

'In this case I think it is. Miss Musthill stressed that she's sure her father wouldn't have countenanced anything illicit. That may be so or it may not.' He tapped a finger on the desk, looking at Jane thoughtfully. 'I've told Miss Musthill that I intend to put a trustworthy officer in charge of it, and that she will have to give us time to make proper investigations. Also that she will have to be satisfied with our findings. And this is where you come in.'

Jane felt the quiver of a very nasty suspicion beginning to take concrete form in her mind. What was he suggesting? That they had to investigate it because Miss Musthill had drawn it to his attention, but that 'discretion' was going to take the form of a private rap over the knuckles, a confidential warning to someone high up in council employ, to avoid scandal? And she was to perform a smoothing-over operation on Anna Musthill? Unwilling as she was to think so, Superintendent Annerley undoubtedly belonged to the same clubs as some of the city's senior administrators. Jane swallowed, and spoke levelly, trying to make it sound like an innocent enquiry. 'If Miss Musthill's sure of her facts, sir, we can hardly do a cover-up, can we?'

'Certainly not, and if you thought that was what I was suggesting, I'd have expected better from you!' The sudden frost which appeared in his eyes was daunting, even if it was also a relief. Jane opened her mouth to make a quick apology, but he was speaking again with a distinct touch of acid in his voice. 'While I'm used to the public leaping to the conclusion that all sorts of things go on under the guise of Masonic handshakes, I do not expect it from my officers!'

'No, sir, sorry, and of course I didn't assume—'

'I trust not.' Something in his look suggested she should have granted him the intelligence not to choose an officer with her record if that was what he had in mind, and that was at least comforting. He gave her one further level look, and then went on, resuming his factual air. 'I'll explain my thinking. You and I both know that you're a former CID officer with the capacity for discretion and the ability to work on your own. However, as far as the public knows, you're a newcomer to the post of community liaison officer and might well want to acquaint yourself with everything about the city, including the workings of the council. This puts you in the position of being able to ask a lot of questions without it appearing that there might be any criminal investigation involved.'

'Yes, I see, sir.'

'While familiarising yourself with the workings of the council, you can be looking to see who awards building contracts and how this is done. You should be able to elicit that simply by showing an interest. Your questions will appear to be entirely innocent, but by the time you've finished we should be able to see who would be in a position to be taking bribes in exchange for fixing council contracts. I don't expect you to be able to tell me who is, only who could be. Then, and only then, can we go further.'

'Yes, I see. You want me to show where to look without warning the guilty party off.' It made sense: if they started investigations immediately from the Musthills' end, too many people would be aware of it. 'You want me to report directly to you, sir?' Jane asked.

'Yes. I want complete discretion on this one for the time being – nothing, even casually, which could cause talk. I'll even ask that you type the reports out yourself without involving the secretarial staff. If there is or has been corruption, I want all the facts and possibilities to be thoroughly in our hands before we make any move, and before anyone has the least suspicion which could make them cover their tracks.' He added, 'Miss Musthill stressed that she has been completely discreet herself.'

'If she's right,' Jane said thoughtfully, 'and if somebody at Musthills has been offering bribes in exchange for contracts, is it recent? Surely if she could spot something odd in the accounts it would have shown up in the firm's usual audit?'

'She thought it might not. She's something of an expert and was particularly looking for anomalies.'

Had she been searching again for some reason for her father's death? Somebody cheating him, perhaps, or something he might have discovered to send him into an honourable despair? Or even to give a reason why he had needed to be removed? No, whatever Anna Musthill might think, it had certainly been suicide.

'I'd like you to have a meeting with Miss Musthill first of all,' the Super said, breaking into Jane's thoughts. 'She's agreed both to co-operate and to leave any further investigations to us. She's staying at her sister's home in Tissingham and I suggest you go to see her there. In fact I'll telephone her myself and set up an appointment. Tomorrow morning?'

'Fine, sir.' As far as Jane could remember there was nothing vital in her diary for tomorrow, and if there was, it could certainly be rearranged. 'Does Chief Inspector Lowell know that—'

'That I'm borrowing you? No. I want this to remain strictly between you and me for now. I'll tell him simply that I've suggested a particular course of action for you as an introduction to your job, as something which occurred to me. Now, is there anything else you want to ask before we close?'

'I don't think so, sir, thank you.'

'Good, then I'll leave all the other details to you.'

So she was now to be on a private CID assignment for

the super, providing him with inside information on how the city council was run. And who might be in a position to be corrupt. That was a turn-up for the book, Jane thought as she closed the super's office door behind her.

The Musthill family really was having a time-and-a-half of bad luck at the moment. A suicide, a disturbed burial and now the possibility that the family company had been involved in offering bribes.

If Anna Musthill's conclusions were right, she was stirring up yet another hornet's nest. And it was ironic that everything, somehow, seemed to be stemming from Tissingham at the moment. For a village which had never entered Jane's consciousness in any particular way until recently, it was now doing a good job at getting itself clearly marked on her mental map. And in all sorts of unconnected ways. You could almost think that the place had suddenly got itself jinxed.

Chapter 8

As Jane drove out yet again to Tissingham the following morning, she had no need to speculate on where she would find the Benbridge house. The address was 'The Laurels, The Street'. That must put them somewhere near Mrs Parrot and her pack of little dogs.

Not too near, as it turned out. The Laurels was a good quarter of a mile further on and its gateway appeared just as Jane was beginning to think she must have missed it. The Street had turned into a winding lane which appeared to be heading on to Seldene and then Leyford. Turning in at the open gate, Jane saw that the high hedges had concealed a good spread of garden with a large, solidly built and attractively designed bungalow in the middle of it. Further back there was the glimpse of a stream running through one corner of the garden, and rough grass with fruit trees, some of them in a froth of pale pink blossom. The bungalow itself was long and low and plainly modern, under a dark roof, with big plate-glass windows and a large double garage as an integral part of the design. If you were the daughter of a builder, Jane thought as she parked on the strip of very tidy and well-kept asphalt which led to the front door, no doubt you had your house built for you to top specifications – and could choose yourself an attractive and spacious site, too.

It was Mrs Benbridge who opened the door to her. She was as tidy as her house, her hair carefully if nondescriptly curled, her clothes a neatly-tucked white blouse worn with a plain pleated skirt. Her eyes, the same light brown as her hair, were small with worry, however, and had dark lines beneath them, not entirely concealed by careful make-up. Her mouth was tight with anxiety (or disapproval?) but was attempting a civil smile as she opened the door. It was replaced by a flash of recognition and a degree of fluster.

'It's you – you're Inspector Perry! I'm sorry, I should have remembered. Please come in, Inspector. My sister and I are through in the drawing-room.'

She led the way into a wide modern room, thickly carpeted and dotted here and there with chintz-covered armchairs and a sofa. There was a big stonefaced fireplace at one end of it filled with flowers. The plate-glass windows here looked out into the garden: a lawn, burgeoning flowerbeds, a child's swing visible to one side. Anna Musthill was standing in front of the window and stepped forward with hand outstretched, after a brief moment when she, too, showed a flash of recognition.

'Inspector Perry? Oh, you're that one. I remember you.' Her handshake was brief but firm and her eyes summed Jane up rapidly. There was that same feeling of likeness but difference between the sisters which Jane remembered noticing at the funeral; a similarity of features, but Anna Musthill's delineated more sharply. They offered a contrast in manner, too. Miss Musthill's was harder and more brisk, and she was dressed in casual trousers and a shirt again, with an air of caring little what she wore. Her hair was shorter and slightly darker than her sister's and definitely more untidy, and her hands were ringless, tanned, and with the nails cut very short. 'Sit down,' she invited brusquely, 'and I'll go through the facts with you which I explained to your superintendent.'

'Would you like some coffee, Inspector? It doesn't seem to occur to my sister that one should start with the civilities!'

There was a fair crackle of hostility in that. 'I'd be very grateful for a cup of coffee, if it wouldn't be too much trouble,' Jane told Mrs Benbridge pleasantly.

'Of course not. Please sit down, it won't take me a moment. And don't start, Anna, until I come back!'

Jane seated herself in one of the armchairs, heavily stuffed and very comfortable. Anna Musthill opened and closed her left hand as if it might be stiff, or as if restlessness required some movement. After several moments of silence she said, her voice a tone deeper than her sister's, 'Do you smoke? No? Probably just as well, since I've given up and Heather doesn't like smoke in the house. We've got the place to ourselves, anyway; both the children are at school and Donald, my sister's husband, is at work. He's a personnel manager with Barnett's.'

'Your sister has two children?' Jane asked politely,

'Yes. Sarah's fifteen – you saw her – and Anthony's eight. He wasn't at the funeral. Heather thought it would upset him too much.'

'It must have upset all of you. Has Sarah recovered from her distress by now?'

'She's still fairly moody, but the drama's getting the better of the— Oh good, if the suitable refreshment's arrived, perhaps we can start!'

That held distinct sarcasm, and caused Heather Benbridge to cast her sister a tight-lipped look as she put down a tray containing a silver coffee pot, matching cream jug and bowl, cups, and a small plate of biscuits. A smaller occasional table was pulled out with deliberate formality to be placed beside Jane's chair and she had to face an elaborate inquiry as to how she liked her coffee.

It had to be with intent to annoy or upset that Anna interrupted with, 'We were making conversation about Father's funeral, Heather.'

'We had a – a very pleasant cremation service,' Heather Benbridge told Jane stiffly. 'It seemed the best thing to do when— You're sure you won't have cream, Inspector?'

'I prefer it black, thank you. Yes, that's fine. I'm sorry you had such a distressing time,' Jane said, offering it with genuine sympathy since some comment was clearly required of her. Had these two always disliked each other, or was it merely the circumstances? She was framing some tactful way of moving the conversation firmly over to the reason why she was here when Heather Benbridge did it for her, with an abrupt and angry tide of colour sweeping up her face to render even her forehead bright pink.

'I think you ought to know, Inspector, that I don't agree at all with what my sister's doing. That the police should be called in on this – this assumption she insists on making! As if things aren't quite bad enough without— No, Anna, I will have my say! It just isn't necessary to stir up a whole lot of extra trouble. You're probably wrong, anyway. Daddy wouldn't *ever*—'

'No, he wouldn't, but what if he found out about it afterwards? What if that's what made him—'

'He was *depressed*, everyone's told you! I – we – everyone thought he'd get over it in time, that it was just normal grieving, and he had his pills . . . We all did what we could. Except you, of course, you weren't here, just like you weren't here when Mummy was ill, leaving it all to me, as usual. Not even because of your important job this time,' Heather Benbridge said on a sneer, the bit well between her teeth. 'Just because you'd decided you were entitled to take a year off and go exploring.'

'You didn't write and ask me to come home, did you? Or tell me how bad things were for him. Just like you didn't tell me exactly how ill Mother was until it was too late, you just made out you thought I'd know, that Daddy would have written and told me.' Both of them seemed to have decided to use Jane very thoroughly as audience, and she was being given no chance to interrupt. 'And this time he was that depressed and you never even noticed? If he was really so bad, if he was down that far, how come his good little stay-at-home daughter didn't see it? Didn't you have time?'

'We had him to lunch every Sunday. And I used to ring him up, and he always said he was fine, that I wasn't to worry about him. Anyway I do have a husband and children to look after.' Heather Benbridge was scarlet with fury by now, and her small neat hands had curled into claws, as if she might forget adulthood and launch herself at her sister physically. 'You've always thought you could be as selfish as you liked, just because you were the clever one who went to university and got good jobs and had the chance to go abroad. And now,' she spat out, 'it's supposed to be clever of you to think you've found out something to show Musthills is dishonest, so you go to the police with it and don't give a damn what it does to all of us!'

With that she leapt up and ran out of the room. Anna Musthill, though as pale as her sister had been red, seemed more able to reach for control, and she swallowed hard, then looked at Jane with a tight apology.

'I'm sorry. My fault. I shouldn't have needled her, but we always have. Ever since she was four to my six. It doesn't seem to have changed, even though I've just reached the big four-oh.' She swallowed again and ran a hand through her hair to leave it untidier than ever. 'You probably – oh well, never mind. I couldn't *not* go to the police, could I? I mean, it's my job, looking for fraud.'

'Is it?'

'Yes. I work for the IRS in the States. Have done for five years, though at the moment I've taken a year's sabbatical.' She sighed, glanced towards the door, then looked at Jane again. 'Heather said she wanted to be here when I talked to you, but perhaps she doesn't. I'll start anyway. I went into the office to ask to look through the books. I didn't see Neville – Father's partner, Neville Pemberton – because he's away, but everyone else took it as a natural request. I say "the books" but the main accounts are computerised, of course,' she added. 'But I'm used to that.'

'And?' Jane prompted as she paused.

'I went through everything thoroughly. All the main

accounts, then the back-up ledgers. Then I started checking contract dates.' Anna drew a breath. 'I'd noticed some – oddities in the accounts. Insufficiently explained payments out. I found they all coincided with the award of council contracts.'

'Exactly?' Jane asked.

'Yes. One I could have taken as coincidence, but all of them—' She broke off, then resumed, her face grim. 'Each of the entries I'd mentally queried showed up just after Musthills had gained a good solid contract from the council. The conclusion seemed unmistakable, once I'd seen it. It had happened four times, going back over a period of two and a half years. The last one was two months ago, which – which would be not long before my father died.'

'Yes, I see,' Jane said into the pause. She glanced at the other woman's face. 'Did your father have much to do with the accounts?'

'No. Well, not normally. I don't think he'd have gone through them without a reason.' Anna said that a little as if the admission was like having a tooth drawn. 'But neither would he have been involved in anything dishonest, if you were about to ask.'

'I wasn't.'

'The accounts were all signed as having gone through an annual audit. The firm of auditors, which is one Musthills have used since the year dot, didn't find fault with anything. But general auditors don't always spot . . . Well, particularly not when it's a company they know, and they're all old friends with each other. And it's the type of thing I'm trained to look out for.' Her mouth twisted and she opened it to go on, but at that moment Heather Benbridge came back into the room.

Her colour had gone back to normal, and if there was a pinched look to her nostrils, she had herself stiffly in hand. She avoided her sister's eyes, glanced at Jane and then away again, and sat down wordlessly, if with an air of distasteful disapproval.

'As I was saying, I'm used to looking out for entries which could be doubtful,' Anna went on, after a brief glance at her sister. 'At first I thought I'd possibly struck some petty pilfering, someone with their hand in the till. But once I started comparing dates . . . I've made out a list for you.'

She passed a sheet of paper across to Jane and leaned over to point an indicative finger. 'Those are the payments. Those are the dates. And those, the dates when contracts were granted.'

'And all of them were work for the council?'

'Yes.'

'How are the council contracts awarded? On the lowest bid?'

'Yes, and by a sealed tender. In an area like this Musthills would know who their competitors were – who's on a tender list is probably common knowledge – but no firm's going to tell another what they're going to bid, naturally. The building trade's a highly competitive business. And you can't risk trying to undercut too far or you'd lose your profit margin. So making the calculations is a risky business. Usually.' Anna was trying very hard to sound objective, though the last word came out with a grim edge. 'Musthills has in fact been doing rather well out of council contracts lately—'

'And gets them because they're a local company with a good reputation,' Heather Benbridge put in sharply, 'not to mention being experienced enough to be able to cost economically.'

'Did you ever work for your father, Mrs Benbridge?' Jane asked politely, trying to ignore the glare she was being offered.

'I did when I first left school. It wasn't very easy though, being the boss's daughter as well as a secretary, so I moved after a year and took a job at Barnett's instead. The agricultural machinery people. I met my husband there.' Heather's expression was tight and she glanced across at her sister, then her eyes came back to Jane and she spoke stiffly. 'I'm certain Anna's mistaken, Inspector, and there's no need for all this.'

'I'm not mistaken. Don't you listen, Heather? I've told you, if anything's been going on, it's all in the three years since Dad took Neville Pemberton on as a partner. You've got no reason to defend *him*, have you? You said yourself you've never liked him. And,' Anna swung round on Jane with angry passion, 'one thing Heather seems to be ignoring is that Neville's been pestering her to sell our share of the firm to him. He started making offers as soon as Father died. He was positively pushing Heather to sell, she told me so, saying that he'd give us a good price, even a bit above market value for a quick sale. And that if we had a lump sum it would be much easier and quicker than having a share of the business assessed for capital transfer tax. And even that Father had promised to make the whole business over to him when he retired, and that as he hadn't been taking much interest, it was Neville's right—' Anna swallowed. 'It seems clear enough to me that he needed to get the whole thing into his hands so that nobody else would look closely.'

'You've got no proof of that.'

'How much more do we need? And this is why we have to call the police in, to nail him. To make sure *his* reputation goes down the tubes, and not Musthills'. I'm damned if I'm going to let him get away with it, even if you want to. When Dad founded that firm and built it up—'

'He would have hated anything that tarnished the firm's reputation. You just don't think, do you? There's the rest of us to think of, Donald, Anthony.' Heather cast an angry look at her sister. 'We have to live here and be the subject of gossip and pointing fingers, you don't. I know I can't do anything about it now, when you've already gone to the police and without even consulting me about it first, but you might have considered that other people get tarred with the same brush.'

'But if the police can prove it was Neville—'

'Supposing they don't? He might have been too clever. All you'll have done then is blacken Daddy's name, and ours along with it.'

'We shan't make any accusations at all without proof,' Jane put in, trying to make her voice as reassuring as possible to stop another quarrel breaking out. 'And we may find Miss Musthill's mistaken altogether.' It certainly was interesting, however, that Neville Pemberton had been pushing to buy the sisters out. Though he might have done that anyway . . . She glanced thoughtfully at Anna. 'You say

Mr Pemberton's away at the moment? When is he expected back?'

'Nobody knows for sure. He makes regular buying trips to eastern Europe since that market's opened up, looking for cheap materials. He's off on one of those trips now – Russia and Poland, I think. I'm told he felt he had too good a chance of shaking hands on a deal to risk losing it by postponing his trip to attend the funeral,' Anna said drily. 'I'd have thought that would have raised quite a few eyebrows – in fact I gather it did, considering the lack of respect it showed. It's all very well to tell the staff that work must go on, but to leave the night before . . . He seems to have thought sending a rather flashy wreath would be enough.'

'So he wasn't there?' That meant Jane didn't have to search her memory to try to put a face to the name. It sounded as if Neville Pemberton definitely put business before sympathy. A surprising absence considering the high-powered turnout that Richard Musthill's funeral had drawn.

'It's always possible he didn't dare face Heather after what she said to him the last time he called,' Anna said, giving her sister a look which was for once approving. 'You told me, remember? That you'd sent him thoroughly to rightabouts.'

'Well, yes, I did. Anyone might have been upset by his coming round yet again pretending it was a sympathy visit, and then pestering me to sell all over again.' Heather looked oddly defensive to be reminded of the incident and added quickly, 'That was two days before the funeral.'

'Heather told him very firmly that he was the last person we'd sell to, and that she'd only communicate with him again through lawyers,' Anna explained. She gave her sister a smile which was not returned. 'That was before I arrived, of course, but I agree with her, it was the best thing to do. After all,' she went on, with a grim note creeping into her voice, 'he was the one who saw the most of Father, so if anyone should have noticed – not that Neville would care about other people's states of mind. Or not unless it was to his advantage. He's a thoroughly slimy type, and I say that even though I've only met him once. When I came over for Mother's funeral he kept putting his arm round me,' Anna added with distaste, 'though God knows why he thought I should find *that* comforting. In fact I could quite see why he's divorced. Ugh!'

'I'm wondering what Mr Pemberton's reaction is going to be when he comes back to find you've been going through the accounts,' Jane said, bringing things back to the main subject, and looking questioningly at Anna.

'He must have expected somebody would on our behalf. And I don't think he knows what my actual job is. Anyway, I took care to make it clear at Musthills that everything seemed to be satisfactory as far as I could see.' Anna cast Jane a bleak stare.

'Mr Pemberton's been away several weeks if he left just before the funeral. Is that usual?'

'Nobody seemed particularly concerned about it. He said he might go on to Sweden, apparently – something to do with finding a quarry for cheap stone near enough to a shipyard to make transportation feasible. He's in charge of the buying side, so they're used to his being away. The general manager runs the place on a day-to-day basis. Dad wasn't – wasn't particularly interested in what went on over the last few months, or so I was told . . .' For a moment Anna's face held a haunted look, the planes of her cheekbones standing out sharply.

So Neville Pemberton was in charge of the buying side. Had he also bought a council employee? Anna clearly thought so, but then it was in her interest to point the finger elsewhere than at her father. Particularly when it was Richard Musthill who was the one with known council connections, from his past as a councillor and then as mayor. It was no wonder Heather Benbridge was so resentful of her sister's actions, so upset about the idea that mud would stick. Jane glanced at her again, but Anna was going on.

'I suppose this trip of Neville's has lasted a bit longer than his usual ones,' she said, giving Jane a direct look. 'I know what you're getting at. He's out of the country after having failed to get full control of the company, but believe you me, I took care to check that there wasn't a large chunk of the firm's capital missing. There isn't. The company seems remarkably healthy, more than I thought it would be, actually.'

'I was just checking all the bases.'

'It'd be a good idea if you could do your investigations before he does come·back so that he can't start covering his tracks.' Anna gave Jane a look of appeal, though it had something vengeful in it. She was holding Neville Pemberton responsible for her father's death, Jane thought. Or desperately wanted to.

Was it actually possible that there was more behind Richard Musthill's suicide than simple depression? Had he in fact discovered he had taken on a crook as a partner but lacked the energy to fight for the firm he had founded? That was probably something they would never know. Though, on balance, it seemed unlikely that he would let his family suffer for consequences he might have prevented; and the note he had left had stated simply and specifically that he felt unable to go on without his beloved wife. It was always possible that he had known all about the bribes; was, in fact, responsible for them. Stranger things had happened with otherwise honest men.

Heather Benbridge was sitting with pursed mouth and hands folded tightly on her lap. A little too tightly, and the frown of seething frustration she was giving her sister suggested another quarrel might break out at any moment, another objection to any investigation being done at all. Jane spoke quickly to pre-empt it.

'Could you go through this list with me again, and more thoroughly?' she asked, her voice polite and deliberately practical, looking at Anna. 'Why did you find the entries suspicious in the first place?'

'Because they didn't seem to be properly covered. I should explain that, like Heather, I've worked at Musthills, though only unofficially. While I was still studying accountancy Father used to let me come in to get some experience of how company books were actually run. He let me do a practice audit one time and explained what all the entries were actually for.' She paused briefly and swallowed hard, memories of her father plainly catching her. 'It's a long time ago but things are still done much the same way, aside from everything being more thoroughly computerised. So you see I do know . . . Anyway, this one,' her finger touched one of the figures, 'was only listed as Miscellaneous Cash. That one was supposed to be Repurchase of Office Equipment but the amount didn't make sense considering there was another similar repurchase just before. This one was Hiring In but it didn't say what for, and should have done. Besides, there didn't seem to be anything going on just then that required it. And the most recent was an order for RSJs but with no sign of any having been delivered, and there's already a yard full of them, so why did they need more?'

'RSJs?'

'Sorry – rolled-steel joists. The backbone of the building trade, they're used to prop up virtually everything. I made a check with the foreman – I did it casually, so he won't have made anything out of it. He hadn't had an order in recently and he wasn't expecting one, said they'd got plenty.'

'And there was nothing to show if any one particular person had authorised those entries?'

'No, there wasn't. And I didn't want to draw attention by asking at that juncture since I'd seen a pattern in the dates by then, and Miss Rawlings, the assistant chief accountant, seems to be the gossipy type.'

'Could you explain exactly what the contracts were which coincided with the payments?'

'One's for building a park. One for old people's flats – council money, not private. One for renovation and extension to an existing hall to turn it into a leisure complex. And one refurbishment contract – that's repairs and renovations to council property. That was the most recent, which they got two months ago.' Heather stirred, her face stiff with hostility, and Anna glanced at her and spoke before she could. 'Yes, I know, it's the sort of thing they might get anyway, as good local employers. But at the same time as an apparently unnecessary order for RSJs? Be your age, Heather!'

She received no answer, her sister merely giving her another hostile look and then turning her face away. Anna went on, looking at Jane bleakly, 'The company might have got by on private work, too, in spite of the recession, instead of concentrating mainly on council contracts as they seem to have been doing over the last couple of years. And four times seems rather a lot of lucky bids. Whoever was running it seems to have been wise enough not to go for massive contracts, just reasonable sized ones. Though the refurbishment one is quite big. Anyway, that's it, Inspector. Is there anything else you want to know?'

'I think that's probably all I need from you for the moment.' Jane glanced at the list Anna had made out. 'Superintendent Annerley did explain to you, I believe, that we'll be approaching this very carefully and discreetly. It would probably be better if you don't even discuss it between yourselves.'

'It's in your hands. I'd like to know what you discover, though. I won't be leaving until I – until you finish looking into it, so you can get hold of me here.'

'We'll be in touch as soon as we have anything we can tell you.' Jane got to her feet, aware that Heather Benbridge had cast her sister a look of acute and martyred dislike on the announcement that she intended to stay for an indefinite period. Or was it just worry in the back of her eyes? 'Thank you both for your time. And thank you for the coffee, Mrs Benbridge.'

'I'll show you out.'

Heather Benbridge escorted Jane to the door. She did so without speaking, until the front step was reached when she managed a stiff, 'Goodbye, then, Inspector Perry.'

The door closed with a soft whump which suggested good insulation. Glancing briefly back at the bungalow as she unlocked her car, Jane decided that whatever else Musthills had been up to, they clearly knew how to build houses.

But the atmosphere inside was very uncomfortable. Jane found herself remembering Senander Baba's comment on families. Families which failed to function, where affection was replaced with intolerable strain.

Since she was here in Tissingham, might it not be a good chance to make a second call at the manor? And kill two birds with one stone? After all, Senander Baba did invite her to come back and discuss his methods of saving the young.

It was part of her job, after all, to know who was doing what on her patch.

Chapter 9

Sense and self-mockery had reasserted themselves before she had driven halfway back along The Street. She would simply be doing her job – oh yeah? How about being honest and admitting that she wanted to see if the man was really as charming as she remembered him? She was too interested in the charismatic Senander by half. In what made him tick. The fact was, he was immensely attractive. And she had no business to think so, nor to be so unwarily fascinated.

She pulled a face, and acknowledged that a return visit to the community was in no way a priority. Certainly not today when she had other things to think about. She slowed for the sharp right turn back into the High Street, firmly indicating that she intended to turn right, not left in the direction of the manor. Equally firmly, she turned her mind back to Musthills. The pattern Anna had seen certainly did raise the possibility of bribery. How did 'sealed tenders' actually work? Jane was hazy about that but no doubt she would learn from her investigations into the council. Some extra fact was tickling at the back of her consciousness, and as she completed her turn into the High Street it came to her what it was. She pulled to an abrupt halt beside the pavement. Was that a point which she should follow up? Should she go back and ask?

No, there was no need to return and brave Mrs Benbridge's further displeasure; one phone call to Anna Musthill from the office would answer the question she had in mind. And the possibility she had come up with might be no more than a flight of fancy anyway. Still, she would check it. That decided, she was about to resume her return to the city when the door of the village shop just ahead of her opened and a figure emerged.

That was surely Martin, the boy from the Spiritual Light Community. He was dressed in ordinary jeans and a shirt and carrying a plastic bag full of shopping, but it was unmistakably him – that profile like something from a Greek coin as he turned his head, the light, balanced walk which reminded her how gracefully if savagely he had moved when instructing the martial arts class. This was one member of the cult, then, who came out and about in the village.

He turned to walk in the opposite direction from the manor, heading away from Jane instead of directly past her. If he had been shopping for the group, he was not going straight back.

Curiosity made Jane set the car into a low gear and follow, driving very slowly. He did not glance back or to either side, but walked lightly and swiftly ahead as if aiming for a particular destination. Perhaps it was his deafness which made him look so shut up inside himself, self-absorbed, in a world of his own. He followed the pavement until it ran out abruptly where the cottages ended, and then ducked into the narrow lane on the left which led to the church.

Jane's route should have taken her on round the right-hand bend and away out of the village. Instead she waited for a moment, then followed Martin into the lane. If he did look back he would probably take her car for that of a stray tourist wanting to visit the church, which was after all an old one in typical Kentish flint with a striking peg-tiled roof. She rounded the corner to catch sight of Martin again, standing still now with his hand raised to the knocker of one of a pair of cottages that stood on their own just here, the high hedge which surrounded the churchyard directly opposite. His moody, beautiful face seemed intent on what he was doing, and as Jane stopped dead and tried to look as if she planned to make the sharp turn which would take her to the churchyard lych-gate, she saw the cottage door open and a tiny old woman appear.

Her face, clearly visible, beamed with delight at the sight of Martin. He held out the bag of shopping with a gesture, and she put out a hand to draw him inside. The door closed behind the pair of them.

A charitable act? The welcome on the old lady's face suggested it might be. Martin somehow seemed an unlikely person to be doing an old lady's shopping for her, yet the beaming smile she had given him and her drawing him inside had indicated familiarity. It would certainly be quite a long walk for that tiny old person to go to the shop herself and carry a heavy bag back. Perhaps Senander Baba had decided to use his young people in this way as a method of softening the village's feelings towards the community.

Jane swung her car and pulled up in the open space in front of the church lych-gate. Were those cottages the ones whose roofs she had seen from the churchyard on the day of the funeral? It looked as if they could be. The old lady must be Mrs Emmett then, the one Kenny Barnes had told her about. The one who claimed to have heard a fight. Curiosity made Jane decide to take a walk in the churchyard and see if those were indeed the same cottages or if there were others in a different direction. It was difficult to orient herself after just that one visit several weeks ago.

The sun caught the russet tiles of the church roof and made them glow a deep amber, speckled here and there with crimson and maroon, the whole sweeping down low above the grey flint wall. The silvery spire at one end rose in its graceful and sharply patterned curves to a tall elegant point topped by a fretted metal cross. And there were the cottages Jane had just seen, their grey slate roofs the only ones visible above the hedge.

The grave which had been intended for Richard Musthill had been filled in, she saw, though not returfed yet. A tidy rectangle of brown earth stood out against the surrounding green. If she walked on she should reach the small back gate to the churchyard which Kenny had also mentioned. There it was, barely discernible for the overhanging hedge; it opened on to the lane she had just driven down.

Turning to retrace her steps, Jane found she was no longer alone. A black cassock topped by a cheerful face was striding towards her between the headstones.

'Hello, Inspector Perry,' the Reverend Michael Mather greeted her in ringing pulpit tones. 'You weren't looking for me, by any chance? The path which would take you through to the vicarage is the other side of the church, with a rather less overgrown exit since it's used more often.'

'I wasn't planning on disturbing you, I was just passing,' Jane told him with a smile.

'You thought you'd like to take another look round and see the place in better circumstances? The church is beautiful, isn't it? We're rather proud of it. I have to admit, it was a relief when your colleagues on the detective side finished here. Such an unfortunate business. Not a very pleasant reminder for the Benbridges, who do come to church of a Sunday, so I was glad to get the place back to normal.' He offered Jane a look which invited her to share his sympathy. 'Poor Heather. It's going to be a little while, I'm afraid, before we see her back taking part in any of our village concerts.'

'Does she?' It seemed a surprising revelation about the stiffly conventional Heather Benbridge. 'I mean, you put on village concerts, do you?'

'Oh yes, we do our best – amateur dramatics. Heather and Donald are two of our stalwarts. He busies himself with hammer and saw building the sets, and also does our stage managing, and Heather has a sweet singing voice as well as being quite a good actress. She takes after her mother, I expect. Mrs Musthill was on the stage professionally when she was young, before she married. We call ourselves the Tissingham and Seldene Players,' the vicar announced with an air of satisfaction. 'You should come and see us next time we put on a show. Though please don't expect us to be West End standard,' he added with a cheerful grin. 'I'm vicar of both parishes, and it's a way of bringing everyone together.'

'You bully both villages into taking part?'

'Oh, certainly!' He accepted the answering grin Jane had given him. 'I'm also quite shameless about soliciting sponsorship in exchange for a name in our programme. I suppose the police wouldn't like to take half a page? You'd be in quite respectable company. I've got Coverhills, the department store, because one of the family lives on the edge of the village, and Rowlands, the retail butchers in the city, since Michael Rowlands is Donald Benbridge's cousin; and Barnetts, of course, and Kington's Farm Shop, and several others. But we always welcome more, and we only charge a few pounds a time. We used to carry a sponsorship advertisement for Musthills too, as a thank-you for the set-building materials Heather managed to beg through her father. I'm very sad that none of us understood how troubled he was,' he added, abruptly sober. 'I've felt I should have. Oh well, that's in the past now, poor man. He wasn't my parishioner, but one still feels responsible.'

Jane nodded sympathetically. 'You've got quite a lot of old people in the village, haven't you?' she said. 'It must mean quite a bit of community care. After some of the remarks I heard, I couldn't help being surprised to notice one of the Spiritual Light people visiting an old lady just near here. She seemed very pleased to see him, too.'

'You must mean the deaf boy. He's Mrs Emmett's grandson. He quite often fetches her shopping for her and I've seen him visiting her in the evenings occasionally too. I do wish the rest of the villagers would appreciate that there's no reason to distrust the whole group.'

'Her grandson?' Jane asked, surprised.

'Yes, she's his mother's mother, I believe. Mrs Emmett was born and raised an Independent Baptist so she won't have any truck with me as a Church of England vicar,' Michael Mather said with the glimmer of a smile. 'And she's a sparky enough old bird to let me know it! However, she does compromise her principles enough to let my wife visit her now and again. I seem to remember hearing that she said it was her daughter's boy. Mrs Emmett's very fond of him. And glad to see him again.'

'Martin originally comes from round here then?'

'Somewhere further north in Kent, I believe. You did make your visit to Senander Baba, then? We may not share the same faith, and I do take care to respect his privacy, but I found his dedication most impressive, didn't you?'

'He certainly seems very sincere.'

'We all have our different methods of service. I was on my way into the church to fetch the baptismal register,' the vicar said with an air of apology, glancing at his watch. 'I have a young mother coming to see me shortly about her baby's christening and I like to show them exactly how we do things. If there isn't anything specific I can do for you, I'd better get on, if you don't mind. But please do stay and go on looking round, if you'd like to.'

'I need to be on my way myself. I'm sorry if I've held you up.'

'Not at all, it's nice to see you. And next time we're doing one of our shows – though it won't be for quite a while, I think – I shall send you an invitation.'

Which it might well be her duty to accept, as part of police relations in the community. 'Thanks,' Jane said, looking more willing than she felt and giving him a smile. 'I'll look forward to it.'

Martin's walk through the village was explained, then. One member of his family clearly held him in affection. Perhaps Senander was right and the boy was only now learning to accept it . . .

Making her way back to her car, Jane knew that she should put the cult out of her mind. She had other things to do. Other things than wonder about Mrs Emmett's story of hearing a fight in the churchyard, too. One factor came to mind anyway: there was no need to suggest someone should ask Martin if he had been visiting his grandmother that night and could confirm her story. If there had been a fight, he would not have been able to hear it.

It was difficult to imagine Heather Benbridge performing on a village stage. It only went to show that one could always learn something new about a personality. Different times and different circumstances. Taking to the boards was perhaps her way of competing with her cleverer elder sister. Though both of them had shown a quite theatrical turn of temper.

Back in her office, Jane remembered the question she wanted to put to Anna Musthill and lifted the phone to dial the Benbridges' number. It might be no more than coincidence; nobody else seemed to find anything suspicious in it, but . . .

She was glad that it was Anna who answered her call; that did at least save her from further colloquy with the resentful Heather.

'Miss Musthill, it's Inspector Perry again. It probably

isn't important, but I'm just getting all my background details straight. You told my superintendent that the chief accountant was called away to nurse a sick relative. When was that, exactly?'

'Evelyn? I'm not sure. It was some weeks back, mother with a slight stroke, I think. I'll just check if Heather knows.' There was a pause, and distant conversation of which only one side was audible. 'Didn't come to the funeral but asked that you should be sent apologies? And Jill Huggins passed them on? Okay . . .' Anna's voice came back at close range. 'Evelyn was called away the day before Father's funeral. I mean the first one. Telephoned Neville to explain the circumstances, apparently. But since Neville was leaving on his trip he gave the apologies to one of the office staff to deliver. Neville didn't have the courtesy to do it himself, or to ring up with his own, either.'

'And what sort of person is Evelyn?'

'Very reliable, pleasant, fortyish, one of those people everybody likes but nobody knows very well. Basically a nice, quiet bachelor. He's been with the firm a while so I've met him a few times in the past. Apparently he's an only child and his mother lives in Cornwall or somewhere, so it was understandable that he'd have to go – and stay, if his mother needed nursing. Why?'

Her description had already knocked Jane's sudden theory on the head. Evelyn, male; not Evelyn, female, with a possible relationship with Neville Pemberton. 'I was just making sure I knew who was who in the firm,' Jane answered.

'A male friend rang later to say Evelyn was sorry but he wouldn't be back until further notice,' Anna said, and added, 'which supports my view that he's probably gay. Wait a minute.' There was a sudden sharpening in her voice, and the touch of a chuckle. 'Did you assume Evelyn was a she? I suppose your superintendent did too when I mentioned the name. And after what we said about Neville you'd started to wonder if he'd cut his losses and run off with the office blonde with whom he was in cahoots?'

That was what had occurred to Jane – roughly. But even if there was no romance involved, there might still be a connection. She was about to suggest the possibility when there was a further murmur in the background from Anna's end, then she came back on the line.

'Heather says nobody would accuse Evelyn of being dishonest, and I have to say I agree. He's been with Musthills for six or seven years, and thoroughly trusted. He also doesn't have anything to do with contracts, so he couldn't . . . I can't honestly see him and Neville getting together on anything either, they're totally different types. I doubt if they even like each other. I'll grant you it could look suspicious that he and Neville seem to have left within hours of each other – if you didn't know the personalities involved. As it is, it has to be coincidence. And anyway, as I said, nothing seems to be missing from the company.'

'Thank you,' Jane said. 'I'll be in touch if there's anything else I have to ask you, if that's all right.'

'Or if you've got anything to report. Oh, in case you want it for your records, Evelyn's surname is Dale. If you want, I can see if I can get the address where he's staying next time there's a message from him.'

'Only if you can do so without showing too much interest.'

And only because Jane had an automatic objection to anyone involved in this case being untraceable. Evelyn Dale's absence was probably as simple and genuine as it sounded, and there seemed no reason for him to disappear abruptly if the company accounts showed no sign of theft. 'It might be inadvisable for you to be asking for any further information at all,' Jane warned, 'particularly if Mr Pemberton's back.'

'It's all right, I'll be careful. I just hope— If Neville's taken off and decided to cut his losses, would that mean you couldn't get him?' Anna sounded weary suddenly, and more than a touch despondent. 'What would he get in this country, anyway, if you can prove corruption against him?'

'It depends.' But very probably not enough to be worth sacrificing a half share in a healthy business, Jane thought cynically. And nothing at all unless the CPS thought there was a strong enough case against him personally. He had the easiest way out in the world, too, in pretending shock and blaming Richard Musthill. That was certainly what he would do, unless a council employee could be found who would finger Neville Pemberton specifically. Even then, what would he get? Two to five in an open prison? Cut down for good behaviour? Probably not even that much. Just a certain amount of scandal, and the knowledge that there would be quite a lot of people who would merely think he had been 'sharp' and happily do business with him when he came out.

She decided not to share these thoughts with Anna Musthill. She made her polite goodbyes instead – and sat staring at the wall for a moment after she had put the phone down.

It was scarcely logical for Neville Pemberton to go away

just now on an extended business trip, was it? Surely the buying of building materials couldn't be that urgent. Now was just the moment when you would expect him to be here, holding his corner against the Musthill family inheritors. And making sure there was nothing for them to find out – if he had been up to something.

Could there actually be anything in the fact that he and Evelyn Dale were both away? The company was healthily solvent, with nothing missing . . .

Speculation would get her nowhere at this stage, and it certainly wasn't getting the next part of her task started. A feeling that things were slightly out of kilter was no help at all when nothing had been proved against anyone yet. Jane let out an impatient sigh and reached for her mimeographed list of relevant local numbers.

The council press and information officer seemed the logical person to begin on with her act as the eager-beaver new community liaison officer whose desire was to learn all about everything. With the city council top of her list.

By the time she drove home at the end of her day, Jane was in possession of the names, addresses and telephone numbers of her ward councillors, together with the advice that the most likely time to reach any of them by phone was in the evening. Although she was welcome to call at the press office at any time, one of her local councillors really would be in the best position to fill her in on all the details of the council's day-to-day operations and would no doubt be pleased to answer any questions she might have. She had also been given the information, with pleasant efficiency, that as she probably knew, full council meetings were open to members of the public to attend (though not to speak unless presenting a prepared petition) and committee meetings were open for public scrutiny too, though press and public were excluded when a committee discussed anything deemed confidential. Oh, would she like a tour of the Mayor's Parlour? If so, the press officer would be delighted to arrange for the Lord Mayor or the Sheriff to invite her. As no doubt she was aware, it was a rather charming house with an interesting history and had been presented to the city some years back for mayoral use.

Jane expressed suitable gratitude for the suggestion, knowing that she would have to take that on board for verisimilitude. The press officer's assumptions about what she knew made her wryly aware of her own ignorance. The Mayor's Parlour, for instance, had previously only entered her consciousness as the building round which she had once chased a teenage thief trying to escape through the public gardens which lay beyond it. Aside from that, she had known where it was on the map, and that it had something to do with the council, but nothing else.

As she pulled into one of the marked parking bays her street had recently sprouted, along with a newly-erected notice marked 'Residents Only', Jane acknowledged guiltily that she ought to have made an effort to learn more about local politics before this. It simply hadn't been her line, but now it ought to be. She knew the law as it applied to local government (or knew where to look it up, if necessary) and had, lately, taken care to catch up with the names of most of the city dignitaries she might be expected to meet, but nothing beyond that.

She let herself into the house, scooping up the post from the mat only to find it contained nothing but a gas bill and four identical circulars advertising loft ladders. Hardly useful for a house that had no loft. Which of her three ward councillors should she approach? she wondered. She had not even known there were three, let alone what party they belonged to. Fine community officer she was.

Dumping her bag and briefcase on a chair, she ran upstairs to change into jeans for the evening. She had just reached the top when she heard Adrian's key in the door.

'Hi,' she called down towards the movements below. 'I've just got in myself. Listen, do you happen to know anything about our local council representatives? Like, are they Tory or Labour or Lib. Dem.? I think I must be about as apolitical as a newt—'

'Are you halfway through changing, or decent? I've brought Fliss round to meet you.'

'Oh, fine, I'll come straight down again.' She was curious to meet the cow-wrestling Amazon. Except that she really must stop thinking of her as that.

As Jane began to come back down the stairs, she heard the murmur of a husky female voice saying something inaudible, and then an amused chuckle from Adrian. They had their heads close together as Jane came round the bend, and then Felicity moved away a pace and looked up at Jane with a suddenly disconcerted expression and an abrupt flush of colour in her cheeks.

She could be nowhere near as disconcerted as Jane felt. She had been expecting somebody tall and muscular, probably trousered and hearty-looking. Felicity Rathbone was no more than five foot four, softly rounded under a long shirt and a flowing skirt, with a cascade of long, wavy, auburn hair. And quite amazing green eyes.

Chapter 10

'She isn't beautiful when you look at her properly,' Jane said. 'She's actually rather dumpy, shoulders too broad for her height, and she's got a long nose and not much chin. You could have knocked me down with a feather, though, when I first caught sight of her. I wasn't expecting anyone so . . . so . . .'

'But did you like her?' Matty asked.

'Well, I can't say I feel we're going to be soulmates. She seems very intense – kept staring at me. And she has a habit of shaking all that hair round her face so that half the time conversing with her is a bit like addressing a wild animal through the undergrowth.' Jane let out a chuckle. 'Mean, aren't I? Maybe there was just something about me which made her nervous.'

'Perhaps she's shy. Were you being daunting?'

They were lunching together again. Matty was looking better, Jane thought; not strikingly happy, but more like her usual self. Work was absorbing her, and must be offering a degree of healing.

'No, I wasn't, I was being thoroughly friendly! She wouldn't stay to supper, said she still had a lot of things to rearrange in the flat. Adrian immediately insisted on walking back with her to help, bless him, saying that although he knew she was as strong as a horse, shifting furniture around needed two, and what were partners for? Oh, that's another thing, she will address him as *Ade*.' Jane wrinkled her nose. 'He didn't turn a hair, mind you. I guess it must be a hangover from when they were at college together. But it sounds fairly yuk to me, I have to say. Oh well. It doesn't actually matter whether I like her or not; the point is that he seems sure she's going to be very good in the practice. I suppose she must tie all that hair back when she's dealing with animals, and presumably she's less jumpy with horses and cows and dogs and cats than she is with people. Or at least as she seemed with me. Anyway, to be fair, Adrian did say when he got back home that she's just come out of a six-year relationship so she's a bit emotional at the moment.'

'You'll probably like each other better when she gets a bit more settled, then.'

The comment was delivered in Matty's normal tones but still brought it back belatedly to Jane that other people's broken relationships were not the most diplomatic subject for conversation. Not that she knew anything more than the bare facts about Felicity's, since Adrian had not elaborated. He had merely produced it, abstractedly, in response to Jane's suggestion that when they invited the Hollingses back for dinner Felicity could be included. Not tactful at the moment to invite her with a couple.

That would apply to Matty, too, particularly a police couple. Jane glanced across at her friend, wondering whether to inquire if she and Steve had been in contact. On balance, better not. If Matty wanted to say, she would.

'This evening I've got to go out and be shown all round the council offices,' Jane said, changing the subject chattily. 'Did I tell you my latest task is to bone up on local politics? It's a large hole in my consciousness.'

'These things are sent to try you.'

Jane nodded. 'It all goes with the new territory. Adrian told me I was a disgrace for not even knowing our ward councillors are Liberal Democrats. I did get him to concede that I wasn't even living in the bloody ward when they had the elections. He voted for this lot, apparently.' And Felicity had mentioned sweetly in passing that she had done some work in her local ward while she was up in Lincolnshire. Then the two of them had lapsed into a reminiscence about some college rag week when they had both stood as candidates for a demonstration parliament and made speeches. It was amazing what you could find out about other people's past interests. 'I'm going to go to a full council meeting next week too, which is apparently a piece of luck because they only come up every seven weeks. Busy, busy, aren't I?'

'You can apply your legal mind to the arguments and hope nobody drones on too long,' Matty told her with a grin. 'Good practice for you for listening to dignitaries with apparently rapt attention. Oh, by the way, you know that cottage out in the country you once told me Adrian had? He's not renting it out by any chance, is he?'

'No, he's sold it, a couple of months ago. To put more money in the practice.' There had been a need at the time, though it seemed a pity when he had put a lot of work into the cottage. 'Why?' she asked. Was Matty looking for a more permanent place to live down here?

'Just interest. Anyway I seem to remember you said it was a long way out.' Matty spoke lightly and abruptly switched subjects. 'I know what I meant to tell you. I had to do some work the other day on your mysterious torso. It's still in our morgue freezer. We were asked for further details on it.'

'By our lot?'

'Yes, the request came from your DI. Dr Kremer wasn't too pleased, actually, got quite huffy about it – "If there was anything more I would already have put it in the autopsy report" – and snarled at me that if they wanted another opinion, they'd better have mine.' Matty grinned in humorous recollection. 'He's not so bad really and I'm learning how to smooth his feathers. This one was a request to know if the deceased could have been diabetic.'

'They must have had a possible ID. Could you give them anything?'

'Had to disappoint them on that. No sign of diabetes, treated or otherwise, A very healthy person, on the whole, your torso. Aside from being dead. Took care of himself quite well, I'd say. Well-fed. Just under six foot tall, unless he had a small head. Reasonably fit, from his musculature. Didn't even have any corns on his toes.'

'A pity, or they might have been able to find a chiropodist who'd dealt with them.'

'Mm. I suppose it's never really dawned on me before that you can tell an awful lot from a body, but not always whose it is if you haven't got the right bits.'

'Are you really taking to it? Corpses? It doesn't turn you off?'

'No, it's interesting. It could be – oh, disturbing sometimes I suppose, if you let it, but it's not that hard actually to see it as a scientific exercise. And like I said, it's certainly no worse than trying to repair live ones.'

'Practical, aren't you?' Jane said ruefully. 'Whenever I talked to Dr Ledyard on the phone I used to wonder how she could be so damned down-to-earth about the details she was giving me. Human beings as meat, you know?' She glanced down at her plate, suddenly extremely glad she had been eating fish salad, then caught Matty's grin.

'Easier for me, dear, being a vegetarian.'

'Doctors!'

'This doctor's got to go off in a minute and do some general autopsies. Not the ones in your field, just the clinically interesting kind.'

She definitely was looking more cheerful, Jane decided after they had parted; getting her balance and her natural tranquillity back. On the surface, anyway. Steve Ryan's treatment of her still rankled in Jane's mind. She had introduced them. Maybe they hadn't been together long enough for things to take proper root. But there had seemed such certainty in that relationship . . .

No use brooding on it.

Jane was due to meet Harry Duckham this evening, the councillor she had picked on out of her choice of three. He had seemed thoroughly willing to initiate her into the mysteries of council administration. It had been his idea that they should meet at five thirty so that he could take her on a tour of the council offices, whose staff would have packed up for the night, and his loquacity over the phone, in a pleasantly cultured voice with a slight cynical drawl in it, had suggested he might be usefully informative for her purposes.

He had said he didn't drive, so would she pick him up from outside his house to save him catching a bus. She would know him without any problem, since he would be the one standing there on the pavement looking like a spare part.

She found him without difficulty, standing in front of a row of terraced houses, a slight man with a bush of curly fair hair which decorated his high forehead in three distinct peaks to show where areas had receded. Perhaps to make up for it, his upper lip sported a thick and luxuriant moustache. Pale skin, a narrow frame. He was clad in tight beige denim jeans and a white shirt. As he responded to her wave and came to get into her car, Jane saw an appreciative stare develop in a pair of slightly bulbous blue eyes. He was older close up than he had looked from a distance, probably nearer forty than thirty. It seemed, however, that he chose to cultivate a deliberately boyish manner, sprawling into the front passenger seat carelessly, giving her a grin.

'Cops get better looking all the time! What do I call you? I'm Harry.'

'Jane.'

'Hi then, Jane. I'm sorry I had to ask you to pick me up, but I'm in the middle of a year's ban for speeding.' He said it as if he enjoyed flinging out challenges.

'Bad luck,' Jane told him in a friendly manner, giving him a smile.

'It's a bit too tempting late at night on the Thanet Way. So you want to know all about how the council works, do you?'

'Part of my new job, as I explained.'

'Well, I'm ready, willing and able. You know we're a hung council, I suppose, after we booted the Tories out last time? We're the largest party, which the Tories don't like at all. They spend their time trying to get their own back. Or to get back into power by making deals with our small and select band of Labourites. Small and select because hardly anyone votes for them in an area like this. Much skulduggery and sacrificing of principle goes on to try and do us down, I can assure you.'

'You make it sound quite exciting.'

'More backbiting than exciting, but some of us do our best to liven things up. If you come to full council next week you'll see us in action.'

'Yes, I'd like to, as I said. I find I'm horribly ignorant about how things are done.'

'Take the next left and then right at the roundabout – sorry, as one of our local police I'm sure you know the way!' He actually stopped talking for a moment or two as they traversed various roads swinging them round the city to its eastern side, each carrying a nose-to-tail line of moving cars in the evening mini rush hour. 'Okay, turn in here and, presto, we've arrived at the so-called hub of things. Not that anyone would really claim it was much of a hub. You can park in the Director of Housing's slot if you like. He's not going to be around at this time of night.'

The council offices, purpose-built in a long, low, two-storey building, covered an extensive site next to the postal sorting office and was surrounded by parking spaces set on a downward slope and liberally divided by evergreen bushes.

More of them had been drilled into tidy lines against the maroon brick of the building. The architectural style could only be described as Modern Municipal, Jane decided, looking at it properly for once instead of merely being aware that it was there. Without the familiar and famous outline of the cathedral rising on the near horizon above a cluster of roofs, they could have been anywhere.

'The public can come into the main building during the day, of course, by the main entrance,' Harry Duckham said, 'but the offices are separate and reached by the yellow doors. The staff ones.' He ducked into a side path which led into a right-angled corner of the building with, immediately visible, the promised yellow door, a bright buttercup shade.

'This way,' he said, pushing open the door. 'Everybody has a key but at this time of day the door's left open for the cleaners. Actually we're all supposed to wear security badges with our photos on, but as you can see, there's nobody here to check.'

There was, indeed, nobody; just a stretch of carpeted corridor and then another yellow door. Harry pushed it open and indicated a wide area of open-plan offices divided up by screens, shelves and filing cabinets. 'Down here's the Housing Department, Planning, part of Treasury. All the offices look much the same, and each of the political parties has its own private room in the building, for the use of its councillors.'

He made for a staircase (with yellow rails) and led Jane up it. On the upper floor, cleaners were beginning to vacuum and polish, moving in and out of areas laid out similarly to those below. 'We contract the cleaning out,' Harry said casually as he followed Jane's thoughtful gaze. 'Everything's bloody privatised nowadays!'

And anyone from the privatised cleaning firm, anyone at all who knew the system, Jane thought, could simply walk in at this time of day.

'The council goes in for open plan for its workers, as you can see. Part of the drive for open government perhaps.' Harry gave one of his cynical grins. 'This, however, is the Chief Executive's suite – secretary's office, then his own inside. And those do have doors. Then this next bit is the press office.' That, as empty of its usual occupants as everywhere else, was a section behind a half-wall, with piles of paper, shelves full of books and files, two or three desks and telephones. 'Half a mo,' Harry said, 'you might as well have a green book if Susie hasn't gone mad and locked them all away. It'll tell you who's who among the councillors and on what committee, and give you all the boundaries – district and parish and ward.'

He dived into the press office area to pull open a drawer. The small booklet he pulled out, in a dark green cover, had the words City Council Membership printed across the front. Jane thanked him for the copy.

'Even if Susie had locked them away,' he said, 'I could have found you one without too much problem. You can get into the filing cabinets with a safety pin.' Harry Duckham's desire to show off was certainly proving informative. 'Desk drawers too, I shouldn't wonder. I know about the filing cabinets because I've done it – but only in the interests of discovering what my own dear party leader had been up to lately!'

'Don't you know? And surely you can't really get into a locked filing cabinet that easily, can you?' Jane was actually well aware that you could, on most standard makes, and that thieves in office premises made a habit of it. However, it was useful to know from his comment that nobody had bothered to fit the ones in the council offices with non-standard locks.

'In answer to your first question, never trust your leader since it's as advisable to watch your back when it comes to your own side as it is with the others. In answer to the second, don't arrest me, officer, I know I dunnit but I'll deny everything! Oh, go on, laugh – you have to, don't you?'

Jane gave him an obediently amused look. 'So what office is this?' she asked, glancing round at the next divided section. All the furniture everywhere was of the same design – wood-veneered desks, grey metal cupboards and filing cabinets, swivel chairs. Much of it was exactly the same as police issue. Government furnishing requirements were obviously produced in bulk.

'This small one's the council solicitor's. He checks that we're not doing anything outright illegal. Here we have Environment.' They walked through another wide office area and on round a corner, past what appeared to be ubiquitous hessian-covered partition walls, most of them with posters or notices pinned to them. One or two small separate offices could be seen here, but with open entrances. Individual secretaries, perhaps, since Jane glimpsed a typewriter on a desk, along with the personal touch of a small vase of flowers, a penholder full of biros and pencils. They passed an actual closed door which had City Treasurer printed on it: he, apparently, like the Chief Executive, was granted his own private office.

They paused to allow the passage of a woman in an overall carrying an industrial vacuum cleaner. Yet another large but desk-crowded open-plan section lay ahead – an enormous number of people seemed to work here – and she flicked over the pages of the booklet, then looked at Harry. 'Tell me what all the committees are and what they do,' she invited, wrinkling her brow and looking at him appealingly. 'There do seem to be a lot of them in here. The Policy Committee, for instance. That deals with – policy?'

'All sorts of things, actually. It used to be called the Finance and General Purposes Committee, which is a bit more explanatory. The Chief Executive and the City Treasurer report to it on, oh, things like budgets and debts and annual pay reviews and so on. The financial nitty-gritty. When you come to full council you'll be able to have an agenda which will give the minutes of each committee. We have to vote them through page by page, with interruptions if anybody wants to make a speech on anything. We're allowed three minutes to hold forth.'

'That doesn't sound long.'

'Long enough if you have to listen to it.' He had propped an elbow on a filing cabinet, apparently happy to stand and chat. 'Full council's mainly a formality. The work's been done in between, in committee. And by all the departments here, of course, day by day.'

'Each department has a director, hasn't it? And the directors are senior council employees?'

'That's right. They're called chief officers, and they're professional civil servants. We – your noble and voluntary band of councillors – get elected by our adoring public. They don't, they're here all the time and are paid to keep local government ticking over.'

'Who makes the decisions? Sorry, but with all these directors—'

'And chairmen, don't forget them. Each committee has a chairman, who's a councillor, and each committee gets reported to by a director, who's a council officer. As to who makes the decisions, well, it's supposed to be us, your elected representatives. Though quite often it's a question of okaying a decision made by a chief officer. Do you really want to know all this?'

'I've got to,' Jane said, giving him a rueful grin.

'Like that, is it? Know your stuff or you'll get pounded back on the beat?'

'You never can tell. How about explaining things to me with an example? Take housing. Supposing you wanted some council houses built.'

'We don't build them any more, we just farm it out to the private sector. And sell off as many of the ones we've got as we can – not that we're allowed to use the money for anything useful.'

'All right then, supposing you want to build something else – an old people's home, a leisure centre? How do you decide who builds it?'

'Oh, that. Local firms – or national ones if it's something really big – get invited to submit sealed tenders. After the relevant committee's agreed that they want it built at all, and council's voted on that . . . Are we assuming we've already got the land? And planning permission's been granted? The Director of Planning has the say on that. Lots of people are involved before you can even start. Yes, I know, complicated, isn't it?' He said that with a grin of satisfaction. 'It's a maze until you're used to it.'

'Yes, I can see. Go on.'

'Policy Committee has to vote the money. Planning Committee deals with the planning. Then the particular committee this mythical building comes under, which might be Housing or it might be Amenities, depending, has to invite tenders. With me so far?'

'Yes. It certainly does seem to involve a lot of people. Tenders, you said?'

'Bids for the contract. They specify work and materials and give the price the firm is offering on a sheet at the front.'

'I get it. I think.' Jane took care to look slightly bewildered. 'And who do these bids go to?'

'I'll show you.'

He led the way round another hessian corner and into another wide area divided by desks, cupboards, cabinets, book-filled shelves. It might have been any of the other offices: a notice tacked up on its nearest half-wall saying City Secretary's Office was necessary guidance. 'The tenders come in to here,' Harry said, 'where they're received by one of the clerks and stamped with date and signature.'

'I suppose there's a deadline?'

'That's right – twelve noon on a particular day. Some might come in as much as a couple of weeks early, but others might arrive with half an hour to go. Then they go in the Tender Box.'

'And that is?'

'Over there.' He seemed to be enjoying displaying his knowledge, and led her between a divider and across the space this took them into. 'See the large black box? That's it.'

It stood on a table between two desks, a deep metal strongbox with a padlock on the front of it. 'Behold the Tender Box,' Harry said, 'probably right this minute half full of thick envelopes if we've got a contract coming up, and I expect we have.'

'So what happens to them next? After the deadline? Someone gets them out and looks at them?'

'Oh, we have a proper ceremony for that. At a convenient time, usually about a week after the deadline, a group assembles, by invitation. There have to be two councillors and two official officers. The Committee Administrator for the committee in charge of the particular contract opens the box and then each envelope, and reads out the bids, which are listed. The councillors sign to say that they've witnessed the opening. Voilà!'

'I see,' Jane said again. Thoughtfully. 'It's always done that way?'

'Oh yes, our own particular piece of pomp and ceremony. To prove that fairness rules okay. And, of course, the lowest bid gets the contract.'

'Fascinating, Wouldn't the chairman of whatever it is have seen the bids in advance?'

'Goodness no. Sealed tenders stay sealed until they're

officially opened. And we don't know who's sent in the lowest bid until then. Not until the box is opened, presto, with all due drama.' He grinned at her and added, 'I hope you're suitably impressed. Look, I'm getting thirsty, so how about a visit to our party office? We're properly equipped with a kettle and tea bags and instant coffee.'

'Sounds fine.'

As they walked, the open-plan layout abruptly ended in a narrow corridor, and Harry pointed out a closed door with the sign 'Labour Group Room' on it. Round the corner was another similar door marked for the Conservatives; then they reached an identical one marked 'Liberal Democrat Group'. 'Our room is the biggest,' Harry said with satisfaction. 'We made them change over when we became the largest elected party.' He reached for a key, but the door gave to his hand without it. 'Someone's already in, so we don't need to unlock. Come in and enjoy our hospitality.'

The room was casually comfortable with padded grey chairs, a long table, a desk, two telephones and cardboard boxes full of leaflets. Cartoons and anti-Tory posters decorated the walls. A large lady sat at the table with a cigarette between her lips and a pile of notes she was apparently working on in front of her, and looked up in a brusque but cheerful manner to be introduced as 'Kath, our group leader'.

Friendly conversation ensued over coffee. Jane inquired whether members of the group often spent the evening working in here. Not the whole evening, she was told, though they sometimes held meetings downstairs in the canteen; then they might stay until eleven, but usually this office was only in use during the day or during the early evening as now. The caretaker double-locked the outside doors at eight and then went home. If you were in, you could get out, but ingress after eight was barred. Another piece of useful information casually offered.

Finally, with a glance at her watch, Jane said pleasantly that she had better move. Harry lounged to his feet and said he would come with her. They retraced their steps through the endless hessian-walled corridors and open offices, passing the cleaners who had now reached the ground floor.

They came out through the same yellow door by which they had entered. Nobody, at any time, had shown any curiosity about Jane's presence. Nor about Harry Duckham's. Given a look of confidence, it seemed anyone could wander in and out.

'Let's go and have a drink,' Harry said with determined hopefulness. 'You will, won't you? The night is yet young, and so are we!'

'Thanks, that's a nice idea. And thanks for being so helpful about explaining everything to me, too.'

'My pleasure. How about the Millers? It's usually quite lively down there.'

Jane agreed to the Millers Arms. She was in the business of being obliging. Maybe she could get him to gossip, loquacious as he was. They drew up in the car park nearest the pub and walked across the road to the sound of the rush of the old millrace.

'I like the way they've done up the old mill into flats without destroying its character too much,' Jane said idly, 'but I'm not sure if I'd want to live right above the water like that. Chilly and misty in winter, I should think.'

'And noisy the rest of the time when all the people from the pub come out and sit on the bank. It's not badly done, though. Musthills did it, I think. Must be several years ago now.'

A lucky and inadvertent bull's-eye. 'Musthills?' Jane said innocently. 'They're quite well known hereabouts, aren't they? Good workmen, would you say?'

'They seem to be. Do quite a lot of our council stuff. They used to concentrate on private work much more but Dick Musthill was on the council then and had to be careful about conflict of interest. Not that I knew him particularly myself, he'd given up his seat by the time I got elected.' He pushed the pub door open. 'I suppose things will go on the same even though the poor sod's dead. There's always the egregious Neville to keep things running. Met him in the course of your social whirl, have you? Neville Pemberton?'

'I don't think so.'

'You'd remember if you had, he'd have been all over you like a rash. Loves the ladies, and they love him back, I've always heard.' Harry gave a half-hearted leer. 'Can't say I've seen him around for a while, so maybe he's gone off to that villa in Spain he's reputed to have. Not that I move in his social circle. What are you drinking?'

'A tomato juice, thanks.'

'Oh, go on, have something stronger. They do a good real ale here, knock your knickers off – if you'll pardon the expression.'

'I'll stick to juice, thanks.'

'Poor little cop-lady has to be careful when she's driving? Tough for you. Wait there, I'll be back.'

Maybe it was her own fault for doing her dumb blonde act a little too well. Or maybe he just believed in addressing female police officers in a patronising manner. There were some even on the force who still addressed WPCs as if they were there for decoration rather than brains, though less than there used to be.

Jane sat looking tranquil and amiable as he did a hail-fellow-well-met act to various people round the bar and leaned across to give the young dark-haired barmaid a smacking kiss. He was a show-off by nature, she reckoned. But he had proved to be a very good choice from her point of view. At last he returned to the corner he had left her in, with his own large pint balanced against her smaller red glass, done up with ice and a swizzle-stick.

'We were talking about Neville Pemberton,' Jane reminded him innocently as he sat down. 'You don't sound as if you like him.'

'He's a flash git and a high Tory. Always got lots of cash to spend – the sort of person who likes to demonstrate a thoroughly bulging wallet, you know the type? Gives large tips after dining in *the* best places. Gets up a party to go to the races when it's the right season.' He took a large swig of his drink and gazed at Jane with cynical amusement. 'Everyone knows everyone in this city, and most people are nasty about each other – don't you find that?'

'Is that the way it goes? Tell me some gossip, I never hear any.'

'I could but I won't. Let's talk about you instead, much more interesting. Are you married?'

'No. I do live with someone though. You?'

'Goodness, is living with someone allowed without having your stripes taken away?' Despite the mocking comment, she had the feeling that her admission of being spoken for had given him a passing twinge of disappointment. 'Me, I'm as single and as free as a bird. You're looking at one of the last footloose bachelors. Makes for an enjoyable life, mind you.'

He really was fond of himself. He had given her clear and lucid explanations, though, and was plainly possessed of a fair intelligence – except for his assumptions about how dumb someone would be who could reach the rank of inspector.

Jane gave him a winning smile and settled down to see if there was anything else she could get out of him.

Chapter 11

Jane got home to find Adrian was out. She made herself a sandwich and settled down to assess what she had learned.

At first sight Anna Musthill's conclusion looked impossible. Nobody could tip Musthills off to put in the lowest bid because nobody was allowed to know what the bids were in advance of their public opening. A bribe might be offered to make sure a company was on the tender list, but how would that help? Some other firm could still undercut.

A bribe to someone working for Musthills' chief competitor in the trade, to know what they were going to bid? That was theoretically possible; except that they must have several. Jane could think of three other building companies offhand who worked in the district. It would be too expensive an operation. A carve-up between the local firms to share council contracts out between them by agreeing whose turn it was to undercut was a far more likely form of dishonesty, but the fact remained that it was Musthills who regularly succeeded in their bids.

Sealed tenders in a locked box, and a formally witnessed opening ceremony – how could you get round that? She would have liked to ask who was actually in charge of the Tender Box key, but that inquiry would have been too direct. Anyway, if the box was opened regularly to put the tenders inside, the key must be kept in a reasonably accessible place, and the official keyholder would know he or she was first in the firing line if there was any suspicion that the tenders had been looked at in advance. Besides, there was more than access to the box involved. All those sealed envelopes inside it would have to be opened without trace and resealed again – steamed open with a kettle? It would all take time. And privacy.

Pulling her notepad towards her, Jane knew she would have to give the super a negative report. She would not give it to him until after she had attended the full council meeting in case anything came out of that, but it seemed highly unlikely that anything would.

Sitting and watching how a council meeting worked would be a genuine piece of community relations anyway, she thought with a grimace. Probably an exceptionally boring one, as Matty had teased.

She made her notes as thorough as possible, and had almost finished when the sound of Adrian's key heralded his return. She shuffled her papers together rapidly to avoid his asking what she was doing. Omission was better than lying, and discretion required that she didn't discuss the corruption inquiry even with him. She looked up to greet him with a smile, only to find him regarding her with an expression which was both tetchy and more than a little sulky.

'Oh, you're home, then? I thought we'd got over the unexpected late evenings bit.'

'I did warn you I was going to be working tonight, meeting that councillor. And a fairly trying character he was too, socially speaking. Busy trying to impress me with what a young blood he is.'

'Oh? Well, you had one man and two women to choose from, and you chose the man.'

Oh dear, one of his sudden and irrational flashes of jealousy. He must be tired. 'I just chose the one who came first in the alphabet,' Jane said peaceably. Never mind if it wasn't true: D did come first but she had made her choice on the grounds that she could get away with playing dumb innocence more easily with a male. She wasn't going to tell Adrian that, and even if she could she wouldn't choose to when he was being unreasonable. 'Had a bad day, love? You seem to have been working late too.'

'No, I came back here after evening clinic but when you didn't arrive I went out again. Fliss and I had supper.'

'Good, I don't have to ask if I can get you anything then. Did you go somewhere nice?'

'She made something in the flat. She's an excellent cook.'

Ouch. 'I'm sure you deserved a decent meal after helping her with her furniture moving,' Jane said, determinedly sunny. 'Is she managing to get settled? Oh, I had lunch with Matty today. She seems to be getting thoroughly dug in to her job. Pathology wouldn't be my choice, and it's always so bloody cold in morgues, but I suppose you get used to it. Sit down and I'll get you a coffee, shall I?'

'No thanks, I'm going to go up and have a bath. Oh, Steve Ryan rang when I was in earlier this evening. He seemed to think Matty would be here. I gave him the address and phone number of her digs since he didn't seem to know it and I found it in your book by the phone.'

'Oh Adrian, you didn't! Damn! If she didn't give it to him it must be because she didn't want him to have it, didn't that occur to you?'

'Why should it? Anyway, if they've had a fight, I can't see anything against giving him the chance to make up.'

'You don't know the circumstances. He's been a right piss-artist. Oh hell, I'd better ring her and warn her he might phone. Or even turn up, since you've bloody gone and given him her address as well!'

'She's a big girl now, she doesn't need you interferring. Let them sort their own lives out. For God's sake, you might give the poor bloke a chance, whatever he's supposed to have done. What on earth help do you think it does taking sides?'

If his words hadn't echoed Matty's earlier ones, Jane might have snapped back instead of opening her mouth and shutting it again. And he was in such an unreasonable mood that she might fume but she wouldn't argue.

'Go and have your bath,' she said stiffly.

'I shall.'

'Well, go on then! Don't stand there being tedious and looking as if you've been rooted to the floor.'

He looked at her, and she looked at him. Then he asked, 'Are you going to be late tomorrow night?'

'Not that I know of.'

'Want to go and see a film? *The Age of Innocence* is on at the university and you said you wanted to see it if it came back.'

'All right. As long as *you* don't get held up late at work.'

'I shouldn't. I'm going to have to work all Saturday though.'

'I expect I'll live.' They were both softening, and Jane could feel the beginnings of an unwilling smile catching at the corners of her mouth. He looked so . . . so *ruffled*. 'Oh, go on, go and get thoroughly warm and thoroughly clean and then maybe neither of us will feel so quarrelsome.'

'I'm sorry if you think I made a mistake about Steve. I still think you should let people have their own head-to-heads, and they won't get the chance if they don't see each other, will they?'

'You're probably right. Okay, I'll just leave them to it. How's Felicity, is she settling in all right?'

'Yes, I think so. Don't be too long coming up, mm? I reckon an early night.'

'Can't think of anything to keep me down here . . .'

If his temper very occasionally went up like a rocket, it didn't usually last. Unlike hers, Jane thought with a rueful grin as she heard the bathwater begin a noisy glug upstairs and stirred herself to put her papers away in her briefcase and tidy up her coffee mug and plate. But she could do without him producing a sudden fit of jealousy over Harry Duckham, of all people. Dear heavens, no contest! She could just as easily start being jealous of Felicity, on the grounds that he spent all day with the woman and praised her capabilities to the skies. He was lucky she had more sense.

For no reason at all Senander Baba slipped into her mind, and the humorous glint in a pair of calm grey eyes. What would Adrian make of *him*?

Nothing at all, since there was no reason to discuss him.

Jane flexed her shoulder experimentally, aware that it hadn't started nagging again at all. Chance, probably.

On Monday morning Anna Musthill phoned. Despite her promise to leave everything in the hands of the police, she was clearly impatient for results.

'Have you got anywhere yet?' she asked brusquely.

'Miss Musthill—'

'Call me Anna.'

'All right then, Anna. I did say we'd get in touch with you if we had anything to report. Is Mr Pemberton back?'

'No. I was talking to Jill Huggins on the phone this morning and she said they hadn't heard anything from him yet. She seems to think he might have gone on to his Spanish villa, to have a short holiday and get over the shock of Father's death. Particularly if the buying spree he was on didn't amount to much after all,' Anna said drily. 'But surely you could start checking on him, couldn't you? Looking into his social contacts and—'

'We can't start investigating Mr Pemberton without anything to give us definite cause.'

'How much more do you need? It's just so bloody frustrating.'

'I'm sorry about that, but we've got no actual proof at the moment that he's broken the law. You really must give us time to make our inquiries.'

'I know, I know. Oh, by the way, Evelyn's friend rang again with apologies for his continued absence but seemed to think he couldn't be got hold of where he is in Cornwall.

His mother's none too well at all. He's spending a lot of time at the hospital and staying somewhere nearby in a holiday cottage without a phone.'

'Inconvenient for the company to have Mr Dale away so long.'

'Yes, but his deputy's managing all right, and everyone understands. He's a nice bloke, Evelyn, and everybody realises he wouldn't stay away without cause.' Anna sighed. 'I haven't been in again since you said it wasn't advisable, but you will let me know when you find out anything?'

Or if. Jane certainly wasn't going to tell her that that seemed unlikely, so far. 'Yes, of course,' she said soothingly.

'Okay. Well, thanks for talking to me. I'll try to possess my soul in patience.'

She was so sure they were going to get something on Neville Pemberton, Jane mused. At the moment it looked far more likely that she had leapt too rapidly to conclusions and the figures she had found so doubtful merely indicated some minor fraud. That could be looked into from the Musthills' end and might not involve Neville at all.

If something else did come up to show that Musthills could after all have been bribing its way into contracts, how was Anna going to feel if those unaccounted-for payments turned out to be traceable back to Richard Musthill? That he was the one who had been involved in something crooked?

Jane sighed, frowned, and made a note to add to her file that Evelyn Dale was still away as well as Neville Pemberton.

Two sudden absences, two men out of touch. It still looked shifty to her. She had a dislike of coincidence. It was difficult not to think that both of them seemed to have gone away a little too conveniently. And stayed away a little too long.

Chapter 12

Full council meetings took place in the Guildhall. In a city with a plethora of ancient churches, it must have seemed natural to convert one of them into the council's formal centre, and as Jane arrived – early, on the assumption that it would be advisable to do so to get a good seat – she looked round with appreciation. It was quite impressive.

At the moment only a few people were present, moving busily about or greeting each other to stop and chat. As far as Jane could see from a double row of empty chairs set along one wall and marked 'Public Seating' on a printed white notice, not many of the citizenry were expected to come along and watch its council's deliberations, and nobody else had arrived as yet. She picked herself a seat from which she would be able to see faces, and sat down to cast a thorough look over her surroundings while she waited.

The walls of the old church were of dark flint; in contrast, the councillors' benches arranged in a hexagon in the middle of the floor were made of pale amber wood. A second row was banked behind the first. A long narrow shelf for papers ran in front of each line, with a small fixed microphone in front of each place. A raised dais at one end completed the hexagon and held three large chairs, in the same pale wood but carved instead of plain, and the middle one was topped with the city arms. Tall curtains of old-gold damask had been hung on a massive pole behind the dais, presumably shutting off what must once have been choir stalls and an altar. As Jane looked up, her eye was immediately caught and held by one of the most impressively beamed ceilings she had ever seen. Its high criss-cross struts suggested extreme age and added an elegance to the scene below.

At the opposite end, facing the dais, reaching only half way up to the ceiling, was a carved wooden screen in dark wood with a door in the middle of it. A murmur of voices and the occasional hearty laugh were beginning to be heard from behind it, as if heralding the gradual arrival of the company. Presumably the door in the screen led to another entrance, the councillors' way in as opposed to the arched stone doorway from the street which was the public access, with a long rubberised ramp running down from it to accommodate wheelchairs.

Jane picked up an agenda from the chair next to hers, a thick wodge of paper stapled together, in a pale green cover roughly stamped across one corner 'Public Copy'. Opening it, she saw that the first page held the signature of the Chief Executive and Town Clerk above a notice which began, 'I hereby summon you to attend . . . for the transaction of business . . .' It was addressed to all city councillors in highly formal language. Jane was about to inspect the order of proceedings when she became aware of someone stopping directly in front of her.

'I recognise you from Dick Musthill's funeral, don't I?

Inspector . . . Perry, the police representative?'

An energetic-looking woman, tall and thin and grey-haired, was beaming down at her with a lot of teeth.

'Yes, I'm police community liaison officer, so I thought I'd come and see how council meetings are run,' Jane answered with a smile.

'What a splendid idea! Councillor Sheila Graham.' A hand was held out and Jane's was shaken with great enthusiasm. 'You haven't been before? You should find it interesting then. And do let me introduce you to some people. Jack, come and meet our police liaison officer. You probably saw her at poor Dick's – well, let's forget about that. Inspector Perry, Jack Kington, our party leader.'

'Yes, I'm Conservative leader, for my sins,' the burly grey-haired man she had summoned over said cheerfully, engulfing Jane's hand in a large fist. More people were wandering in now, though they seemed to be treating the idea of a council meeting with a lot less formality than suggested by the official summons. Some of them were even carrying bags of crisps and, apparently, other provisions. One person walked by with a bunch of grapes sticking out of a paper bag, and several clutched cardboard cups of coffee. 'You'll find us sitting over there,' Jack Kington boomed, waving a hand towards the benches opposite, 'with Labour in the middle there, and the Liberal Democrat lot this side. If we can ever get them out of the coffee room. Oh, excuse me. Before we start I must just have a word with one or two people,' and he shot away to buttonhole somebody.

'We've got a lot to get through tonight,' Sheila Graham said brightly, giving Jane another beam and noticeably checking who was coming in with her other eye. 'Has anyone explained to you how it works? Well, if you look on page two you'll find a list of committees and what page each one starts, so that you can follow. The Lord Mayor and his deputy and the Chief Executive will process in first, of course, with the mace, and then we'll have a prayer . . . Betty! Just book me that seat, will you? Put your bag down on it or something. And then come and meet our police liaison officer who's come to watch how we do things.'

'Maybe we should pass that information round and see if it makes some of the little darlings behave better,' Betty called merrily, giving Jane a grin as she arrived beside them. 'Oh yes, I remember your face. Awful business that, at poor old Dick's funeral, wasn't it? Have you caught the person who did it yet?'

'It's not my side of policing, I'm afraid, but I gather they're still pursuing inquiries.'

'Tough on the Musthills. That kid used to be in my class when she was at primary school. Nice to meet you – Tony, I must just have a private word . . .'

She, too, bowled away rapidly, catching the arm of someone who was passing and drawing him aside. Sheila Graham gave Jane another smile and then left her to join them. A lot of private business seemed to be going on all around and the noise level was rising. Several men in dark suits had arrived in a clump and seemed to be settling themselves quietly into seats which flanked the Lord Mayor's dais each side. Two other members of the public had arrived to join Jane in the public seating now but, in true English fashion, sat down separately with several seats between them and well away from Jane.

The council benches were gradually filling up. Jane caught sight of the Liberal Democrat leader whom Harry Duckham had introduced to her at the council offices as 'Kath'. She was deep in conversation with a companion. Then Jane's eye was caught by Gavin Levitt, recognisable from the funeral. Tall and solid and with that rather brutal mouth, he was easy to pick out. He was also noticeably unsteady on his feet. A certain glassiness about his eyes suggested he might be on the edge of being drunk. As Jane watched, he shook off somebody's hand impatiently, then went to plump himself down heavily on a bench.

Councillor Mrs Levitt appeared not to be with him. No, but that was surely her slim figure and blonde pageboy hair coming in now – and rather deliberately choosing a seat well away from her husband after one brief and apparently cold glance in his direction. Both of them were sitting on the side Jack Kington had pointed to as being the Conservative benches. If Gavin Levitt looked drunk, Tina Levitt's petite and pretty face had a wracked air, all bones and large eyes.

They had been at odds last time Jane had seen them, in Tissingham churchyard, and it looked as if things were no better now.

A further gaggle of people came filing in, with Harry Duckham at the tail end of it. He looked round and gave Jane a careless wave, but then slid into a nearby seat to go into an immediate huddle with the person next to him. The set of his shoulders looked as if he was telling one of his cynical jokes. He had been extremely useful, Jane reminded herself, even if his information had given her negatives rather than positives. He would hardly have been so open about his ability to pick locks if he had been secretly raiding the Tender Box, she thought with a flash of amusement.

All the same, his revelations had set up a line of thought which had been brewing in the back of her mind. Councillors seemed to have little real power, but – on the other hand – just as much access to the council offices as the administrative employees. And councillors would know exactly how the tender system worked; probably, too, where the Tender Box key was kept. They could come in and out after hours, on legitimate business; could, in fact, stay on after the eight o'clock deadline unnoticed, safe in the knowledge that nobody else would be coming in through the double-locked outer doors. They had their own private and well-equipped party rooms. It would be possible for a councillor to choose a night when nobody else was having a party meeting in the canteen – if he or she wanted to carry out some particularly private business . . . It seemed a more open scenario than any other she had considered, even if it involved a certain degree of risk-taking. If one particular councillor had been involved in all the suspect deals Musthill had won . . .

More latecomers were making a hurried entrance. Then, on the dot of seven thirty, a voice boomed out, 'Be upstanding for the Lord Mayor!'

In his robes and in solemn procession, the Lord Mayor managed to look thoroughly ceremonial, despite being a small, round, twinkly man. He entered, preceded with due gravity by an official carrying the glittering, ornate shape of the city mace, and was followed by his deputy in a lesser chain of office, then by the sheriff in his, then by a slim white-haired man in an ordinary suit, whom Jane recognised as being the Chief Executive. A black-robed chaplain completed the procession. The mace was decanted onto a metal stand set into a stone flag in the middle of the chamber floor. So that was what it was for; noticing it earlier, Jane had wondered if it was the remains of some torture instrument placed there by old tradition. The Lord Mayor took his place on the dais, taking the carved chair in the centre, his deputy and the Chief Executive flanking him. The sheriff slipped into a bench at floor level, while the chaplain lurked in front of a chair on the other side. Everyone was requested to bow their heads while the chaplain intoned a short prayer.

Formality definitely crumbled once the opening ceremony was completed, Jane decided some time later. Almost as soon as the main proceedings began, people started slipping out of their seats and going to whisper to friends. Some left the council chamber altogether for a while and then wandered back: others made a habit of talking to each other deliberately during other members' speeches.

A bell sounded loudly to interrupt anyone who spoke for more than the permitted three minutes: it appeared to be set automatically, a green light on a metal box changing to amber and then to red with the pealing of the bell.

'Come out and have a coffee to leaven the boredom.' Harry Duckham had appeared in front of Jane. 'Coffee room's outside – come on.'

The minutes of the Environment Committee which were currently being voted through, with various councillors springing up to put forward arguments and opinions, seemed to offer little Jane could not find out simply by reading them. They were also extensive. She joined Harry as he led the way out of the chamber through the door in the rear screen. Several other people were moving to and fro, out of what Jane had decided was a remarkably mixed bag; members of the council seemed to come in all sizes and most ages, from solidly senior grey hair to surprising youth. There was a more or less even division in gender, too, and a fair sprinkling of accents, from outright local, to classless, to distinctly posh, with even the odd Scottish burr.

They passed into an outer lobby. Harry opened an unobtrusive door to one side, bringing a hum of conversation and laughter, then a cry from the woman named Betty to whom Jane had been introduced earlier.

'Shut the door, Harry, you know this is the only bit that's soundproof! I see you've nabbed our police inspector. You're in bad company, dear, he's a right little horror, that one!'

'She can't help it, I'm her ward councillor. We took the whole of that ward off you, remember?' Harry said smugly. He made for the coffee machine in one corner, saying, 'Black or white, Jane, and sugar or no sugar?'

'Black, no sugar, thanks,' Jane told him. Tina Levitt was sitting with Betty. Why had she flinched when Betty said the words police inspector? It had been a tiny movement, but noticeable.

'How are you enjoying it?' Betty inquired, giving Jane one of her merry looks. 'Oh, are you off, Tina? I'll come back in with you, then. And don't worry, love,' she went on sympathetically as the two women began to move towards the door, 'I'll sit on bloody Gavin if he looks as if he might make a fool of himself. You would do well to try and keep him off the sauce, though, if it's starting to turn into a problem. He wasn't at his best last time at committee . . . Harry, if you're listening with your long ears again, and if you dare make capital out of that, I'll find some really nasty way of getting you thrown off everything, you see if I don't!'

Nobody else in the room seemed to find her suddenly raised voice or her instruction surprising, and Harry looked amused. He said, 'She probably would, too, she's more dangerous than she looks, is our Mrs Adams.' He settled down to tell a few more people who Jane was and what she was doing there. One of them was the leader of the Labour group; he and Harry had been slagging each other off regularly in the chamber, but relations out of it seemed remarkably friendly. Jane took care not to tell either of them that a lot of the cross-party banter seemed very childish to her, and if, as they both said with satisfaction, the atmosphere was 'as much like Parliament as we can make it', that was no recommendation for national government either.

One or two more people recognised her from Richard Musthill's funeral and inquired whether the police had solved the case of the extra body yet. Jane offered the same response as previously. There was a general air of sympathy over 'poor old Dick' and the miserable business of his interrupted funeral, but nobody seemed inclined to dwell on the subject of his death and the manner of it.

Harry escorted Jane back to the chamber after a while, where the business of the meeting was still grinding on. Shortly after that, she saw Gavin Levitt stagger out of his seat looking abruptly green about the gills. He left and did not come back. After a while his wife followed him, and several minutes later the sound of a private quarrel erupted all too audibly above the rear screen.

'No I don't, you silly cow, and whose fault is it anyway? Tell me that? Oh, I'm the one to blame, I suppose, nothing at all to do with you, or that you can't keep your hands off other—'

'Would somebody please go and remind those in the lobby,' boomed the Lord Mayor's voice with sudden authority, 'that the coffee room is the only place for private conversation? Thank you.' Someone from the Conservative benches was already moving, fast, while heads endeavoured not to turn. 'Councillor Mays, please continue and I'll see that you have extra time to make up for the interruption.'

A brief and quieter colloquy from beyond the screen culminated in the forceful slamming of the outside door. Gavin Levitt failed to reappear, though after a minute Tina Levitt did, looking pale and avoiding all eyes, but with her chin set.

A brave return, Jane thought, and was irritated to see Harry Duckham make a very obvious mime of putting a bottle to his lips with an air of satisfied amusement. He did stop, however, when several people including some in his own party cast fierce glares at him. A sympathetic solidarity apparently ruled.

The minutes of a final committee worked their way through without further interruption and were voted on by the usual show of hands counted by a clerk from a table below the dais. Then at last they were all upstanding for the Lord Mayor again, the mace was retrieved, the clerk whose job it had been to count the votes was shuffling his papers together, people stretched and shifted and began to file away. It was over.

Jane took herself off before Harry Duckham could catch up with her again, should that have been his intention. There was nothing further she could immediately learn. If there had, by any chance, been a guilty party present, that person would scarcely have it stamped across his or her forehead. As she reached the fresh air and crossed the road beside the tall bulk of the West Gate, its tower blotting out the stars, she frowned thoughtfully.

Had her observations on the meeting given her anything new? Not really. She had seen the councillors going about their ceremonial duty . . . but behind that was the work of a multitude of committees where the real decisions were made. And the work of each committee was interlocking, which meant, in the end, that everyone had a finger in everything. Certainly as far as the councillors were concerned.

It was still true that a councillor was the most likely person to be able to make a quiet and unobserved scrutiny of the contents of the Tender Box. The party group rooms were really the only private spaces in the building, and memory told her that the windows of each of them must look out on to the building's central courtyard. Which meant that somebody could be there late into the night without displaying an obvious light into the outside world. The rooms were equipped with kettles, which could be used to steam open envelopes . . . and, if someone were going to that amount of trouble, could surely be resealed again afterwards with equal care. There were even telephones there so that the information could be phoned out. And councillors worked voluntarily, unpaid, and might be anything from independently wealthy to unemployed: surely that made more sense of a bribe of a few thousand pounds a time? That still seemed to Jane an unlikely amount to offer a career civil servant in a steady well-paid job – given the risk . . .

There was still one major snag, though, which seemed to put paid to the whole idea. The tampering with the Tender Box would have to be done at night. So there would still be at least twelve hours to go before a noon deadline. Some other company might tender just as late as the one which had illegally bought the information, and might still put in a lower bid. It would be too chancy by half; nobody, surely, would pay good money for those odds.

No, it didn't work. She would have to let it go.

She would give Superintendent Annerley her conclusions in detail, but then it would be up to him to decide if continued investigations would get them any further.

Chapter 13

'Thank you, Jane. You seem to have covered everything comprehensively,' Superintendent Annerley said. He had read her report before calling her in to talk it over, and they had already gone through it. He frowned now as he went on, 'I still don't like the coincidences of the dates – if Miss Musthill's right about them. What we could really do with is someone from Musthills to go through the accounts with us and see if there really is an alternative explanation but I'd prefer not to raise speculation there until I've considered everything further.'

'I looked up corruption cases in other districts and the most common one is bribery in exchange for planning permission,' Jane offered. 'But that doesn't apply here. They were council contracts which would have planning already granted.'

'And as you say in your report, there doesn't seem to be any way anyone could influence the actual destination of a contract outside the tender system either at committee stage or beyond.' The super frowned again. 'Glad as I'd be to think we aren't actually faced with a case of corruption, I can't let it go until we're totally sure there isn't something we haven't spotted. Just in case. It may be that our only course of action is to wait and see if it happens again. But that gives us a problem too, doesn't it? If it doesn't recur, we've got a choice of conclusions. That Richard Musthill was somehow responsible for influencing contract decisions by some means we don't know. Or that the guilty parties have decided it's no longer safe. And then we'd be allowing them to get away with past actions, which is an idea I don't like at all.'

'No, sir.'

'Anyway we can hardly ask Miss Musthill and her sister to keep away from the company indefinitely so that we can set up a trap. Musthills landed a contract only two months ago so they'll be unlikely to be tendering for another one just yet.' He sat looking thoughtful, and tapped his finger against the sheaf of papers Jane had given him. 'I'll have to brew this for a while.'

'Yes, sir.' Jane hesitated, then added, 'Miss Musthill was very keen for us to start investigating Neville Pemberton. I told her we couldn't, without due cause. There is his protracted absence, of course . . .'

'We've got nothing at the moment to indicate that those possibly falsified entries in the accounts are down to him, whether they turn out to be an indication of corrupt practices or not. We can hardly start investigating him just because he's away on business.' The superintendent paused, frowning into the middle distance. 'No, she'll have to accept that it's not enough. We've got no grounds to investigate either him or his inconveniently absent chief accountant.'

'If Miss Musthill rings me again, shall I stall her?'

'Leave that with me, I'll telephone her myself. She'll have to accept that our hands are tied unless or until we have more to go on.' With that definite statement made, he looked up to give Jane a smile. 'Thank you again for the thoroughness of your report, though it's no more than I would have expected of you. Did you find it interesting – from your own point of view?'

'Yes, thank you, sir. And I suppose you could say I've shown the flag very thoroughly.' Jane tried not to let her voice sound ironic – or to remember that she would still have to make that tour of the Mayor's Parlour if it was offered. 'You were right, nobody seemed at all surprised that I was taking an interest, and it's all grist to the mill and useful for future contacts.'

'I don't believe I've actually asked you: how are you enjoying your new post?'

'Very much, thank you, sir.' It was the answer he would expect. Not the wistful comment that it had felt good to be doing something investigative again. 'Particularly the European side,' Jane added, with more truth this time.

'Yes, that promises to be a growth area, and a liaison officer with linguistic skills should prove very valuable to us. The plans are that every Kent division should have a language specialist before long.' He gave her one of his approving looks, then added, 'I must let you get back to your own work, and thank you again for letting me borrow you.'

'Any time, sir,' Jane said obediently but gave him a grin along with it. She had worked for him enough in the past for him to be well aware she would have found leaving CID a wrench. It was no use, however, finding the thought of returning to a steady diet of public relations unappealing. She had given him the report he wanted, including every possibility and every conclusion, so that was that.

At least it was coffee time, to give her an excuse to go down to the canteen instead of settling back at her desk. She might hear if there was any further news about the torso.

As she made for the stairs, Jane tried to detach her mind from a sudden moodiness, brought on by the sour thought that at least she could show an interest in murder here, if not at home. Not that she had the chance to talk to anyone about anything at home, considering she and Adrian barely seemed to have seen each other for days. What on earth was the use of her switching to a job which gave her more free time if all that offered was an empty space? He had not only been out all Saturday, as warned, but all Sunday too. He and Felicity had had to go through the practice records so that she could familiarise herself with their regulars.

And when Jane had looked in at the practice to see how they were faring, or if they would like to stop for lunch, she found they had already stocked up with sandwiches and coffee from the flat upstairs. She had had the distinct feeling of being *de trop*, and that Adrian would rather she didn't stay.

Then on Monday night Felicity did a call-out but rang for Adrian to go and help because it was a horse with a condition which was apparently too complex for her to manage alone. Tuesday night Jane had had to go to full council. Instead of choosing to do it then, Adrian had elected last night to take Felicity round to meet various farmers so that they would know her and she would know the route to their farms . . . It was all necessary, and inevitable, but they did seem to be having a positively minimal private life at the moment.

He had had to put up with as much from her, Jane reminded herself, when she had been busy in the past with CID surveillances. It was just – a nuisance. And she had the uncomfortable feeling that he didn't want her to make friends with Felicity, either. Jane had made a point of suggesting that they should invite her round for an evening some time soon. All he had said was, 'Oh, I don't think so,' and then finished his breakfast in a hurry and gone out.

Jane managed a rueful grin at her lapse into self-pity and pushed open the canteen door. At once she found herself part of an audience. Dave and George – PCs Mason and Doyle – were clearly in the middle of describing some very recent arrest to an assembled group of their colleagues.

'And the little bugger had only broken the man's arm with a kick, hadn't he? He got one in on my thigh, too, right there,' Dave expostulated with remembered injury, rubbing a point on his extremely solid leg. 'I was lucky it was only a glancing blow and that George'd grabbed him from behind by then. It took both of us to put the cuffs on him. We had to restrain him round the legs with straps, too, before we could shove him in the car.'

'Sounds like a definite case of resisting arrest,' Jane said and gave both the constables a grin as they turned round to acknowledge her presence. 'What size was this violent character? A giant?'

'It wasn't size, ma'am, it was the way he could move! I

tell you, I wouldn't like to have that one coming out at me from nowhere on a dark night.'

'I hope you didn't get too damaged. Where did all this happen – full daylight in the High Street?'

'No, Tissingham. We were out there on a call about somebody's stolen hens.' George Doyle's expression, though it tried for blankness, showed what he thought about having to chase missing hens. 'Anyway, we were just starting back when we spotted this fight and stopped to intervene. I tell you, ma'am, he'd got two grown men cowering. Anyway, once we'd got him they went off to hospital, said it would be quicker in their car than waiting for an ambulance. And we brought him in. Not that he'd give his name. Or anything. Wouldn't say a word. He's in the cells cooling off until he decides to be more co-operative.'

'Whereabouts in Tissingham?' Jane asked with a frown.

'Just outside that manor on the edge, where the funny cult is. Wouldn't be surprised if he doesn't come from there.'

'Yes, he does,' Dave put in, '‘cause he'd been wearing one of those robe things, I saw it on the ground just inside the gates. There were some other kids in the background in robes too but they ran away when they saw us. Just left this one boy – well, by that time we were trying to restrain him anyway. Weird-looking kid really and he moved like, oh, like Bruce Lee in those Kung Fu films.'

'Wait a minute. You said he didn't speak? When you brought him in?'

'Wouldn't speak, wouldn't listen. Sarge just said put him in a cell to cool off and see if he comes to his senses.'

'If he's the one I think he is, he's deaf. And probably

can't speak either, since I was told he's been deaf from birth. It's all right, you obviously didn't know.' Jane gave the constables a look to show she wasn't allocating blame, but turned rapidly back towards the canteen door. 'Who's on the desk, Sergeant Morris?'

'Yes, ma'am.'

'I'd better go and have a word with him then.'

Martin. It had to be him. And fighting outside the manor – what the hell had been going on? Jane's steps took her rapidly to the charging area where she found Sergeant Morris ensconced behind the desk, though luckily not booking anyone else in at the moment.

'I've just heard from Mason and Doyle about their bringing a boy in after a fight. Wouldn't answer when spoken to, and you've got him in the cells.'

'Yes, ma'am. Thoroughly uncooperative, so we put him in to cool off. Is there a problem?'

'I think he's someone I know. And if I'm right, he's stone deaf. Not very tall, about twenty, chunky, short hair, face like a Greek statue?'

'I don't know if I'd've said that about his face, but it sounds like the same lad. You'd better take a look, ma'am.'

He moved to join her, his face concerned, his mind obviously moving over the fact that a deaf prisoner presented a different problem. 'We'd better get someone from Social Services who can sign or get him to lip-read or something, if you're right. Here, in number three. I did take a look at him a moment ago to see how he was doing or if he'd answer.'

He flicked up the metal panel on the cell door so that Jane could peer in. The figure crunched up on one end of the bench at the far end of the cell had his face half turned away, one arm curled protectively over his head, and made no movement to acknowledge the sound of the panel opening. He looked as if he was making himself as small as possible in his corner. Jane turned her head to the custody sergeant.

'Yes, it is him. Look, I think we'd better be careful with this. He won't have been able to hear the caution so we may be on dodgy ground for locking him up at all, even if we had to for his own and everybody else's protection.'

'Thank God I didn't chuck him in with the restrainers on. I nearly did. Does he know you, ma'am? I don't think I'd better let you in, anyway, he may look quiet enough now but he was like an animal when he was brought in. I'd better get Inspector Henderson to come down,' he added.

'Yes, I'd suggest that. Leave the panel open. What is the actual charge?'

'Affray, bodily harm, resisting arrest. I've sent Della – WPC Maxwell – up to the hospital to check on the victim. Doyle and Mason said his friend was taking him straight there.' They had returned to the desk and Sergeant Morris picked up the internal phone, requested Inspector Henderson's presence in the charging area as a matter of urgency, then turned back to Jane. 'Didn't occur to me that he might be deaf. He just seemed, well, out of it. We can't exactly let him out, though, can we? Doyle and Mason said he broke this man's arm. We're going to have to—'

He broke off as Inspector Henderson came round the corner. 'Hello, Ron,' Jane said, 'sorry to interfere in your department, but I've recognised a prisoner of yours and he's going to need a special approach. He—'

Her words were interrupted by the buzz of the desk phone. She continued with a rapid outline of the problem in a lower voice while Sergeant Morris answered it, then found he was waiting to intervene. There was a peculiar expression on his face and he raised his eyebrows in Jane's direction.

'Front desk says there's a man in robes saying we've arrested Martin Jones and he's his guardian. Says you'll vouch for him, ma'am . . . Sir what?' he added into the phone. 'Sir Nanda?'

'I was just going to suggest it might be a good idea to send for him. Senander Baba,' Jane told Sergeant Morris and Inspector Henderson. 'And yes, I can vouch for him. He's someone I've called on, to do with community relations.'

So Senander had come after Martin. She should have expected that. She gave a quick explanation – Tissingham, the cult, its guru – and was half amused to see Ron Henderson trying to look deadpan about the whole situation. You really never did know what police work was going to throw up next. Gurus, asking to be vouched for by police inspectors, were certainly out of the common run.

'We'd better both go and talk to him in an interview room. Can you give me the charge sheet, Sergeant? Yes, all right, I know it's temporary and you couldn't get any name and address. We can't even think of charging him when he can claim not to have been properly cautioned anyway.' Inspector Henderson gave a dire look, then applied his attention to the sheet Sergeant Morris handed him. 'Hm. Well, Doyle and Mason had to apply restraint if he was committing that kind of violence, deaf or not. And they couldn't have known if nobody told them. Where's the victim?'

'Hospital, sir. Della Maxwell's up there with them to see what the damage is.'

'Let me know as soon as she reports back. Meanwhile, we'd better go and talk to this – what did you say his name was?'

'Senander Baba.'

'Right. In the meantime, Sergeant, see who we've got listed for communicating with the deaf and try and get hold of someone. We'll need to have done that. Oh, and keep a regular eye on the boy to make sure he's all right, will you?'

Senander was waiting in a relaxed stillness in the front foyer, his composure apparently unruffled by the stares which were being offered to his shaven head and long white robe. He looked just the same, Jane thought, and as if it was perfectly natural to be dressed like that in these surroundings. Despite the outer air of tranquillity, however, there was an immediate impression of – urgency? – in the grey eyes as they caught sight of Jane. It was lost behind a brief smile of greeting and a look of grave concern.

'Inspector Perry. I'm glad you were in. Your officers brought Martin in here, I believe. May I see him? If he's been shut up—'

'I'm afraid he had to be, for his own safety. And nobody realised at first that he was deaf, which is natural, I think. This is Inspector Henderson. If you'd like to come this way, we can have a talk in the interview room.'

'I want to reassure myself that Martin's all right. As well as his deafness, which is profound, he had an abused childhood which included being locked in cupboards as punishment.' Senander addressed that politely to Inspector Henderson, mingling charm with firmness and apology. 'So I'm sure you can understand that locking him away when he can't understand what's going on could be damaging.'

'He's being carefully observed, sir, and I'm afraid it was necessary.' Inspector Henderson sounded equally firm. They had reached an interview room by now, the door closing behind them. 'He has actually injured somebody—'

'Yes, I'm aware of that. Are you aware of the reason for it? Two men came into the manor grounds and tried to kidnap one of the girls. Martin went to her defence.'

'Ah, I see.' Inspector Henderson's expression as he glanced down at the charge sheet in his hand showed that point had not been raised. Jane had not heard that side of it either. 'Have you got proof of that, sir?'

'Yes, certainly.' Senander sat down calmly on the chair he was offered, the white robe falling tidily around him. 'Perhaps Inspector Perry hasn't had time to explain what we are. A community, with voluntary members who are adults. The men who tried to snatch Elena, the girl concerned, had no legal right to do so, nor to be on our private grounds. The fact that they're undoubtedly employed by her father makes no difference: Elena is twenty-two years old.'

'Could you tell me exactly what happened?'

'A group was raking the drive and tidying the bushes when two men came in through the gates and tried to drag Elena out to their car. Martin went to her aid, was attacked, and reacted. I can provide you with witness statements to show that's what happened. Oh, and I'd like the men charged with attempted kidnap – if you can find them.'

'We'll need to follow that up, sir. The men are at the hospital at the moment and I gather one of my officers is with them.'

'I'll be surprised if you find the men at the hospital or prepared to make a complaint,' Senander said drily. 'I should explain. There was an attempt to snatch Elena before, at one of our previous addresses. The men concerned that time certainly weren't prepared to be interviewed by the police.' He offered Inspector Henderson a grave smile. 'All my young people are protective of each other, and I find it understandable that Martin should have gone to Elena's defence. If you feel he overreacted . . . Personally I find that understandable too. She's a slight young woman, and there were two of them, manhandling her. Elena is prepared to say so, and also that, when Martin went to her aid, he was attacked. First.'

Jane wondered if that was true. She had seen Martin in action teaching his class. She kept silent, however. Ron Henderson was frowning. 'Where is the young woman now?' he inquired.

'She's very distressed so I left her in the charge of Mrs Mather at Tissingham vicarage – the vicar's wife. That's why I wasn't here sooner.'

Jane found herself wondering how he got here at all. Perhaps he had borrowed Michael Mather's car. He had certainly assembled a formidable defence for Martin's actions and taken care to include a pillar of the community in it in the shape of the vicar's wife. No, perhaps she was being unfair; who else could he have gone to with a distressed and frightened girl?

'May I see Martin?' he said. 'He'll be very confused,

since he won't know what's going on. He can lip-read, but only when he concentrates, and I doubt he's in any state to do so. I can communicate with him by sign language, and explain.' Senander was bringing the full force of his considerable persuasion to bear in a way which, at least to Jane, was almost palpable.

'That might be useful, sir, though we have sent for someone who knows sign language in the hope that—'

'Good, I'm glad to hear you've taken the trouble. It'll need to be someone who knows American sign though – which isn't much used in this country,' Senander said with apologetic charm, 'but happens to be the one I know and taught him. He's twenty years old and therefore legally an adult, but in view of his disability I must ask to be there when he's interviewed. I called myself his guardian at your front desk as I consider myself that to all my young people. In the circumstances, and since he might react violently, out of bewilderment, towards anyone else, I think it's fair to ask if I could be taken to him in his cell or wherever you've got him. Now.'

It was unusual. But then so was the situation. Jane could see that the hint of underlying steel in Senander Baba's calm manner was not lost on Ron Henderson. The suggestion was there that Senander would, if necessary, make trouble. A deaf boy, police brutality – Doyle and Mason had made no secret of the fact that they had trussed Martin up fairly thoroughly to bring him in – police attitudes towards the leader of a religious cult . . . Jane did not relish the thought of having to deal with the public relations fallout from that one if it turned bad.

'That sounds like a very good idea, sir,' Henderson said after the briefest of deliberations. 'You do understand, however, that we can't just let it go. We'll have to keep the young man here at least until we've sorted out what actually happened.'

'As long as I can see him.'

Senander got to his feet with his usual grace. He even offered Jane the glimmer of a smile as Henderson led the way out of the room. Since they were taking him through into the non-public areas, Senander had to be given a visitor's badge. He gave it a quizzical look as he was offered it, but pinned it to his robe.

Jane was abruptly deflected as soon as they got inside the inner door by someone from the general office signalling to her, wanting to deliver the message that Chief Inspector Lowell had been looking for her – something to do with a telephone call from one of her French counterparts. By the time she had sorted that out, Ron Henderson was coming back frowning and looking as if something was giving him the uncomfortable feeling of crumbs under the skin.

'Someone get me the FME,' he said. 'I want the boy in three checked over to make sure he hasn't got any bruises that couldn't have been caused by fighting. And hasn't anybody heard from Della Maxwell yet?'

'She radioed in to say she was up at the hospital, sir, but she hadn't been able to find anyone with a broken arm who'd been brought in by a friend. Or not so far. She's still looking.'

'And nobody's turned up at the front desk with their arm in a sling and wanting to lay charges, I suppose. I want

Doyle and Mason. If they've gone out again, call them back!'

'What have you done with the guru?' Jane asked.

'What he insisted – locked him up in the cell with the boy. Well, he would have it. I left him sitting there as calm as ninepence, just waiting for the boy to stop crouching in the corner and notice him. This has been badly handled. *Somebody* should have spotted he couldn't understand what was being said to him!'

'Dave and George said he was struggling too much for anyone to tell,' somebody protested, only to receive a glare.

'I want a WPC out to Tissingham to take a statement from a girl called Elena at the vicarage. And then from the rest of the bunch at the manor. Yes, what?'

'I don't think they'll answer the door if they see a uniform,' Jane said apologetically. 'House-to-house had that trouble on the Tissingham murder inquiry. In fact if the story Senander Baba told us is true, I doubt if they'll let anyone in just now. Not even me, and they've seen me before. Particularly with him not there.'

'All right, just the girl at the vicarage then. Elena something. The vicar's wife is supposed to be looking after her. I suppose we should be able to count on a vicar's wife being co-operative.'

That order given, he turned back to cast a look of apology at Jane. 'Sorry, didn't mean to snap your head off. Look, I've got to chase up the whole of this story. Then eventually we'll have to find some way of questioning the boy himself. I'd be grateful if you'd sit in on that when we get to it, since you seem to know something about these cult people.'

'Okay. Just let me know when. And let me know if there's anything else I can do.'

'Thanks for alerting us to the boy's deafness. We don't want any comebacks on the way he's been treated. I'll buzz you when we get any further, then— Ah, Mason and Doyle, there you are. I want a word with you.'

Meanwhile, Senander Baba was sitting quietly locked in a cell with Martin. Jane would dearly have liked to go and look through the flap and see what he was doing.

Chapter 14

The scene in the interview room felt slightly unreal.

Martin, quiet now but with a tension in his muscles which showed itself in the occasional very faint shiver, sat still in the chair to which he had been led, with Senander beside him. His face was blank, with a shuttered lack of expression which made that classical profile look even more like a statue.

Ron Henderson had removed his uniform jacket at Senander's request and replaced it with a tweed jacket he must have had in his locker. He looked rather bizarre, casual above, official below. Jane was in civilian clothes anyway today, despite the fact that she was nominally attached to the uniformed side nowadays; and Senander sat there in his usual folds of white, draped like a toga over a white T-shirt. One arm, slightly tanned and with a dusting of light brown hairs, lay tranquilly across the table, and the overhead light caught the smooth sculpture of his shaven head.

A young woman from the local Deaf Association was in attendance. She had said apologetically that her skill was in English sign language, not American, though she should be able to follow most of what was signed nevertheless. She sat to one side, looking as if she was trying not to feel confused.

A statement had been taken from Elena Georgiadis and brought back to the station. This confirmed that two men had tried to kidnap her from the manor grounds and that Martin had been attacked first when he went to her rescue. She was too distressed to be asked to come in to the station. There was a confirmatory statement from Mrs Mather to say that the girl had been brought to her sobbing and with red marks all the way up her arms which were already turning into bruises.

There had been no sighting of the two men. Della Maxwell had failed to find them at the hospital. A ring round to local doctors had not shown them up either. They appeared to have vanished.

Martin still had to be interviewed, since there certainly had been an affray. Arrangements had been made to solve the problem of taping an interview with someone who was unable to make audible answers. Senander would speak aloud at the same time as he signed to Martin, and would then speak Martin's signed replies. It was complicated but necessary, and the formalities had to be gone through. Senander had made another request: that it should be Jane who asked the questions. Martin would more easily be persuaded to trust her, since he had seen her with his guru.

Inspector Henderson had agreed to that too, to make sure it was seen that the police were doing all they could to be fair and reasonable. He started the tape now, spoke the required official description into it giving date and time and those present, and indicated to Jane that she could begin.

'I'm addressing Senander Baba, who is acting as Martin

Jones's translator. Would you ask Martin to tell us in his own words – I mean terms – what happened, please?'

Martin fixed his eyes on her as she spoke – though only, Jane thought, because Senander had made a clear indication to him that he should. They were hazel eyes with gold flecks in them, adding to the boy's extraordinary beauty; and as they watched her warily but with distinct intelligence, she was sure he understood what she had said. As soon as she stopped he looked at Senander who signed a question with graceful fingers.

'Senander Baba is signing to Mr Jones,' Ron Henderson put in quickly, and added, 'Aloud, sir.'

'Yes, I'm sorry. I said, "If you understood, answer."'

Martin's fingers began to fly, roughly at first, then with more care as Senander made a restraining gesture. The light baritone voice with its faint Australian twang began a calm translation.

'We were tidying the garden. Two men came in very fast through the gates. They must have been watching us. Waiting for Elena to go near the gate.' Senander paused with a gesture to Martin to stop and glanced politely at the young woman from the Deaf Association. He said with a friendly smile, 'I don't know if you want to confirm . . .'

'It does seem to be what he's saying,' she said, looking at Jane and seeming slightly flustered by the sudden attention. Or perhaps by Senander's extremely charismatic smile, Jane thought drily. 'Do you want me to try and translate as well?'

'Only if there's any query, I think.' Jane looked at Ron Henderson for confirmation, and he nodded. 'I'm speaking to Senander Baba again. Please would you ask Mr Jones to go on.'

'I saw them catch hold of Elena. Erik was nearest but they knocked him over.' Senander put up a hand to stop Martin, flickered his fingers in a question, spoke it aloud before Inspector Henderson could intervene again. 'I asked Martin to confirm that. That they knocked Erik down. He's saying that Erik could have tripped, because of his leg.' He stopped again with a quick smile at Jane. 'Inspector Perry can confirm that we have a young man with a lame leg, she's met him.'

'Yes, that's so. Please ask Martin to go on.'

'I went to help Elena.'

'And?' Jane asked, as the boy's gestures stopped. She saw Senander spread his hands in a querying gesture which needed no translation. Then he was speaking again.

'They were hurting her. She was frightened.' Martin's gestures were quite forceful now and these, too, required little translation, save for the fact that it was needed for the tape. 'I tried to stop them. One of them came for me. I was trying to get to Elena. I made them let her go.'

'How?'

Martin gave her a hostile look. After a moment, and after a calm reminder from Senander, he made a brief gesture in return.

'He says you know how.'

'All the same, I'd like him to tell us.'

Martin made some very quick gestures, his face scornful. Senander said placidly, 'He chopped one man and kicked the other. He means you to understand by martial arts fighting. As you know, he's good at it.'

'Did none of the others come to help you?'

'They knew I could do it and they were better out of the way.'

'Did you hit the men first, or did either of them hit you?'

Senander gave her a thoughtful look but apparently translated her words, since that was what he said aloud. And the young woman from the Deaf Association offered no denial. If she was following. Martin gave an angry look, turned his head to Senander, received a calm look and a small gesture in return. 'Mr Jones is pausing to think and is being instructed by his translator to answer,' Ron Henderson's voice said flatly beside Jane.

'I meant them to let Elena go.'

'Please answer the original question.'

'One of them tried to hit me. He missed.' Martin's scornful look showed that he wouldn't have expected anything else.

Jane asked carefully, 'But you felt he intended to attack you?'

'Yes.'

'And then what?'

'They let Elena go.'

'And after that?'

'The police came.'

'What were you doing when the police came?'

There was a pause again; a glance from Martin to Senander. Finally Martin broke into another bout of gestures, fingers and arms moving, hands coming up to his face then down again. It was very expressive, much more so than the calm translation his guru offered.

'I wanted to make sure they didn't come again. At least I wanted to frighten them. They were trying to harm Elena. So I went after them outside. That's when the police came.'

'Why didn't you stop once the police were there?'

'I really don't think that's a fair question, Inspector,' Senander said mildly, speaking for himself not Martin. 'He has had no reason to trust the police in the past. As I once told you, I think. He was probably afraid they might just hand Elena over and only check the true facts afterwards, when it might be too late. He had no means of putting his side of it, after all.'

'Would you ask him all the same?'

He did, though he gave her a reproachful look first. Martin frowned as if he didn't understand. Perhaps, literally, he didn't. The glance he gave Jane was inimical and she saw that tremor in his muscles again, the faintest of shivers. Finally, after a wait, he made a small, sulky gesture with his hands.

'He says he didn't see them,' Senander translated.

'I see. Is he telling us he wasn't aware who they were when they grabbed hold of him? They were in uniform.'

Senander's hands spoke that, while his voice repeated it. There was another pause. Then Martin's fingers answered, unwillingly.

'I knew who they were, but I was afraid of them.'

Jane was aware that the young woman from the Deaf Association had stirred and turned her head towards her. 'Miss Clary has a comment,' she said noncommittally for the tape.

'I'm sorry, I – I thought what he said was, "I didn't like them."'

'I'd say he meant both, and that in his case it's much the same,' Senander replied.

'Well, yes, it's only that I thought—'

'Very well. Does Mr Jones agree that he had to be restrained in order to be brought into the station?'

'He didn't know why they were taking him!' Senander protested.

'Very well, we'll grant the probability of that.'

'Will you also grant the probability – the *fact* – that he was doing everything he could to stop someone he looks on as a sister from being kidnapped? Taken away by force? Should any member of the public simply stand by and allow that? And a further point: we have a boy here who, due to an abused childhood, reacts badly to male authority. Two large policemen could certainly be said to represent that authority, don't you think?'

Jane glanced at Ron Henderson and saw him give the tiniest shrug. In the absence of the victims, they had no charge besides affray and resisting arrest. And the arrest, in the circumstances, had its problems. 'We'll stop the tape here while I have a word with Inspector Henderson,' Jane said. 'Would you excuse us for a moment?'

Outside, they looked at each other, then Ron Henderson shrugged again. 'There isn't anything else I can think of to ask him. You've covered the basic points. He went for the men intending to hurt, that's clear, but in view of the girl Elena's statement we can't make too much of that. Doyle and Mason – well, we don't want an argument about how much they had to manhandle him. Will this – what's-is-name Baba accept it if we go with a caution and release the young man into his custody? Since the two so-called kidnappers do seem to have taken off, we haven't got a complaint from them to back up a charge of bodily harm. And the girl's story confirms everything. I don't see there's much else we can do.'

'And there are reasonable grounds for saying he tried to fight Doyle and Mason because he didn't understand what was going on.'

'Yes, they'd be bound to go with that, wouldn't they? And I'm not sure I'd altogether like to cross that guru if he wanted to be difficult, for all he looks so calm. Odd character, and you never know with these religious weirdos, do you? Shaving your head and going around in robes is the least of it. Still, when you met him before, you thought he was all right, you said.'

'Seemed to be. Up to now, all they've been doing out there is keeping their heads down and living quietly.'

'Well, it's your job in community liaison to keep an eye on that, thank goodness, not mine – unless anything else comes up. Let's hope it doesn't. This is what we'll do, then. We'll let Jones go on a caution and tell both of them the boy's got to keep the peace in future or he will get charged. Fair enough?'

'Fine.'

'Good. And I'll point out that they should let *us* know if they see any other strange men hanging about.'

They went back in. Inspector Henderson duly explained the police decision. Jane could sense his relief when Senander merely nodded his head and appeared not to want to raise a complaint. He had apparently spent the last few minutes showing Miss Clary some of the American signs and where they were different from the English ones, and the young woman was looking slightly flushed and definitely charmed.

Inspector Henderson requested that Senander should put his signature to the tape – and that Martin should too, after Senander informed him tranquilly but with a lift of the eyebrows that Martin could read and write. A caution to keep the peace was delivered, via Senander. He did seem to have the boy well in line, though with a gentle affection; Martin was looking withdrawn again and faintly sulky, but obedient. Ron Henderson left, taking Miss Clary with him, and Jane was left behind to show Martin and Senander out.

'You were quite tough on us,' Senander said, but with a glint of humour in his eyes as he looked at Jane. 'But thank you all the same.'

'I have to do my job. Will Martin be all right?'

'I think so, now.'

'And the girl, Elena?'

'I hope Mrs Mather has been able to keep her reassured, but I must get back to her. To all of them. We can go?'

'Yes. Oh, could you . . . No, perhaps not. Perhaps it doesn't matter.'

'What?'

'I wondered if you could ask Martin something? About his grandmother, Mrs Emmett? There was a night several weeks ago when she thought she heard a fight in the churchyard. I'm not suggesting Martin was involved,' Jane said quickly, 'I just wondered whether he happened to be visiting her that night and might have seen something.'

It was purely impulse that had made her ask. Senander raised an eyebrow but turned to touch Martin on the arm to get his attention, then signed a fairly long question to him. The boy, however, seemed to have had enough; Senander had got barely halfway through when Martin deliberately ducked his head and stopped watching.

'I'm sorry, he obviously doesn't want any more questions. It's a way of cutting the world out not to look.' Senander said that with quiet patience and a thoughtful glance at the boy's face. 'Is it something important?'

'Not really. I'll show you out then. Have you got transport back to Tissingham?'

'Yes, thank you,' he told her as they arrived back in the station foyer. 'It's outside. At least I hope it still is after all these hours. You don't wheelclamp strange cars in your forecourt, do you?'

'Not usually, but I'll come out with you and check.'

The large grey Saab which was parked at an angle next to a bollard looked new and luxurious and had a notice stuffed under its windscreen, but no clamp. Senander handed the notice to Jane with a grin – it was signed by the station sergeant and required the car to be removed – and produced a key from somewhere under his robe. He signed to Martin to get in, shut the door on him, and turned back to Jane.

'Be thoroughly kind and don't let anyone turn that into a fine, will you? Or I'll have to make cringing apologies.'

'Is it the Reverend Mather's car?' Jane inquired. It looked distinctly expensive to belong to a vicar.

'My landlord's. Well, I did need to get here without any

further delay, so I borrowed it.' Just for a second, the light in the grey eyes was remarkably like that of a mischievous small boy, and so was the quirk of his lips. Then he sobered and became all adult again, the concerned man of peace. 'I hope you understand Martin's reaction to your policemen, but will you give them my apologies if either of them was hurt?'

'Sure. I don't think they suffered much.' The apology would certainly surprise them. It might also reassure them, since they had been given the rough side of Inspector Henderson's tongue on their handling of the whole affair. 'If they'd known he was deaf they'd have treated him differently,' Jane said, to make sure the mitigating point went home. 'But they had no way of knowing.'

'Yes, I understand. Martin just can't take anything he thinks is bullying – now he's strong enough not to. His father, as well as his experiences in that damned children's home . . . He sought out his father, you know, when he was sixteen. Even went to work for him. His father owns some big company in the wholesale food trade. Martin was asking for nothing but the chance of contact. He worked hard, too – he's told me so, and I believe him.' Senander spoke abstractedly, his mind and his concern obviously on the boy. 'At the end of six months he was simply told to go and when he wouldn't, his father sent for the police and had him thrown out. So you see . . . Well, I must take him home.'

He gave Jane one of his glimmering smiles, glanced up at the police station with an oddly quizzical expression, then smiled at her again and walked round to let himself into the Saab. It made an unconventional picture as he drove away, back to his community and his following, to soothe them all, no doubt, and set them back on their path of simplicity and discipline. How did someone like him, with those often amused eyes, turn into a guru?

Jane shook her head and went back into the station.

She had lost the whole of today from mid-morning onwards. It had all taken hours, while the victims were sought, Elena Georgiadis's statement was solicited, a translator for the deaf was found; and while Dave Mason and George Doyle were asked again for a detailed account of exactly what they saw, exactly how they behaved. And through it all Senander had sat tranquil and uncomplaining in a cell with Martin until the police were finally ready to interview him.

It was all over now, anyway. And it must practically be time to pack up for the day. In fact a glance at her watch showed Jane it was actually past time.

She went upstairs to make a check on what was on her desk, what she should have been doing but had rapidly rescheduled during the day. Nothing else too vital had come up, luckily. Except for a message which had been brought up and left on her desk. It said the council press officer had rung to say that a tour of the Mayor's Parlour had been arranged for her for eleven o'clock next Monday morning, when the Lord Mayor would be glad to receive her.

Damn. She was stuck with that one. A community liaison inspector could not, on any account, stand up the Lord Mayor.

Jane pulled a resigned face, entered the appointment in her diary, and gathered her things together. She would go home. Perhaps Adrian would be in this evening.

He wasn't.

Chapter 15

'The tower is much older than the rest, and would have been a section of the original city wall,' the Lord Mayor said, pausing in the doorway of the irregularly-shaped upstairs room which now appeared to have been turned into a pleasant office. A man working behind a desk had been introduced as the mayor's administrator. 'As you can see we've had modern windows put in, though we've tried to keep them in character. Originally they would simply have been open slits.'

'For firing arrows?' Jane asked with a smile.

'I'd imagine so,' the Lord Mayor answered with a twinkle. 'The tower must have been in a good defensive position if anyone tried to cross the river and storm the walls. By the time the present house was added on, the rest of the medieval walls round this part of the city had gone and life was rather more peaceful. As I told you downstairs, the gardens were originally private and belonged to the family that lived here. Nowadays of course they're part of the city's public facilities but they do give us a nice view.'

The long vista of tidy lawns, bushes and trees visible from the end window certainly was pleasant. And directly below, between the tower and the river, wide municipal flowerbeds blazed with neat ranks of flowering plants in a variety of summer colours, flanking an asphalted path. The Mayor's Parlour had an enviable setting. Its original residents must have owned a lot of land, too, since the public gardens were now a feature of this end of the city and stretched for a good half mile along the river's meandering banks.

Jane had already been shown round the rest of the beautifully kept, highly polished house where the Mayor had his official offices. It was no mansion, merely a medium-sized residence built of brick and flint with pleasantly proportioned rooms, portraits hanging on the walls and wide Edwardian-style windows. An elegant curved staircase led to the upper floor. Apart from the tower and another office, rooms up there were empty, used only for storage. Downstairs, a sitting room, a central dining room with a long polished table, and a panelled area which served as a coffee bar formed the showplace where the city's chief dignitary, elected annually from the council's largest party, received official visitors.

They returned below, the Lord Mayor keeping up a flow of knowledgeable chat. He was not clad in his robes today but in a plain grey suit, which made him look more ordinary though just as round. He had greeted Jane with great amiability, and with such an apparent pleasure that the city's police should want to make a show of forging contacts that she felt slightly guilty.

As they reached the gleaming dining area again, the Lord Mayor summoned the hovering housekeeper who apparently ran the place, then turned to Jane with a smile.

'You've seen everything. Now, what can we offer you, coffee or tea? Coffee? Thank you, Marjorie, if we could have two coffees in here? I was explaining what the house looked like originally, Inspector Perry. If you look over here, this is the old photograph I mentioned . . .'

Other photographs were displayed all along one wall, and Jane drifted over to inspect them as the coffee arrived: fine china cups brought with a tall coffee pot.

'This one might interest you too,' said the Lord Mayor. 'You were asking upstairs about the improvements to the tower. That was done during Richard Musthill's tenure as Mayor. It was Musthills that did the work on the windows, as a gift to the city, and this is a photograph of the reopening. Dick Musthill, as you can see, and various other people from the firm, as well as official dignitaries.'

Jane leaned forward to look more closely at the colour enlargement. So that was Richard Musthill, a solid, cheerful-looking man at that time, wearing his chain of office with obvious pride. She looked for a likeness to his daughters but saw none; they must both take after their mother. 'Sheila Musthill wasn't well enough to come even then,' the Mayor said gravely behind her, 'though it wasn't realised then just how serious her illness would become. Very sad, they were a devoted couple.'

'Yes. Would that be Neville Pemberton, Richard Musthill's partner, standing half behind him?'

'No, this was five years ago so it would have been before Pemberton's time. That's . . . Oh, what is his name? Evelyn Dale, that's right. It must be, because you can see his hand, quite clearly.'

'His hand?' Jane asked, looking at the photograph in puzzlement.

'Yes, his right hand, with the birthmark all across the back of it. You probably took it for a glove – it's quite dark and extends right up to his fingers. One shouldn't notice such things, I suppose, though whenever I've met him he hasn't seemed at all self-conscious about it. He works for Musthills, some senior post on the accountancy side, I believe. The company did a very good job on the windows,' the Lord Mayor went on with approval as he bustled Jane on to the next photograph, 'and they do seem to have stayed nicely draught-free as well. These aren't in any order, I'm afraid. This one's Jack Kington, whom you probably recognise. He was Lord Mayor the year before last. Ah, now, here we have a painting rather than a photograph.'

A roundfaced, grey-haired man; the same chain of office; an oil-painted portrait in a gilded frame hung against the panelling with a dignified space round it. 'This painting was done to celebrate our first *Lord* Mayor since medieval times by crown petition, four years ago. We were demoted to being allowed no more than a mayor after an early predecessor was publicly hanged in the Buttermarket for disagreeing with the King.' The Lord Mayor offered that with a cheerfully twinkling look. 'It's a piece of city history I occasionally remind myself of and hope nobody decides to repeat it.'

'I should think you'll be safe,' Jane told him with an answering smile. What she really wanted to do was go back and look at the picture of Evelyn Dale but the Lord Mayor was leading her to the table and dealing with the cooling coffee pot. What she had been able to see of Dale had looked ordinary: tallish, light brown hair, glasses; generally nondescript. Except for a birthmark on his hand.

No picture of Neville Pemberton, which was a pity. She was beginning to feel it might be quite important to know what he looked like.

After coffee the Lord Mayor civilly escorted her outside and cheerfully waved her off as she backed her car round on the gravel parking space. He really was a very pleasant man, thought Jane as she returned his wave and drove off. Her visit had been both interesting and useful.

Her thoughts turned to Evelyn Dale. Had anyone from the firm spoken to him, personally, since he went away? According to Anna, nobody had; there had been messages from 'a friend' but the office staff had been told that Evelyn himself was not available by telephone. In person, he had talked to nobody – except, by report, Neville Pemberton, to explain the reason for his sudden absence.

Suppose something had been going on at Musthills – fraud, corruption or whatever – and suppose the chief accountant had spotted it and raised a query. And had then, rather suddenly, become absent. If Evelyn Dale had become a body, what would identify him, besides his face? One of his hands.

Jane pulled up at the nearest phone box. She punched up the number for Directory Enquiries and asked for Musthill and Pemberton's telephone number. Then she dialled again, was put through to the company switchboard, and asked to speak to Evelyn Dale.

'I'm afraid he's away at the moment. Can anyone else help you?'

'It's a personal call. Do you have a number where I can reach him?'

'I'm sorry, I'm afraid I can't give out staff home numbers, and anyway he's not there, he's away. I'm not sure when he'll be back, but would you like to leave your name and a message?'

'No, it's all right, thanks. I'll try again in a week or so. Oh, unless Mr Pemberton could tell me where to reach Mr Dale?'

'I'm afraid Mr Pemberton's away at the moment too.'

'Oh dear, then I'll have to wait, won't I? Thank you.'

So both men were still absent.

Jane reached into her bag for her diary and flicked through the back pages. Matty's work number was one she did have. It would be awkward if Dr Kremer answered since she had no official status on the case, but luckily it was Matty's familiar voice that answered.

'Autopsies, Dr Ingle here.'

'Matty, it's me, Jane. Can you talk?'

'I'm on my own at the moment, yes. Solo, but busy. So if it's about giving Steve my address—'

'It's not, actually, but while I've got you I'll start there. I'm sorry about that. It was Adrian and he didn't know. Should I have rung and warned you? I would have done, but—'

'It's all right. We had to be in touch with each other sometime. He's going to come down, but don't ask me for any conclusions because I haven't got any.'

'All right, love, I'll keep well out of it as promised. I just didn't want you to think I'd been interfering. Anyway, what I actually rang for was something different. It's not my case but I need some information on the torso.'

'You mean you can't get a look at the path report but will I recite it to you? Have a heart, girl, there's pages of it.'

'I don't need pages, just a small bit. Was there any trace of the edge of a birthmark on the right wrist? I don't actually know if the birthmark went that far, but it was quite dark and covered the back of the hand. Even if it didn't reach to the wrist, would there be any sign of it? A thickening of the skin or something?'

'Not very likely if it started lower down, and I don't remember anything being mentioned. All right,' Matty said with audible patience, 'hold on and I'll go and dig our copy of the report out of the files. Getting involved in things which aren't your brief again, are you?'

There was the faintest touch of resigned amusement in the question, but she went away without waiting for Jane to answer. There were moments of silence on the line during which Jane fed in more coins as the indicator panel showed her time was running out. Then Matty was finally back.

'We haven't noted anything that would suggest it. But, as I say, if it was surface pigmentation which started lower down . . . All we've got on both wrists is that they seem to have been severed manually with a single blow, with something very sharp like a chopper, and it was obviously done by someone who knew their anatomy well enough to know exactly where to strike. A fairly expert butchery job. Though not as violently bloody as it would have been on a live victim, of course.' Matty's voice was crisp and practical. 'Nothing special about the skin or, as my boss would say, we'd have said so.'

'Okay, thanks.'

'It helps, or doesn't help?'

'Neither really. It might have been conclusive if there had been something, but as I'm not sure about the position of the birthmark, it isn't conclusive if there isn't. It's just something that came up and I wanted to check it before I took it to Chris Hollings. Thanks, anyway.'

'My pleasure,' Matty responded drily. A smile came back into her voice as she said, 'I know what you're like once you get a bee in your bonnet. A good murder and you can't leave it alone.'

'Don't, you sound like Adrian.' If she ever bloody saw Adrian, Jane thought. An hour here and there if she was lucky. Even this last weekend, yet again . . . Felicity did seem to require an inordinate amount of his time. 'Shall we lunch again sometime?' she asked with deliberate cheerfulness. A grumble about her relationship was not the sort of subject to raise with her closest friend at the moment.

'Yeah, let's do that, but I don't know exactly when yet. I'll ring you, okay?'

The torso could be Evelyn Dale. Jane was back on to that as soon as she had put the receiver down. Possible enough to take to the DI? Yes, she had better. Tentatively. Maybe there was nothing in it, but she did know the man had not been seen since a date which fitted the facts, and she also now knew of a reason why someone might cut the hands off. It would explain Neville Pemberton's absence, too. If Neville had committed murder, he might well have calculated it was better to get out fast.

It was all speculation, but as Jane's mind ranged rapidly over the theory, it did seem to fit. And as far as she was aware, CID hadn't come up with anything at all, speculative or otherwise.

She went into the station on swift feet and began to make for the CID room, then paused. No, she would have to clear it with the super. It would be necessary to explain the corruption inquiries to Chris Hollings, and the super was still cogitating on that and had not said the imposed confidentiality could be broken. When he had stressed so firmly that no hint of the inquiry was to be let out, she could scarcely discuss it even with the DI without asking first. She turned back and went upstairs to his secretary's office.

'Has Superintendent Annerley got someone with him? I'd like a word, if I can?'

'He's away all today, Inspector, at a conference in London.'

'Oh. Will he be back later?'

'I'm not expecting him in until tomorrow morning. He's got a meeting at ten, but I could put you in for a few minutes before that, if it's urgent.'

'Yes, would you? Thanks.'

Jane managed a smile and went off to her own small room with its planning chart and public relations paraphernalia. It was frustrating but she supposed the torso could wait. It had waited several weeks already, after all. Even if she should turn out to be right, the difference between today and tomorrow could hardly be significant.

It was annoying just the same, she thought, looking round her office with irritation. What the hell was she doing here, in an area of policing she had sworn she would never allow herself to be pushed into? The sort of work women officers were supposed to go into, according to male thinking, the dull, non-dangerous, administrative, downright *secretarial* side of things.

She had to remind herself that she had only seen a photograph of Evelyn Dale because she had been doing her administrative duty. And had only been brought in on Musthills' problems because she was in community liaison. So she had better swallow her sour bile. Even though, once she handed things over to Chris Hollings, she would be out of it yet again. Oh hell, why was it so difficult to settle for what she had chosen to do?

She made herself sit down to work; pick up the phone to talk to someone about the Crime Bus they were planning to park in the shopping precinct with the logo 'Come and talk to your police'; go and see Chief Inspector Lowell with some suggestions for flyers they might have printed. He complimented her on her ideas and expressed pleasure at the council links she had been forging. They discussed an extension to the schools campaign. Then a late lunch, eaten without appetite. She fancied no more than soup and an apple.

Nobody from CID was in the canteen while she was, and for all she knew they had come up with an identity for the torso anyway. But station gossip would probably have been buzzing with it if they had. Jane was offered, instead, some teasing about being an expert on gurus, though Senander and last week's events had gone so far out of her head at the moment that she was hard put to it not to offer a genuinely blank look to the amused comments.

Back in her own office, she was just convincing herself,

very firmly, that Neville Pemberton was hardly likely to do anything between today and tomorrow, when her phone buzzed. She picked it up and snapped, 'Inspector Perry.'

'Jane? Chris Hollings here. Sorry to disturb you if you're busy, but could you come down? I've got someone in interview room one who's asking for you, says you'll know what it's all about. A Miss Anna Musthill.'

'Yes, I do know her. How did she land up with you?'

'She says someone's just tried to kill her.'

'What? Does she say who?'

'Someone called Pemberton.'

'I'm on my way,' Jane said.

Chapter 16

Anna was looking rumpled, grass-stained, and filled with a tension which made her eyes gleam feverishly. She jumped up as soon as Jane came into the room and leaned forward with her hands on the table.

'You'll have to do something now, won't you? Damned Neville took a shot at me! Several!'

'It's okay, Anna, sit down. You've met Detective Inspector Hollings, I gather. Maybe you could just run through it again for both of us.'

The constable who had been waiting quietly by the door slipped out, and Jane and Chris Hollings took their places behind the table. Anna sat down unwillingly on the other side, her restlessness palpable. 'All right,' she said on a breath, clearly reining herself in. 'I went for a walk in the woods. It's beautiful up there and I wanted to get out of the house. I'd been out for, oh, I suppose about half an hour and I was just going to start back. Then there was a kind of a ping, like an insect flying past my ear, and then I heard the crack of a rifle.'

'How far away from you?' Chris Hollings asked.

'Quite close, the sound wasn't much delayed. People do

go rabbiting in those woods so my first thought was that someone was being careless, and I let out a yell to show I was there. But then there was another shot and that one certainly only just missed me. If I hadn't suddenly moved, it would have got me in the head!'

'Where from this time?'

'It came from the same sort of angle and I thought it must be from behind a particular patch of undergrowth. The shot went slap into a tree. I went back afterwards and you can see the bullet, so that's proof for you. At the time, I ducked and yelled again and ran towards the bushes I thought it had come from, because I still thought it was carelessness. I stopped being so bloody unsuspicious after there was a third shot.'

'Close again?' Jane asked.

'Yes, but it got a tree again, I think. After that I made sure I kept behind them. I wasn't far from the road. It's quite steep there and the road's almost directly below, so I started to run towards it, as best I could. That's when I saw the car.'

'On the road down below?'

'Pulled off it into an opening where there used to be an old quarry. Parked. It gave me a – I don't know, an odd feeling. Something to do with the way it had been pulled right round the corner so it'd be out of sight. Anyway, I started yelling and shouting and making out I was talking to someone and I went zigzagging back up the hill instead of going down. Then I heard someone. Moving away from me, quite noisily, downwards, a bit further along. In a hurry. So I yelled again, still as if I was talking to someone, saying something like, "I don't know who it is but I think it came from over here." And then I ducked back – got some fieldglasses with me, did I say that? I'd been planning to look at birds, and the glasses were still on their strap round my neck. So I saw him quite clearly when he jumped down off a bank and ran to the parked car. It was Neville.'

'You're quite sure?'

'Yes, of course I'm sure! Good God, what do you need, a video tape? He was carrying a hunting rifle. He chucked it in the back of the car and jumped in in a hurry and backed out very fast. But it was definitely him.'

'He's back in the country then. Did you know that? Has he been into the company?'

'No, he hasn't. I rang Jill Huggins this morning and she said they still hadn't heard from him. But he's certainly back in the country, and taking potshots at me. He must have guessed I'd been in looking at the accounts.'

'Can you be sure he was deliberately shooting at you?' Chris Hollings asked seriously. 'That it wasn't just accidental?'

'It was no accident,' Anna said grimly. 'He must have known someone was there after I shouted, and he went on firing in the same direction, didn't he? If I had to guess, I'd say he must have seen me on my way there, walking along the road. Looking back, I think I did hear a car behind me, though I didn't take any notice. So he must have thought he'd take his chance and followed me up into the woods and waited for a good moment.' Her face was defiant. 'Afterwards, I can only suppose he must have thought I'd met someone else up there and that was who I was talking to, so he left it and ran. It wouldn't have looked like an accident any more if he'd moved in and finished me off!'

'It seems rather a rash move on his part, to try, and then leave it.' Chris Hollings was playing devil's advocate, though with careful politeness. 'If he'd actually meant to kill you, as you say—'

'He didn't know I'd be able to see him when he took off. He'd have thought I was still crashing about up above looking for a careless hunter. And whether he meant to kill me or frighten me, I've got a legitimate complaint against him. Though I'd lay a fair bet,' Anna said between her teeth, 'that if he'd had the chance, I'd have been found up there later, dead due to some accident. Inspector Perry knows why.'

'Miss Musthill found a problem in Musthills' company accounts,' Jane told Chris Hollings, 'and Neville Pemberton's the surviving partner in the firm. He's been out of the country and out of touch for some weeks. I'd better give you the details on it. Anna, we're going to leave you for a few minutes, but I'll get someone to bring you a cup of tea. Will you be all right?'

'Yes, as long as you're going to do something!'

'Of course we are. You've made a complaint and we're bound to follow it up.'

The next interview room was, luckily, empty, and after she had organised the tea for Anna and a constable to stay with her, Jane shut the door. 'Sorry about this,' she said apologetically to Chris. 'It's just that I've been on a highly confidential inquiry for the super, with strict instructions not to discuss it with anyone at all. He's off at some damned conference in London today, so could we keep what I'm going to tell you now between the two of us? And only give out the basics about someone taking a shot at Miss Musthill?'

'Yes, sure. So?'

'Anna raised the possibility of corruption between her father's building firm, Musthills, and the council. She took it to the super. It's still at a very confidential stage because he wanted to see first who could be doing it, from the council end. He asked me to find out a few things, which I did, and he's still brewing it. Neville Pemberton could be the suspect at the Musthills' end, but he's been out of the country on a buying trip and it hasn't been possible to look at him at all thoroughly yet. Anna Musthill is one of the heirs to the Musthill company and she's also a top accountant. Are you with me so far?'

'Yes. The Musthill funeral – would I have seen this man Pemberton there?'

'No, he didn't attend. He'd just gone away.'

'There's more, from your expression.'

'Well, yes . . . No, I won't raise that with you at the moment, it might just be a distraction. I'll fill you in on that a bit later, but I do think Neville Pemberton might be dangerous.' Jane frowned. 'It's an outside chance because I can't see that he'd be as rash as that, but maybe we ought to have a squad car hanging around very obviously outside the Benbridge house at Tissingham, as a precaution. Heather Benbridge is the other heir.'

'Okay, agreed. And meantime you want us to keep Anna under wraps while we check out her story and look for Pemberton, as a matter of urgency?'

'Yes. Look – oh hell, I may be quite wrong, but I'd better

bring it up after all. I came into a piece of information a couple of hours ago which I would have brought to you if it hadn't collided with the super's inquiry and if I could have got hold of him to clear it, but it's just possible that Pemberton may have something to do with the torso. Your Tissingham body.'

'Right. We'll deal with that when we've found him.' One thing you could always say for Chris Hollings, he knew when to cut through to current essentials. He gave her a sudden smile. 'I'm going to ask a favour of you now. You're obviously in on this anyway, but will you stay in, and let me borrow you back? I've got Doug Phelps out looking into a container hijack and a DC out with him. And Peter Pettigrew's up at Faversham on a meeting about car crime. So for this afternoon I could really do with you.'

'Fine by me,' Jane said happily.

'Good, thanks. I'll go and organise that squad car for the Benbridge address – watching brief. I'll also round up some bodies to start looking for Pemberton. Will you go back to Anna and see what else she can give us on him? A good description, his home address, anywhere else he might go. We'll have to take her back up to the woods and see where it all happened too, get a SOCO to dig out those bullets from the trees. Oh, and ask her for as close a description of that car as she can give us, will you?'

After the months she had spent working for him as his sergeant, it was easy to follow his line of thinking, so Jane was already well ahead of him. She went back to Anna feeling suddenly invigorated and light of heart.

* * *

'So, what have we got? No sign of Pemberton. Rifle bullets in the trees, just as Miss Musthill told us – those have gone to forensic. Car tracks in that quarry opening but as there are several different ones it may not give us much. You took Anna home, Jane?'

'Yes, I did – at least I followed her. She drove here in her own car, or rather the one she's hiring, if you remember.'

Anna had stumbled back from the woods to the Benbridge house to get it apparently, and she had then driven off without bothering to go inside to tell her sister what had happened. And Heather Benbridge had looked startled when Anna had arrived back with Jane in tow. When told what had occurred, she had seemed bewildered and disbelieving. 'Oh, but—'

'Tell Inspector Perry anything you can remember about Neville,' Anna interrupted. 'You know him better than I do.'

Heather had claimed to know little, looking confused. The way she eyed her sister was, for once, full of doubt rather than anger, and she showed surprisingly little concern for her safety. She was flustered by the idea of a police watch outside her house, perhaps, Jane thought, because it brought home to her that the police genuinely did think Neville might present a threat.

Chris Hollings was speaking. 'Kenny, you say they haven't seen Pemberton at the building firm? And there was no sign of his presence in or near his house?'

'No, guv. The staff at Musthills say they haven't had any word from him, and his house has got all its curtains drawn, as I said. A bit too obvious a sign of being away if you don't want to be burgled! There's mail piled up on the mat inside the front door, too. Rachel had a peer through the letter box.' He grinned at WDC Welsh, acknowledging she was younger and thinner than he was, therefore more able to bend double. 'The neighbours say they haven't seen him,' Kenny went on, 'and that he's been away for weeks. Nobody's spotted him coming back. Nor seen a white car like Miss Musthill described. Pemberton's usual car's a dark green Jaguar,' DC Barnes added, with the merest touch of envy in his voice. 'A flash new one. Bought it a couple of months ago. The woman who lives opposite him told me that.'

'I wonder where he's staying then. A second address we don't know about? Or maybe he's just come back and whipped out again. He may even be on his way back to this villa of his in Spain by now. It's all very well to alert ferries and airports, but if he decided to use the tunnel which is the most likely from here, he could be through already by now. Somebody make a note to remind me to fax the Spanish police if we don't find him here. We've got his description circulated?'

'Yes, guv,' WDC Jennie Cullen put in. She added helpfully, 'I managed to find a news photo of him as well – I remembered seeing it in with some stuff we had on local businesses. It's from the local paper a couple of months ago when he was hosting an industry dinner. Should I get the print from the *Gazette* so we can have it copied?'

'Well done for finding it. Have you got it there?'

Jane looked over the DI's shoulder as he took the folded paper Jennie Cullen held out. A grainy print showed a man with slicked-back hair, muscular body, a wide and toothy smile. A man well pleased with himself. A man who would kill and chop up the corpse? Who could tell?

Jane stirred a little, aware that she should soon tell Chris her speculations about Evelyn Dale. There had not been time so far, but they had reached a point where there might be.

'A useful find,' he was saying now, 'but we'll save it for the moment. We'll search that house of his first: the warrant should be here soon. We've got sufficient grounds to be granted one. Right, while we wait, can we have a private word, Jane?'

They moved into the privacy of his small glassed-in office in the corner of the CID room. Familiar territory. 'You had something else about Pemberton?' Chris asked. 'And the torso?'

'Yes. It's only a possibility, mind. There are two people missing from Musthills, not one. They both went away just before the funeral. The other one's the chief accountant, name of Evelyn Dale. Evelyn, male.' She explained the given reasons for his absence and the fact that only relayed messages had been had from him. 'It's been bothering me that the chief accountant was absent as well, though nobody else seemed worried about it, and he's been described to me as a completely honest man. When Anna was going through the accounts, she didn't find anything apart from the corruption possibility. No money missing.' She drew a deep breath. 'Anyway, this morning I happened to see a photograph of Evelyn Dale. He's around forty years old and must be about six feet tall. Normal build. One striking identification point was a large birthmark on the back of his right hand.'

Chris's eyes showed instant alertness. 'When did you

say he went absent?' he demanded.

'The day before Richard Musthill's funeral. He's supposed to have rung and told Neville Pemberton the reason for it.'

'And where's he supposed to be?'

'Cornwall, in a house without a phone.'

'And the only word from him has been through a third party with a male voice? I see why you thought Pemberton might be dangerous. But what the hell has he come back for? You'd have thought he'd have stayed well away. He must have had a good reason.' Chris flung open his office door. 'Hasn't that warrant arrived yet? Kenny, Rachel, I want you out again to Musthills. You should just get there before they shut up for the night if you step on it. I want the home address of Evelyn Dale, their chief accountant – official request. When you've got it, go round there and make the same sort of inquiries you did at Pemberton's address. See whether the house looks shut up, find out when the neighbours last saw him, ask if anyone's got an address for him – all that. Move, now!'

The two DCs were gone in a scramble and without further inquiry. The door had no sooner shut on them than it opened again and Mike Lockley came in with the sworn warrant in his hand. And straight after him DS Phelps with Gary Peters in his wake.

'Oh, Doug, good, you're back. You can tell me about the hijack later, for the moment we've got a search to do. Premises of an attempted murder suspect. He may be on the premises, and he may be armed, but I'm going to suppose he doesn't know he's a suspect at the moment so isn't likely to start a siege situation. We'll take it carefully all the same. Gary, you can stay here and mind the store in case I radio back with further instructions. Jennie too. Mike, Doug, with me. And Inspector Perry will come with us. I'm going to take someone from uniform as backup and with a sledgehammer in case we need to break in. Here's the address. Everyone know where they're supposed to be?'

Jane was grateful not to have been sidelined by the return of DS Phelps. She would have fought tooth and nail against it.

Chapter 17

'It certainly looks quiet enough.'

Chris Hollings leaned forward, inspecting the exterior of Neville Pemberton's curtained house. It was detached, modern, brick, with a cream-painted up-and-over door to its integral double garage; one of a group of similar but not quite identical executive homes which had been built to form a semicircular close. There were half a dozen of them in all, each with a small unfenced front garden and a tidy concrete path leading up to the front door. Between the houses, to emphasise the fact that they were spaciously detached, wide paths led round to what must be back gardens. Each house had well-polished windows and sound paintwork, none of it in garish colours. Muted respectability obviously held sway, and front lawns had been neatly mown, flowerbeds tended. Except for Neville Pemberton's, where a growth of grass flanking the concrete path showed several weeks' neglect.

Only Chris Hollings's unmarked car had driven into the close, a complement of four people inside, the squad car which had accompanied them waiting outside on the road.

'There's no way out round the back, is there?' the DI said

now. 'It looks from here as if they've all got gardens with wood-panel fences to block them off from the next close. Jane, does Pemberton know you?'

'No, I've never met him.'

'Good. Are you on for walking up to the front door and knocking? We'll watch for any movement of the curtains, but even if he is inside, he's not likely to see a passing female as a threat.'

'If I don't get any answer from the front, shall I try the back? I could be a canvasser or a market researcher or something.'

'You'll look less like a possible burglar casing the joint than one of us would,' DS Phelps put in, giving Jane a surprisingly friendly grin. 'One of the neighbours might decide to dial the station and start a whole new confusion!'

'Okay, but don't take any risks,' Chris Hollings decreed. 'Just look normal and see what you can see and then come back.'

Jane swung her legs out of the car and stood up, smoothing down her skirt. The close lay quiet in the early evening sunshine, its other residents indoors somewhere out of sight, behind walls too satisfactorily soundproofed to emit the noise of television or radio. She walked without haste up the concrete path to Neville Pemberton's dark blue front door and gave a calm rat-tat to its polished brass knocker. Then she tried the bell, hearing a muffled chime from within. The window curtain nearest to her, showing a pale lining with a dark blue edge, certainly gave no twitch. Kenny was right, she thought absently: to leave all the curtains drawn like that really was a rash advertisement when going on a business trip. She would have expected Neville Pemberton to be the sort of person to be more careful than that.

After a normal wait, she allowed herself to look dubiously up at the house windows, then stepped back and took the extension to the path which led round the side of the house. The back doors here were at the back, not the side; she found one with a frosted glass panel next to what was probably the kitchen window, though it had a closed Venetian blind down over it. Next to that, a broad plate-glass window, curtained again. An unused barbecue stood on a stone-flagged patio and there was a stretch of not very tidy garden with a small pond in the middle of it and a half-grown willow tree. The garden was fenced round with tall bark panels and, as the DI had surmised, there was no rear entrance.

Her quick look round had taken quite long enough for verisimilitude. An uncurtained upstairs window showed no movement that a casual glance upwards could see. Jane walked back round to the front again and, for good measure, rang the front door bell again. As she did so, a female voice from somewhere on the opposite side of the close let out a clear call.

'Hello? Yes, you, at number five. He's away, dear, you won't get any answer.'

The voice came from a curly grey head sticking out of an upstairs window in the house directly opposite. Its middle-aged owner had clearly been waving to attract her attention. The arm in a padded peach housecoat stopped flapping and withdrew. The head remained and the face regarded Jane carefully. 'Are you a friend of Mr Pemberton's?'

'No, but I was hoping to find him. You haven't seen him?'

'We all look out for each other, and I would have if he'd been back.'

'Thank you,' Jane called politely. So much for not looking like a possible burglar. Neville Pemberton's neighbour was obviously out to make it clear that Visitors Would Be Seen. Jane sent a smile upwards and walked back to the car, to lean down and speak through the window.

'Did you hear that? I suspect she thinks we might be a gang of miscreants and that's why Kenny was making inquiries earlier on. I couldn't see any sign of life round the back. It'd be the easiest way in, though – glass panel in the back door.'

'Right. No movement this side. I'll just bring the squad car in so the neighbours know we're legit.'

The head opposite was still keeping watch as the police car drew up behind them. 'We're police,' Chris Hollings called out to the woman reassuringly as he got out of the car. 'There's been a report of an alarm being tripped inside Mr Pemberton's house. It looks as though we're going to have to break in. I'm glad to see your Neighbourhood Watch scheme's active!'

'Oh, I see. I didn't know Neville had had any alarms put in. He does usually leave his curtains drawn back and his lights on an automatic switch when he goes away. We thought he must have gone in rather a hurry this time and forgotten.'

'Don't worry, we're dealing with it. Right,' Chris said in a lower voice, 'that should satisfy local curiosity. Let's go and have a look at that back door. Jane, stay this side, will you, and sit inside the car for now, just in case. One of you two stay in the squad car; the other one, bring the hammer. And Doug, Mike – with me.'

The four men disappeared round the back of the house. The minutes stretched, then Mike Lockley opened the front door from the inside and beckoned to Jane to join them.

'Couldn't have been easier getting in, there's a couple of bolts on the back door but he hadn't bothered to slide them in, just left it on the Yale lock. And there's nobody here. What are we looking for, guv?' he asked as Chris Hollings appeared on the stairs, obviously from checking the upper floor.

'Any sign that he's been back. Any weapon. Anything bloodstained. Jane,' he drew her aside as Mike Lockley went off, 'are you after bank books, that kind of thing?'

'Might as well, though I'd imagine he'd have taken everything with him.'

'So would I, but come and look upstairs.'

She followed him up the carpeted staircase and into a front bedroom. He had left the curtains closed and switched on an overhead light. Modern spotlights were built in to each side of a double bed. The room was untidy, a leather suitcase open on the bed, half packed – the sort that opened out flat. 'What strikes you first?' Chris asked.

'Dusty.'

'Yes, isn't it? Even the case.'

That was true. A thin layer of undisturbed dust lay on every surface and could be seen as an almost invisible film across a half-folded white shirt.

'It looks as if he was packing the suitcase to go, then

something happened which made him decide to leave in a hurry without it, doesn't it? It certainly isn't one he's brought back and started unpacking.'

'No, it isn't. What does the rest of the house look like? The same?'

'Yes, what I've seen of it. No sign that he's been back here.' Chris looked thoughtful. 'Maybe he had a change of clothes somewhere else.'

'He could always buy more, I suppose.' Jane frowned round at the room. A built-in wardrobe with one sliding door open, suits hanging, polished shoes on a rack below. A chest of drawers with one drawer partly open. 'He was in the middle of packing. Then what? He made or got a phone call and decided something else was more urgent?'

'Or someone came to see him and things became urgent after that.'

'No car in the garage, guv,' Doug Phelps said, appearing in the doorway. 'The door through from the house wasn't locked. He keeps a freezer in there and it's half full of convenience meals, nothing else. And there aren't any stains in the garage which could be blood.'

'Thanks. Okay, go through the rest of the upstairs rooms, then the downstairs ones.' Chris Hollings stood still, looking ruminative. 'He went off in his dark green Jaguar then. But when he was next seen, today by Anna Musthill, he was driving a white car. Because he'd used the Jag to transport a bloodstained body?' Chris looked at Jane with a query in his eyes. 'Possibly. If so, I wonder where it is now. Burned out somewhere or otherwise disposed of would be the obvious guess.'

'If he did murder Evelyn Dale, I wonder why he's come back. There must be something vital he left behind. If not here, then at Musthills. If he's going in there, it'll probably be at night since he doesn't seem to want to be seen.'

'I radioed back for Gary and Jennie to get over there and keep covert surveillance.' Jane might have guessed he would already have thought of it. 'And if he did murder Evelyn Dale, I wonder where he did it?' Chris went on, obviously thinking aloud. 'Cutting up the body ought to have left traces, and we haven't seen a sign of that so far, not even of a very comprehensive clean-up. So, somewhere else.'

Neville Pemberton must know that the body in the churchyard had been discovered, Jane thought. It had been a gory enough circumstance to make the national papers as well as the local ones, and they would be obtainable abroad. If abroad was where he had been. But what had he left behind to make him return in such apparent secrecy? It was not as if there had been any publicity to say the torso's identity had been discovered.

And why risk shooting Anna Musthill? Shooting and missing, what's more. And then running away. If he needed to get rid of her that badly and had already committed murder once . . . For that matter, why should he have been driving about at Tissingham armed with a hunting rifle? He could scarcely have known he would find Anna conveniently wandering in the woods. That factor was something which had been exercising Jane's mind off and on for the past hour.

The search of the house continued, quickly and thoroughly. The rooms were stuffy with disuse and showed nothing but the signs of an ordinary, interrupted life. A couple of dirty plates lay in the kitchen sink, an unwashed whisky glass on the draining board; the one untidy bedroom upstairs was the only one of three that showed any use; the main sitting-room was tidy but as dusty as everywhere else.

'Ma'am? I've just finished going through that attaché case while you were doing the desk. No bank books, but there's a handful of statements.'

'Thanks, Mike.' Jane glanced down at the top sheet of the papers he had handed to her and drew in an involuntary breath. 'Did you look at this?'

'Yeah. Seriously rich,' DC Lockley said. 'I'm not surprised he keeps it in a bank in Jersey!'

'Neither am I.' And if Neville Pemberton had not been milking Musthills, he had certainly been getting money from somewhere. A current balance of almost a quarter of a million pounds. Payments in of ten thousand, twenty thousand, fifteen thousand, quite close together, and all of them over the past year. The account was in a company name, NP Associates.

'Pity he didn't leave his chequebook and a specimen signature in his luggage,' Mike Lockley said with a grin. 'If I had that kind of bread, I'd have gold-plated bath taps at least, never mind the latest state-of-the-art hi-fi, though he has at least bought himself that.'

'Mm.' The attaché case Mike had been searching had been pushed out of sight under the desk. Forgotten? Jane glanced up as Chris Hollings came round the door.

'We're finished,' he said briefly. 'Nothing useful from our end, and we've even checked the loft. Anything from your end?'

'Possibly.' Jane passed him the top bank statement and saw his eyebrows go up.

'He's planning on being comfortable, wherever he is,' he said drily. 'Right. I'm going to leave someone here on watch. Somebody make that back door secure, and we'll be off.'

As they reached the front door Jane bent down and picked up a folded sheet of paper lying on top of the other post and thrust through the letterbox without an envelope. It was on thick cream notepaper. No address at the top but a message written in a large and dashing hand saying, 'Neville, where *are* you? Ring me! Sara,' with several crosses underneath for kisses. A lady friend, one who was also finding his absence inexplicable, apparently. Jane put the note back since it bore no address to help them.

As they came out into the close and pulled the front door shut behind them, one or two heads could be seen peering through neighbouring windows. A couple of cars were drawn up on front drives now, suggesting some of the owners of the other executive homes had returned from work. A door opened and a male figure appeared, to walk with brisk steps towards them.

'Doug, just go and tell him there's no panic and the alarm we were answering must have been tripped accidentally,' Chris Hollings instructed, 'but that we'll keep an eye on things, okay?'

His sergeant duly went off to deflect the curious neighbour. As the rest of them reached the cars the constable who had been left outside in the squad car leaned out to speak to the DI.

'Sir? Control's just come on to say DC Barnes is trying

to get hold of you. Do you want them to patch him through?'

'Yes, please. Into mine.'

Kenny's voice came through clearly across a crackle. 'We're outside Mr Dale's address, guv, but we haven't managed to gather much. It's the sort of area where everyone goes out to work and none of the neighbours knows each other. Dale's house doesn't look particularly shut up. We rang the bell and didn't get any answer, though. Nets at the front window so we can't see inside. What do you want us to— Hang on a minute. Someone's just arrived and is letting himself into the house with a key. I'd swear I know that face, but I can't remember where from.'

'He's gone inside?'

'Yes. As if it's what he's used to doing. What do you want us to do, ring the bell again? And if that was Mr Dale, what do you want us to ask him?'

'Where are you? Longley Street, isn't it? That's not far from here. We've finished this end so I'll come and deal with it. Hold on a minute. Did you notice the man's hands when he was letting himself in? Any sign of a noticeable birthmark on one of them?'

'Not that I saw. No, Rachel didn't, either. Wish I could think where I recognised him from.'

'Keep thinking. Otherwise, wait there and keep an eye out but don't do anything.' Chris turned to Jane. 'You heard?'

'Yes.'

'Let's go and see what this means then. Doug, you and Mike go back to the station in the squad car. Ashton, you stay here on foot keeping an eye on the house. We've made enough of a public splash so we may as well leave a uniform. I'll see you're relieved later.'

If it had been Neville Pemberton letting himself in to Evelyn Dale's house . . . No, surely then Kenny would have made a definite ID. They had all taken a look at the news photo. Jane joined Chris Hollings in his car, wondering if she was going to turn out to be totally wrong. But it had been a fair assumption to make. Evelyn Dale had certainly been absent too long for comfort. Had been too thoroughly out of touch, too. If he had genuinely been away nursing his mother, however distant and however sick, surely he would have rung Musthills himself at least once to check with his deputy that all was well after his hurried departure.

Longley Street was a row of small terraced houses off the wide road which led into the city via the West Gate, less than half a mile from the suburban development of which Neville Pemberton's modern close was part, but entirely different in character. The narrow houses were whitewashed and attractive, probably built in late Georgian times as workmen's cottages but now done up as small but comfortable residences for professional people. Kenny and Rachel were parked just up the street outside the pub. The DI drew up behind them.

'Nobody's come out again,' Kenny said as the DI bent down to his window. 'I still can't remember where I've seen that face, but I'm sure I do know it from somewhere. Around the station, too. Someone known to us.'

'Right, thanks. Stay here while Inspector Perry and I go and see if we can get any answer to the door this time.'

'If we do, what are we going to say?' Jane inquired as they crossed the road together.

'As a reason for wanting to see Mr Dale? I'd suggest that if necessary we go for the straightforward approach and say someone's reported him missing.'

They rang the bell. It was answered after only a moment's delay by a pleasant-looking man in shirtsleeves. And Jane was immediately aware where Kenny's sense of familiarity had come from. Jane knew the face herself, but it wasn't a known criminal: quite the reverse.

Recognition was mutual and brought her a greeting. 'Hello, it's Inspector Perry, isn't it? We were at the same meeting only the other week. Jim Callow. From the probation service,' he reminded her with a smile.

'Yes, I do remember. This is Detective Inspector Hollings – I don't know if you two have ever met. We're actually looking for a Mr Evelyn Dale,' Jane went on as the two men shook hands. 'We were given this as his address.'

'Yes, it is. Is there – is there some reason why you want to see Evelyn? He's actually away at the moment.'

The hesitation before he said this was puzzling. 'We really want to talk to him personally,' Jane told him with a smile. 'Do you have an address for him?'

'Well, I – can you tell me what it's to do with? I'll be in touch with him, you see. I could get him to contact you.'

'It's to do with Musthills.' She instinctively abandoned the plan of saying Evelyn Dale had been reported missing; she had also reached the conclusion that Jim Callow was probably Evelyn's partner, or housemate. It would fit in with Anna's comment that he was probably gay, and she remembered making that assessment of Jim Callow – one of the quietly unobtrusive ones, but he had given her that feeling.

'We do rather need to talk to him face to face,' she said politely.

'You'd better come in.'

Jim Callow said that with sudden resignation and an oddly wry look. They followed him through the small hall inside the front door and into a long room which stretched from front to back and must once have been two rooms. Someone was sitting in a high-backed chair next to the window which looked out onto a small enclosed garden at the back. A man with a pale, thin face, turned half away; glasses; a rug over his knees. And a bony hand lying along the chair arm, with a dark birthmark across the back of it.

'Eve,' Jim Callow said in a gentle voice, 'you haven't dropped off again, have you? There's a couple of people who need to see you. Inspector Perry and Detective Inspector Hollings, and it's something about Musthills, apparently. So I thought you'd be bound to want to see them, knowing how you worry about the place.'

The man who looked round towards them from the chair clearly had other things to worry about. He was skeletally thin and dark purple marks were visible on the skin of his face as he turned towards them, all too clearly recognisable as the stigma of Kaposi's sarcoma.

The eyes regarding his visitors were weary but intelligent. 'Will you excuse me if I don't get up?' he said politely. 'I'm actually rather better today, but . . . Is there trouble at Musthills? Police trouble? Unfortunately, I've had to be rather out of touch lately.'

But not away nursing a sick mother.

They had found Evelyn Dale alive – at the moment. But not for long, if his appearance was anything to go by. He was clearly seriously ill with Aids.

Chapter 18

'I'm sorry to have had to disturb you, but there was a suggestion that you were missing, so we had to check it out.' Chris Hollings spoke in polite but practical tones, and glanced at both men.

'Oh dear, was somebody worried about me? I suppose I should have guessed it wouldn't work indefinitely.' The sick man in the chair gave a tired smile. 'I was hoping day by day to be well enough to go back to work, but with this face . . . I haven't been in Cornwall nursing my mother, of course. She's thoroughly healthy, I hope.' He paused to let out a painful cough, making Jim Callow hover concernedly until Evelyn gave him an impatient wave away. 'So there isn't actually any trouble at Musthills? That was just a front?'

'As far as I know everything there is functioning normally, so there's no need for you to worry.'

'But he does, naturally,' Jim said with an air of resignation. 'I told you they'd be bound to be managing, didn't I?'

'Somebody ought to be getting the accounts ready for audit after Richard's death.'

'Then I expect somebody is, Eve. You said yourself that Miss Whatever-it-is could do it just as well as you could.'

'Yes, she can. I only think I'm necessary. Actually I'm not.' Evelyn Dale gave a smile, a tired stretching of his thin face. 'Musthills will run under its own steam, it always has. Though I, for one, will miss Richard. And wish I'd known his depression was so bad. But then, so does everyone.'

'Thank you for seeing us. I'm sorry again for disturbing you.' Chris Hollings gave the man in front of him a kindly look. 'We had to see you for ourselves, but now we have, we can stop bothering you.'

Evelyn Dale lifted his birthmarked hand in a gesture of polite denial, though there was a mocking touch in it, Jane thought. And if, faced with anyone else so clearly ill, one might have offered civil wishes for a quick recovery, here it hardly seemed appropriate. They said their goodbyes and Jim Callow showed them back to the front door. There was really nothing to say to him either, except to give him a smile.

Once they were a safe distance away from the closed door, Jane looked at Chris with an abject apology.

'I'm sorry. I set you off on a possibility and it turned out to be a fool's errand.'

'It was a fair guess. He and his partner were obviously too busy trying to concoct an excuse to cover things to realise it might set up an alarm about his absence. He must have gone down with a sudden infection but hoped against the odds that he'd be able to recover enough to go back to work, and without too many people asking too many questions. I guess I wouldn't want the world knowing if it was me,' Chris added. 'You never know what attitudes people are going to take up.'

'No, though he's very well liked at Musthills, I gathered.'

'So perhaps it wouldn't be too bad. But I doubt if he's going to make it back, from the look of him.'

'No.'

'Making the tie-up between Pemberton and the torso may still be valid,' Chris said thoughtfully. 'He's clearly been up to something, hasn't he? And from what we found at the house, it's worth following through.' They reached Kenny's car and he leaned down to speak through the window. 'Okay, you two, we've finished here for now. In fact you can both go off and I'll see you first thing in the morning. Doug and Mike can relieve Gary and Jennie later on the surveillance at Musthills, and I'll ask uniform to go on keeping an eye on the Pemberton house.'

'Right, guv. You found Mr Dale, did you?'

'Yes, we did. No further problem there.'

'And the face you thought you knew is a probation officer, not somebody off the cards,' Jane told Kenny, giving him a grin.

'*That's* it! I knew I'd seen him somewhere, though he hasn't been around the station for a few months.'

'Doing something a bit more administrative maybe. I came across him at a liaison meeting recently.'

'Thanks, ma'am, that's set my mind at rest. We'll be off then.'

'You can leave the paperwork until morning,' the DI said. 'Come on, Jane. If you don't mind my picking your brains again, I'd like to go through what we know about Pemberton when we get back. And we'd both better see the super in the morning,' he added as they got into his car, 'to explain what you've told me, and why.'

Back at the station, they spent more than an hour discussing the possibilities of a tie-up between something fraudulent at Musthills and the dismembered torso in the grave, with Neville Pemberton as the pivot. His behaviour seemed inexplicable unless something very serious was involved. The manner of his departure certainly suggested something out of the ordinary had happened, and then there was the large sum of money in the NP Associates account in Jersey.

By the time Jane went home her head was buzzing with possibilities. A memory there too of Evelyn Dale, poor man. Anna and Heather had both described him as thoroughly nice. But what the hell was Neville Pemberton doing taking random shots at Anna?

Jane let herself into the house with her mind turning over the missing pieces of the puzzle and stopped dead at the sight that met her eyes.

Steve Ryan was sitting on the sofa, Adrian in an armchair, both of them companionably drinking beer. It wasn't Adrian's usual tipple, so one of them must have gone out and got some.

'You're late,' Adrian said mildly, but with the sort of look in his eyes which suggested there might have been an accusation in it if they had not had company.

'Yes, I got involved in something. I couldn't ring, sorry. Hello, Steve.'

He had come to his feet and stood looking at her as she offered that level greeting. Typically Steve, with those neat muscular looks and an expression on his face which managed to mingle penitence, charm, wariness, and a touch of little-boy-lost.

'Hi, Jane. I've just been hearing about your promotion. Congratulations, you made it, then.'

'Into something I didn't ideally want, but yes. To what do we owe the honour?'

'Well, I was down here so I thought I'd look in. And it's been good to meet Adrian.' He cast an amiable look at Adrian who responded by lifting his glass in salute. It had been an all-boys-together chat, had it? 'He's been kind enough to say you can put me up overnight.'

'Has he? I'd have thought somebody might have asked me first.'

Steve let out a sigh. 'I know I've been every kind of stupid idiot, and if you cuss me out it won't be worse than I've done to myself. But you helped me out once before, and I'm asking again. Put in a word for me with Matty. Tell her I mean every word I've been saying. That I know I made a lousy mistake but it'll never, ever happen again.'

'Talk to her yourself.'

'I have. I just need something extra to help her make up her mind. You could.'

'Oh no. No way. If you want to know what I think, it's that she could do a lot better than you if you can't keep your hands off passing women just because they're available. But if she decides she wants you back in spite of everything, that's up to her. If she decides she doesn't, that's up to her too. And don't you start telling me I ought to speak up for him either,' Jane said furiously, rounding on Adrian as she heard him stir. 'You're the one who told me not to get involved, remember? Or is it different when you want me to smooth the way for your new drinking buddy? Maybe you reckon it's all right for someone to carry on with an old girlfriend on the side, and even get her pregnant. Or didn't he tell you that bit? Oh, go to hell, the pair of you! I've had a long day and I'm going upstairs to change, and if I've got a choice about it, I don't want him here when I come down again!'

She stormed off up the stairs. It was a less dignified exit than it might have been because she was carrying a bag of fish and chips, bought in a reversion to old bad habits of relying on takeaways because it was late and she'd half expected Adrian to be out yet again. He had been out so often lately, nurturing Felicity, that she had stopped counting on his presence.

Jane reached into the package for a chip and put it bad-temperedly into her mouth. She was bloody hungry, and Steve Ryan was the last person she wanted to have a sociable evening with. And to ask her to go and plead for him to Matty – the nerve! What was she supposed to say? Boys will be boys?

She crammed another chip into her mouth and went and turned on the bath. The noise of that should make it clear that she had no intention of being sociable. If she had thought Steve was genuinely penitent she might have, well, not gone and had a jolly evening with him, but she might have put it to Matty. But there had been something calculated in the way he had tried to charm her into it, something almost smug, as if Adrian had told him, 'Don't worry, I'm sure Jane will try and talk her round.' A show of male solidarity. The two of them, sitting there . . .

She pulled a piece of fish out of its batter to eat; it had gone cold and wasn't very nice. She muttered a cross 'Yuk!' and dumped the whole lot into the bedroom waste basket. To hell with the fact that it would make the room smell. She stamped off to try to console herself by pouring some perfumed oil into the bath. Which would have been all right if her hand hadn't slipped so that she got twice as much as she wanted. Now the bathroom would be awash with bubbles. Blast!

When Adrian pushed the bathroom door open, it definitely was not the moment for him to get a conciliatory reaction. His opening words didn't invite one either.

'I asked him to stay and he's staying,' he said, his voice low but a stubborn expression jutting his jaw.

'Oh, really? So you do think his behaviour's quite all right? And I can expect the same from you, can I?'

'Don't be so stupid. What's between him and Matty is up to the two of them.'

'Quite. So why do you think I ought to rush out and persuade her to take him back?'

'You'd be perfectly happy if someone was telling you to rush out and persuade her not to.'

'No I bloody wouldn't! I may get a bit feminist sometimes at the way females are treated by the police hierarchy, but

I've never been an anti-men radical in my private life, and you know it! Or you should. Or do you really just want someone who'll walk two steps behind you saying "Yes Adrian, no Adrian"?'

'When you're in this unreasonable mood, there's no use talking to you. And why were you so bloody late back tonight anyway?' he added. 'I was beginning to worry.'

'No you weren't, you were having a nice matey time with dear Steve.' And if he hadn't been, he would have been having an equally matey time with dear Felicity. She was probably an ex-girlfriend of his, come to think of it. The two of them certainly seemed to know each other very well. The Fliss and Ade show. And, just like Steve had been with Matty, he all of a sudden didn't like her popping in at the practice. His body language, if nothing else, made that clear.

She wished she hadn't thought of that.

'Considering how often you've been out, I'm surprised you have the nerve to complain because I'm late *once*,' she said stiffly.

'I've had to be out, you know that. And where were you, anyway?'

'I had to be out. Work. CID work. The sort you think I shouldn't want to be involved in any more. Oh do go away, I've run this bath and now I want to have it – in privacy!'

He gave her a level stare and withdrew. She promptly locked the door. If they wanted the loo they could damn well go and pee in the garden. She intended to stay in here for precisely as long as she liked. The only part of the house where she could have any peace . . .

Her thoughts were highly unsatisfactory. If other things

had been equal, she thought bleakly, she would probably have told Adrian how much it had shaken her to stand and look at a perfectly ordinary, perfectly nice man who was clearly dying of Aids. Not that she hadn't seen worse, in different ways, during her police career. Murder victims. The frightened, the vicious, the insensibly violent. Old people who had been battered for the theft of the few pounds of their pensions. Teenagers destroyed by drugs.

Adrian's view would probably be that she shouldn't stay in the police when it gave her a view of the lowest side of life. He had been so bloody unsympathetic lately – when she saw him, when he wasn't busy with blasted Felicity.

At least Senander's followers had a safe place to be, a roof over their heads, a discipline to follow. And his affectionate care. None of them were on drugs any more, he had said.

It wasn't as if Evelyn Dale was someone she knew, just a man she had heard others talk about. And a statistic.

She stayed in the bath a long time, and when she came out, she got into bed. She could have done with a cup of tea or coffee, but she wasn't going to go down and get one. She picked up a novel instead, one she kept beside the bed because she was always intending to make herself read it, though the first few pages which were all she had managed so far were extremely heavy. As far as she could hear downstairs, the men had the television on.

She had nothing against Steve on her own account, whatever Adrian thought. It was up to Matty to decide if she wanted to forgive him and take him back. It was just that she was not going to look as if she was taking any kind of side with him against Matty. No way. Adrian should surely be able to understand that.

She was still reading, with a forced concentration on some very dull text but at least with the advantage that it shut everything else out, when Adrian appeared in the doorway a long time later. She made herself look up, though keeping one finger deliberately on the page.

'Steve's in the spare room, is he?' she inquired stiffly.

'No, he decided to drive back to London. He said he didn't want to cause a quarrel.'

'Big of him.'

'There's no point in talking about it. You plainly won't give him a chance.'

'It's not up to me to give him a chance. Just because he's obviously charmed you—'

'We enjoyed each other's company. If you'd been a bit more civilised, we could all have had a reasonably pleasant evening. What the hell's that smell?'

'Mouldering fish and chips in the waste basket.'

'God, I'm not sleeping with that.' He picked up the basket with distaste and disapproval and walked out of the room with it. As she heard him go downstairs, Jane felt like shouting after him childishly that at least he had had something to eat which was more than she had; and that he didn't have to be so bloody prim either.

Instead she threw her book on the floor, switched off the lamp on her side of the bed and hunched down under the covers facing the wall with her face buried in the pillow. She was *definitely* going to look as if she was asleep by the time he came back, if only to save any further arguments.

He got into bed carefully without touching her and turned away on his own side. Annoyingly, he was asleep before she was.

Chapter 19

Chris Hollings joined her for her appointment with the super in the morning so that they could both tell him about the developments. There had been no sightings of Neville Pemberton overnight, either at his house or at Musthills.

Superintendent Annerley listened to the explanations thoughtfully, with the occasional question, the occasional nod. He gave the bank statements Jane handed over a long moment's consideration; then a brisk, 'Yes, that will have to be checked out, won't it? So we appear to have Neville Pemberton running amok in the district with a rifle but he hasn't been seen again?'

'No, sir,' Chris Hollings said, 'but we've got an APB out on him. And we're keeping up the watch at the Benbridge house, just in case.'

'Yes, that would seem to be necessary. His behaviour appears to be irrational, doesn't it?' The super gave a small frown. 'A tie-in between Pemberton and the Tissingham murder does look as if it could be possible,' he went on, 'and may explain what he's doing now. Something certainly seems to have panicked him. See what leads you can come up with in that direction. Try the Jersey police too, since you've discovered that bank account there.'

'Yes, sir, I'm already on to that. And on to Spain, in case he's on his way to his villa.'

'Good. Now, Evelyn Dale.' The super looked at Jane. She waited for him to tell her that she had jumped too quickly to conclusions. Instead, he came up with an entirely different comment. 'You saw him. Would you say he was well enough to help us?'

'He's clearly ill, but his mind's working. What did you have in mind, sir? The Musthills accounts?'

'Precisely. He's the one person who could tell us in confidence whether there's actually a reasonable explanation for what Miss Musthill found, and if there isn't, then who exactly would have authorised the payments. We can't rule out his own involvement in that, of course, but I'd say you're probably right: his general attitude suggests innocence. He'd be extremely useful to us as a source of information without having to alert the rest of Musthills staff, if he's well enough.'

'I'd say he'd be thoroughly willing to help us if he can. I had the impression that he cared quite a lot about the firm.'

'Well, we can only ask him, can't we? He might also be able to tell us whether anything actually is missing, though I don't think we could put him through the strain of going through the entire accounts looking for fraud. But he might be able to suggest what Pemberton may have been up to.' The super looked thoughtful, and turned back to Chris. 'I suggest we still try to keep the two strands of the investigation separate, for the moment. CID will continue to try to find Pemberton, as a matter of urgency. And meantime, I'm going to borrow Jane from community liaison again and she and I will see if we can solicit Evelyn Dale's help on the Musthill accounts. Everyone agree on that?'

'Sir.'

Neither inspector was likely to disagree; certainly not Jane. While Chris Hollings went away to continue the Pemberton investigations, Jane remained, and after some discussion rang Evelyn Dale's telephone number. Jim Callow answered, apparently not at work today. And, after a few moments, Evelyn himself.

She handed the receiver to Superintendent Annerley in response to his beckoning finger, and heard him give a brief and extremely partial explanation for his request. Then, 'If you're sure? It would certainly be very helpful if you could. Yes, I see. My inspector did explain that you weren't well, but if it really wouldn't be too much trouble . . . Yes, that would be the best way of handling it from our end, too. Very well, then, we'll pick you up this evening. Thank you, it's very good of you to help.'

He put the receiver down and looked at Jane. 'Let's hope he doesn't immediately alert someone. No, I think I'll go with the judgement that he's genuine. He's offered to go into the company with us this evening, after the staff have gone home, and go through everything we can find.'

'Right, sir.'

'You and I will pick him up at six forty-five. We won't involve Miss Musthill. Yes?' His raised eyebrow suggested he had picked up something from Jane's expression.

'I was just hoping Mr Dale would be well enough, that's all,' she said.

'The time was his suggestion, and he said he'd rest this afternoon. He certainly seems keen to help us all he can, and sounded concerned at the thought of trouble. Now,' the super glanced at his watch, 'I'm almost half an hour late for my meeting, so we'll deal with the rest of this tonight.'

By evening, there was no word from CID that they had had any success in finding Neville Pemberton. Not a sighting of him, not a hair or a whisker. Jersey had been alerted, Spain had been alerted, and all points in between, so if he did stick his head above the parapet . . . Jane, who had worked through the day on her normal tasks, had also managed, this time, to put a call through to the practice to say she would be late home tonight. She had left the message with the practice secretary without asking if Adrian was free to speak to her, but at least he couldn't say she had not given warning. They had both tried for normal civility over breakfast, but that wasn't her most sociable time of day anyway.

She pushed all such thoughts away as she went to meet Superintendent Annerley, and thence to collect Evelyn Dale from Longley Street.

They went in the super's car which was large but anonymous. Collecting Evelyn turned out to mean collecting Jim Callow as well, looking mutinously resolute to be one of the party if his sick partner insisted on going out. His presence was accepted without comment. The super shook both men by the hand and thanked Evelyn again for agreeing to help. He did look a little better today, Jane thought, or was it just that the shock of his condition was diminished on second sight? He certainly seemed determined to appear as normal as possible, his mind fixed on concern for the affairs of the company.

The entrance to Musthills' offices lay in a side road with a small car park opposite. Jane saw the unmarked observation car parked innocently up the street, but they had been warned of the visit. 'We have a night caretaker on security patrol for the yard,' Evelyn said calmly, 'but he won't come round to check this side until about ten.' He produced a key to let them into the building.

It was like any office building anywhere: a reception area with soft chairs and receptionist's desk, corridors, doors. Evelyn led the small procession upstairs to an office which was, plainly, usually his. It contained two desks, filing cabinets, ledgers, a large safe set into the wall, and the inevitable screen and keyboard of a modern computer.

'What do you want me to look for, Superintendent?' Evelyn asked, moving towards the latter. He sat down a little heavily on the desk chair in front of the screen and let out a ragged breath which made Jim Callow stir a little and look at him anxiously. 'I'll just boot up the system. I imagine everything's up to date. All the main accounting is run from here, and ordering from stores comes into the same system. Could you tell me what the actual problem is, now that we're here? Or – Jim, maybe you'd better wait in the reception area if this is confidential.'

'You might need me,' he objected.

'I'm fine, you've no need to watchdog me.'

'It's all right if Mr Callow stays. I'm sure we can rely on his discretion in the circumstances. Particularly since he's used to police work,' the super intervened tactfully, offering

Jim Callow a small smile which acknowledged his determination to stay with the sick man, and a possible need for it; there should perhaps be experienced help available when the police were, basically, trespassing on Evelyn Dale's health and well-being by asking for his help.

Superintendent Annerley described what Anna Musthill had found, flatly and evenly, which made Evelyn Dale draw in a sharp breath which turned into a cough. Nobody, Jane thought, could doubt that he was appalled. He looked at Anna's list and then went into action, discovering where to look, checking; moving around with a slight unsteadiness but a definite energy, into a connecting office to boot up another computer, to ledgers kept in a cupboard. 'She's right,' he said after a while, concealing another hoarse cough, 'and I had no business to have missed it. I can't have authorised that. No, I certainly didn't. We didn't make that order. Nor this one for RSJs.'

'Can you say who did authorise them?'

'Either Mr Pemberton or the stores foreman. But it shouldn't have passed me by. How could I have missed them?'

'The auditors did too,' Jane put in, since he was showing obvious distress.

'Because they trust my accounting! They wouldn't have lined them up with the dates, either.' He paused to cough again. 'What put Miss Musthill on to it? What she must think of me . . .'

'Don't, Eve, nobody's going to blame you.'

'Well, they should. I – I could do with a glass of water. There's a kitchen just out in the corridor.'

Jim Callow disappeared quickly and came back with a brimming glass. 'Miss Musthill only picked up on the figures because she does that kind of job in America,' Superintendent Annerley said, his voice very calm, when Evelyn Dale had got over his paroxysm of coughing. 'You say all these authorizations would have been done by Mr Pemberton?'

'Or the stores foreman, for ordering. Not for hiring in. Not for office supplies either. It wouldn't have been Richard – Richard Musthill – not on those dates. He passed that kind of thing over to Mr Pemberton or the general manager. I should have double-checked. How did I let this go by me?'

His distress was so patent that Jim Callow put a hand on his shoulder, only to have it shrugged impatiently away.

'Was Mr Pemberton in charge of putting in sealed tenders?' Superintendent Annerley asked. The query seemed to bring Evelyn Dale out of his shaken guilt with an effort.

'Richard did a lot of the costing. Though not in the past year. It was always one of the partners who settled the final bid.'

'And sent it in?'

'Yes.'

'And did Musthills make a habit of tendering late?'

'I'm afraid I haven't the least idea. It isn't my department. Tendering was always dealt with by the partners.' Evelyn paused, then said raggedly but with patent sincerity, 'Superintendent, I can assure you it wouldn't have been Richard Musthill who was responsible for – for what these dates and figures appear to mean. He is – was – the last person in the world . . . I assume, since we're here clandestinely, that you haven't already spoken to Mr

Pemberton about it. That he hasn't accused—'

'We haven't spoken to Mr Pemberton. He appears still to be away on his buying trip, and nobody's heard from him.' The super obviously thought it best not to mention Anna Musthill's sighting, thought Jane. She observed surprise in Evelyn's face, then swift comprehension.

'In the circumstances,' the super went on, 'it would be helpful to know if there's anything else in the accounts which immediately strikes you as – unusual,' adding quickly, 'I don't suggest that you should go through them in detail, but with your experience and knowledge of the company, something might strike you as having been tampered with.'

'I would have to make a thorough check for that. I haven't seen anything so far.' Evelyn began to scroll figures up rapidly on the screen, with such an air of someone who planned to settle down to several hours of work that Jim Callow stirred again, an objection clearly visible in his face. Superintendent Annerley intervened quickly.

'I was only asking for your immediate impressions. There is something else you could tell us, though. Miss Musthill checked to see if any of the company's capital was missing but seemed to feel that it wasn't. It would be helpful if you could confirm that.'

Evelyn's hands moved swiftly and a different set of figures came up on the screen. 'Yes. Yes, the balances look normal. At this time of night I can't do more than check for unusual withdrawals, but there don't seem to be any. Excuse me.' Evelyn got up awkwardly from his chair and limped across to the safe. The thin hand with the birthmark across it fed various figures in on the heavy safe door; then he was swinging it open. 'The cheque-books are all here,' he said on a note of relief. 'And the certificates. Including the Lennox Holdings certificate. That's an investment Mr Pemberton brought in a few months ago, in exchange for a small shareholding. I don't think Richard was very keen but Mr Pemberton persuaded him it was to the company's advantage.' There was a doubtful note in his voice as he went on, 'I can't see any way he could have removed any lump sum without the relevant papers. You thought he might have done?'

'It was just a line we were following up,' the super said, smoothly uncommunicative. Evelyn opened his mouth to say something else, but it turned into a stifled cough. When he recovered from that he cast the superintendent a determined look.

'In view of what we've already found, I shall take it on myself to open this.' He pulled an envelope out of the safe. 'It's sealed as confidential with Mr Pemberton's name on it, but I don't recall its being there before, and in the circumstances . . .' He tore one end off the slim, square envelope before anyone could agree or disagree. 'Ah, I thought that's what it felt like, a computer disk. It doesn't seem to be marked anything except "Trefoil", but perhaps it'll give us some figures Mr Pemberton would rather we didn't see.'

'No, wait!' It was Jane who interrupted, urgently, as he moved back towards the computer. 'Could I see that?' she asked quickly.

He handed it to her after a brief hesitation, and she was aware that the super's eyebrows, too, were raised. As Evelyn had said, the small, normal-looking disk bore nothing except the handwritten word 'Trefoil' on its label, but it was that word that had given Jane pause. She looked across at the super.

'I don't think we'd be wise to put this in the machine, sir. There's a computer virus called Trefoil. One of the more destructive ones. Whoever invented it gave it that name because it takes out every third letter. Or figure, presumably. And then when it's finished doing that it switches all the remaining letters round until they're incomprehensible.'

Evelyn Dale was staring at the disk in her hand with almost comical dismay. She could see him imagining what that would have done to the accounts. And she could see a very thoughtful look dawning in the super's eyes, as she and he both wondered if that was what Neville Pemberton had come back for. To do just that, feed the virus he had left in the safe into Musthills' accounting system. And if that was so, there really was something to find.

'We'd better take it away with us for testing,' the super said into the silence. 'And if—'

He broke off as the clear sound of breaking glass reached them from somewhere outside along the corridor.

Superintendent Annerley made a rapid sign for silence. And stillness. Out of it came another brief rattle of glass, then a scraping noise which could be a sash window being pushed up.

It was still daylight, a summer evening barely dusking down. And the observation car was supposed to be on watch.

The super made another hushing sign, then moved on very silent feet to the door which they had left half open. He beckoned Jane to join him, then edged the door until it was only just ajar. If Neville Pemberton was out there, this was surely the logical place for him to come. Either here, for the disk Jane still held in her hand, or for some other reason to his own office, further down along the same corridor. Jane had noticed his name on the door as they passed it and had meant to suggest to the super that they looked in there after they had finished in Evelyn Dale's office.

Soft footsteps were approaching now, audible to straining ears. And the door began an inward movement.

The super was instantly round it, wrenching it wide to pull someone off balance, then reaching for an armlock with a speed which showed his senior position had lost him none of his skill. Jane, ready to give backup, stepped aside to avoid one wildly flailing foot, and was startled into an exclamation by the face which met her eyes above the disabling grip of an arm across the throat.

'Anna!'

At least the sight of her stilled the terror in Anna Musthill's face. As the super abruptly let his prisoner go, she stumbled forward, then regained her balance.

'Miss Musthill, what on earth are you doing here?'

'I—'

She might have said more in response to the coldly angry sound of Superintendent Annerley's voice but her eyes had caught sight of Evelyn Dale where he stood in the corner, and the shock in them was clearly visible. 'Evelyn?' she brought out on a half breath.

'Good evening, Miss Musthill.'

The words were courteous, but there was a blankness in

the thin face with its betraying marks. That was just the kind of instant, horrified reaction he had wanted to avoid, Jane thought. It was a relief when Superintendent Annerley spoke again, a cool distraction.

'Miss Musthill, what are you doing here? I'm sorry if I gave you a shock, but if you choose to break into the building—'

'Thank God it was you. I thought for a moment it was Neville.' Anna Musthill was reaching for composure and getting it back fast. 'I wanted to take another look at the accounts, and you told me to stay away. Yes, it was stupid of me, but I've known ever since I was a child that there was a way in across the flat roof of the building next door. And since it's empty, I wasn't exactly trespassing.'

'Inspector, would you go and take a look at the window Miss Musthill broke to get in, and see if it can be made secure? And see if there are any others which could be used in the same way.'

'Right, sir.'

As Jane hurried to obey, she heard the super's deep voice continuing, with a caustic note in it. His view of Anna's idiotic behaviour would definitely be making itself felt. The woman was obsessive in her inability to let the police handle things. And surely she had a key. There must be one among her father's things. She would hardly have refrained from using a key because of the observation car since she would not have known it was there.

The broken window, round one corner in the corridor, had a middle pane shattered; clearly to let a hand come in and undo the screw of the sash fastening. It looked out over a small tangled garden with the flat roof of next door's extension directly under it. If you knew about it, and knew that this window wasn't fitted with any kind of alarm, it was an easy way in. What the hell had the detectives in the obs car been doing? At least one of them knew Anna Musthill by sight from the other day. Why hadn't they noticed her in the street as she made her way to the side entrance of the building next door?

Jane went carefully round all the windows in the rest of the building but found no other which would have easy access. Most, in fact, had a more modern design and proper locks.

Anna was talking quietly to Evelyn and Jim Callow when Jane returned, with the super standing to one side, grim-faced. She crossed to him.

'The broken window could do with being nailed shut, sir, which should make it safe. Or we could simply warn the obs team that it's there. I'd like to check from outside that you can't get to it from any other direction. None of the other windows would be a possible way in.'

'Thank you. I suggest Miss Musthill takes you round to the yard to ask the caretaker to secure the window while I check this other way in and speak to the obs team.' His voice boded ill for the watchers. 'Then I'll take Mr Dale and Mr Callow home. I'll leave you to make your own way.'

'We've finished here, sir?'

'Yes, there seems to be nothing further we can follow up tonight. Miss Musthill has agreed she has no need to look at the accounts again. And Mr Dale's clearly tired,' he added quietly with a glance at the three in the corner. 'I shall take that disk out of the safe with me – I've already put it back in its envelope, the one with Pemberton's name on.'

And if it did turn out to be what Jane thought it was, it would give a basis for having Musthills' accounts double- and treble-checked. When? Jane wondered. A fraud check would certainly set the cat among the pigeons. But there had to be some reason for that disk, kept in a sealed envelope in the safe and marked as confidential in what was probably Neville Pemberton's own handwriting.

Anna led Jane on foot round to the yard which backed unseen from this side onto the office building. There were large gates, a small locked postern gate within them, and a bell to one side with which to summon the night caretaker. Jane had already seen that there was an observation car this side too, and one whose occupant was clearly wide awake since she received a covert acknowledgement from Mike Lockley as she looked his way. The caretaker arrived with a large Alsatian on a chain, knew who Anna was, and accepted her story that she had noticed a broken window while making a late visit to the offices. He said he would go in and deal with it straightaway.

As the two women walked away, Anna glanced at Jane and said in a subdued voice, 'God, Evelyn looks bad, doesn't he?'

'Yes.'

'I wonder how long he's known? It's intrusive to speculate, I suppose.'

'Probably.' Jane turned her head to look at her. 'He confirmed your suspicions about those figures and assured us that it wouldn't have been your father who authorised them. We've already started investigating Neville Pemberton, so you didn't have to pull tonight's stunt as well.'

'I don't know what you mean.'

'Yes, you do. You got just what you wanted from us with that rifle story. Tonight was to make us think Neville had been into the company, wasn't it? Just in case we let things slide after a few days had gone by. But all it did, in fact, was to point up all the holes in your first story!'

For a moment Jane thought Anna was going to stick with it and reiterate that Neville Pemberton had been there in the woods shooting at her. But, abruptly, her resistance crumpled.

'All right, do me for wasting police time, or whatever the phrase is. But I had to do something and it worked. As you said, I got what I wanted from you.'

Jane met the defiant stare she was being offered grimly and with angry exasperation. All that time and manpower wasted, all those theories which would now need disentangling all over again. Anna had the grace to shift under her gaze, though her chin remained at its defiant angle.

'So what happens now?'

'Now, Miss Musthill, you stop behaving like a spoilt child and come back to the station with me and tell the truth!'

Chapter 20

Jane found Chris Hollings in his office off the otherwise empty CID room, working late too. He looked up as she came in and spoke before she could.

'We've got progress of a sort. A dark green Jag was pulled out of a water-filled gravel pit not far as the crow flies from Tissingham a couple of weeks ago – no plates, nothing left inside, but the wreck hadn't been sent off to the crushers yet and the chassis number may give us a trace back to Pemberton. We're waiting on that, and meantime the car's gone to forensic to be gone over by the inch. Oh, and you know that Jersey bank account? It's been cleared. I was going to pass that info up to you in the morning. Nothing off the APB yet.'

'No, there won't be,' Jane told him grimly. 'I've just brought Anna Musthill in. She's admitted she made up the story about seeing Pemberton.'

'What?'

'Yes, I know.' Jane drew a breath. 'She's got sone kind of obsession about Pemberton being responsible for her father's suicide, so when the super told her we couldn't start investigating him without more to go on, she decided to give us something and rigged the whole thing – the rifle bullets in the trees, everything!'

'Bloody hell!'

'I've got her down in the interview room. She broke into Musthills while we were there this evening – another move to make us think Pemberton was around – and I didn't reckon the excuse she gave, so I challenged her on it and got an admission. She's had us running around like blue-arsed flies.' She stopped, her face disgusted. 'I ought to have guessed sooner from what I know of her, but she's such a bloody good actress. She borrowed her brother-in-law's hunting rifle and set the whole thing up – told me so on the way here. She hasn't seen Pemberton at all.'

She could see Chris rapidly reorganising his thoughts, trying this, testing that. 'He's off on his toes, then, and always has been. Via Jersey, to judge from the bank account being cleaned out. He could be anywhere by now. I'm going to talk to her.'

'Yes, I knew you'd want to. If I hadn't been told you were still in I'd have called you. Just to catch you up on our side of things,' Jane told him as they both made for the door, 'we think he was probably in on some kind of corruption, and there may be more to be found out from Musthills' accounts. But so far it still seems as if there's nothing missing from the company funds. It certainly looks as if he's been up to something but the question is, what?'

'Quite. You don't leave home in that much of a hurry for no reason. At least we know that much, so Miss Musthill's done us a favour, in a sense. Not that I shall tell her that.' His voice was extremely grim.

'Do you want me in on your interview with her?' Jane asked politely, and saw him pause as if surprised by the question, before he gave her the flash of a wry grin.

'Yes, please. Sorry, I'm getting so used to having you back. You're the person she made the admission to anyway, so come and sit in while I do the rest.'

Anna was looking a little more subdued after her wait in an interview room in the charge of a constable. Jane had been tempted to let her cool off in a cell. Her lies might have brought to light some interesting facts about Neville Pemberton but that didn't excuse the sheer waste of police time and manpower she had caused. It was satisfying to see that she plainly found the DI's manner daunting, and the fact that she was given a formal caution, then taken through a taped interview, with witnesses, none of whom showed her the least sympathy.

Jane was surprised to hear her offer a swift defence against blame for her sister. Perhaps some family feeling did exist on Anna's side. 'No, Heather didn't know anything about it at all, she wasn't in on it before I did it, or after. She didn't know I'd borrowed Donald's rifle either, and then put it back.'

'You don't think she'd guessed?' Jane asked, putting her word in.

'No. The only thing she didn't say to you was that I went out by car, not on foot, and that was because I interrupted her.' Anna's confirmation was swift, and without apology. 'The whole idea was mine and I didn't tell her about it. She's too much of a—' She broke off, and her expression suggested it was, after all, less family feeling than scorn for Heather's co-operation that had motivated her. 'In fact I thought she was going to blow the whole thing wide open by looking so surprised, and say "Don't be silly, you never go out for walks" or something idiotic like that. I'd planned the whole thing pretty carefully,' Anna went on, cockiness resurfacing. 'It's really not that difficult to put rifle bullets in trees if you know how to shoot. And I do.'

'So you lied to the police from start to finish. At no time did you see Mr Neville Pemberton. There was no question of his presence, nobody took a shot at you, and you arranged the whole event in order to make us believe something which was untrue,' the DI said coolly.

'Yes, I've said so.'

'You're aware that you can be charged with wasting police time?'

'I had to—' Anna subsided again under the DI's inflexible gaze. 'Yes,' she said with sulky resignation.

'It's a more serious charge than you may imagine, Miss Musthill, and I hope you appreciate that. That's why you were cautioned at the beginning of this interview, and offered the presence of a solicitor, which you refused.'

'One more question, Miss Musthill,' Jane said. She could see Chris was preparing to wind things up. 'When you were at Musthills on your previous visit, did you then or at any other time put something in the safe?'

'In the safe? No. Why? And what?'

The puzzlement in her answer seemed genuine. 'I'm just making sure you haven't left us any other false clues,' Jane said coldly. The Trefoil disk wasn't down to Anna then. Jane glanced at Chris to show him she had no more to ask, and he went through the completion of the interview.

They left Anna to wait again after the formal signing of the interview tape. The DI raised his eyebrows at Jane once the door was closed behind them, disgusted exasperation clear on his face. 'I've a good mind to hold her overnight and see if that teaches her a lesson,' he uttered abrasively. 'And hope for several noisy drunks to keep her awake!'

'At least she told us the truth this time and didn't try to get out of it. Or demand a lawyer.'

'She's too pleased with herself for that. What I'd really like to do is send her the bill for all the surveillances! At least I can cancel them now.' He gave Jane a suddenly dubious look, though there was a touch of humour in it. 'Oh hell, am I going to have to count you on my overtime budget too?'

'You can always refer it to the super, since he's the one who pulled me into this in the first place,' Jane suggested with a grin.

'That's the best idea I've heard all evening. I'm going to have the DCI on my back enough as it is.' He gave her a rueful smile, then let his breath out in a sigh. 'Right, what I've got to do now is call all my wasted manpower off duty. God, that woman. She gave us a thoroughly theatrical performance to get us moving, didn't she?'

'Maybe it's in the genes. Her mother was an actress.'

'Well, she can stew while I'm disentangling all the extra work she's caused. Then, I suppose, I'll have to let her go, though not before I've made it clear to her that she'll hear later about charges, after I've consulted with my superiors.'

'Need me any more?'

'No thanks. And thanks for getting the truth out of her.'

'Don't. I keep thinking I should have guessed sooner.' What she knew of Anna should have pointed the way. Nobody else had queried it, not even the super, so that was some comfort. Jane saw the friendly shrug Chris gave her, hands spread wryly as if to say, 'How could you?' and he went away looking thoughtful rather than despondent.

Jane went home, to a quiet house. Adrian was, in fact, in bed. There was no reason why he should have waited up for her. She crept in quietly beside his sleeping form and was obscurely comforted when he rolled over with a mutter and tucked an arm round her. He could, of course, have spent the empty evening with Felicity. No, she was not going to think like that. He was usually the one who showed jealousy, not her. She had to acknowledge that it was a highly uncomfortable emotion.

Breakfast saw them behaving with careful politeness towards each other. As Jane went in to work through the summer morning, she made herself leave home thoughts behind, contemplating instead that yesterday had not been unconstructive, after all. It had given them at least one step forward in the case as well as a step back.

Chris Hollings had virtually admitted missing her in CID too, which somehow made it easier not to feel wistful for having left it. In fact she barely had, lately. Signing in, she found herself subduing a grin as she wondered how DCI Morland would feel about that when he heard. His pet anathema proving herself useful – oh dear!

No sooner had the thought entered her mind than he

appeared on the stairs going in the opposite direction. She gave him an angelic smile with a deliberately pleasant 'Good morning'. With any luck that might spoil his day.

She knew Chris Hollings would already have sent up a report to the super about Anna Musthill, so unless or until Jane was summoned, she should get on with her own work. She bent to it, trying to push speculations about Neville Pemberton out of her head. Though she still couldn't see how he could have made the bribes work from the council end. A study of Neville's social contacts might shed some light. But why should he keep what must be an illicitly purchased computer virus in his safe? Presumably so that he could cause general disruption and distraction in the accounts department if ever whatever he had been up to seemed likely to blow up in his face. But then apparently something had come up which was far more urgent. Something which had made him flee abruptly without even gathering his possessions. It had to concern that money in the Jersey bank account surely. A quarter of a million pounds might well be enough to kill for. But kill whom?

Who was the torso? If they only knew that, everything else would probably fall into place.

Her internal phone buzzed, but it was only CI Lowell wanting a conference. Jane sighed, wrenched her mind back to community relations, and went obediently along to his office for a discussion on further moves to cement public good will.

Later in the morning she had a call from Superintendent Annerley's secretary – but not to summon her to a meeting. 'The superintendent asked me to tell you that you were right about something called "Trefoil",' the secretary's pleasant voice told her.

'Oh, thanks. Does he want to see me?'

'He hasn't said so, Inspector. He just asked me to pass you the message and to thank you for giving a warning about it.'

'Thanks,' Jane said again. She gave another sigh and decided that she might as well take up the rest of her morning with a tour of youth club premises, since CI Lowell seemed to feel it would be valuable if they made an assessment of what was on offer to keep the city's young occupied.

Or she could make another call at Tissingham Manor. She probably ought to check that everything was all right after the attempted kidnap of Elena. And see that Martin was causing no more trouble. Both gave her the perfect excuse. It was tempting to remember, too, that Senander had made it clear she was the only police visitor who would be welcome at the centre. The prospect of seeing him again quickened her interest far more than a survey of the city's more mundane youth facilities.

Still, the youth club premises had better come first. The cult this afternoon perhaps. A lollipop as a reward for good behaviour, she thought wryly. Nobody else seemed to want her for anything.

Jane drove her car across the police station forecourt and paused to check the turn into the road. She should concentrate on what she was doing *now*, not—

Afterwards, she was sure it was not her own inattention that had caused the accident. Memory told her that the car that turned abruptly and too fast into her path had no indicator flashing. She just managed to avoid a scrape along the wing but there was a sharp twang and her wing mirror produced an instant starring which suggested it had caught the mirror on the other car. She swore under her breath, backed carefully, pulled to a halt, and leapt out to speak to the other driver. And found herself looking into the white face of Councillor Mrs Tina Levitt.

'I'm – I'm terribly sorry,' Mrs Levitt said through her open window before Jane could speak. 'I wasn't – I didn't . . .' She swallowed hard. 'Oh look,' she said on a high note, 'I've broken my mirror. Probably yours as well. I suppose that's fourteen years bad luck rather than seven.'

There was a distinct edge of hysteria in her voice, and if she had seemed racked last time Jane had seen her, today she looked even worse. Surely her overwrought state wasn't entirely due to what was only a minor collision. 'Are you all right, Mrs Levitt?' Jane asked quickly and with concern, looking into eyes which were huge. 'I think you'd better get out and come inside and sit down. You look as if you could do with a glass of water.'

'I was coming in. I need to talk to someone. Seven years wouldn't be enough for murder, would it? Oh God!'

'Come inside, Mrs Levitt. That's right, come on.' The poor woman was babbling and her colour was dreadful. 'It's all right, there's no harm done, but you've had a bit of a shock. I'll get someone to bring us a cup of tea.'

'I don't want anything. Just someone I can talk to. I – I need to report a crime. Someone – someone's been killed. Please?'

'In here.' Luckily there was an empty interview room.

'Could you wait just a minute?' Jane asked soothingly, and put her head round the door to catch a passing constable. She asked him to fetch Inspector Henderson, plus a WPC.

Mrs Levitt had sunk down on the nearest chair. 'I've been so afraid,' she said, looking up with those haunted eyes. 'I've left it and left it, but . . . Oh God, I've been more sure every day that that's what must have happened!'

'It's all right, try to calm down. Are you feeling all right? You're sure you wouldn't like a glass of water?'

Ron Henderson came round the door before Tina had time to answer, a WPC following him. Mrs Levitt flinched at the sight of the uniforms, which brought Jane a sudden and vivid reminder that she had done just the same when Jane had been introduced to her at the council meeting as a member of the police. She was struggling for control as Jane introduced Inspector Henderson, though after offering him her hand as if without thought, she let out a deep sigh and seemed to collapse in on herself despairingly.

'Mrs Levitt wants to talk to somebody,' Jane explained to Ron Henderson's inquiring face, 'about something that has happened, apparently. So I'll leave her with—'

'No, please don't go! I'd rather you stayed. You were there before and you saw what Gavin was like.' She clutched at Jane's skirt like a frightened child.

'All right, I'll stay, if you want me to,' Jane said soothingly. She exchanged a look with Ron Henderson, Tina's words clearly spelling the Domestic Violence Unit to both of them. However, she spoke again before anyone could suggest it, the words coming out with jerky desperation.

'I think my husband's murdered somebody.'

'All right, Mrs Levitt,' Ron said quietly, 'try to keep calm. Your husband?'

'Gavin Levitt. Councillor Levitt. We're both councillors . . . Oh please, do listen, it's taken me all my courage to come!'

'We are listening, Mrs Levitt. And there's no need for you to be afraid, you're quite safe here.' Ron Henderson was being at his most paternally soothing. 'Who do you think your husband may have killed?'

'My – my lover. Gavin found out about us. He's got a terrible temper. He went out saying he was going to meet him. Have – have it out with him. Then he came back covered in mud, and – and – Oh God, it has to be! He's been drinking ever since. And he barely speaks to me. And nobody's seen – the man I'm talking about – ever since . . .'

Jane and Ron Henderson exchanged another look. Tina was weeping now and fumbling helplessly for a handkerchief. Jane reached quickly for the box of tissues which was kept on a shelf and handed it to her. 'When was this, Mrs Levitt?' Ron asked, his voice still soothing.

'Almost seven weeks ago,' Tina managed, her voice shaking. 'I kept telling myself it wasn't – that he couldn't have – I didn't want to believe it! But I do! I would have heard from him. I know I would. And then there w-was . . . Oh God, it's so awful!' She looked up at Jane with desperate appeal, her small pretty face streaked with tears and angular with strain and clutched involuntarily for her hand. 'You saw it,' she brought out with a shudder. 'In the grave. I didn't even think of it at first, and then I didn't w-want to think about it, but it has to be . . .'

Jane's every nerve had suddenly gone on the alert. 'The body in the grave? At Tissingham?' she asked swiftly.

'Yes! And Tissingham's what I heard him say on the phone! "All right then, Tissingham, if you must. Bloody silly place but I'll meet you there" – that's what Gavin said! And my – my lover, the man I'm talking about, he wasn't at the funeral next day when he should have been; and he hasn't been seen since, and, oh God, Gavin was so angry when he found out about us, and he's got such an awful temper! And he's got an uncle who's a surgeon, too, so he knows about cutting up bodies. In f-fact he got Gavin a holiday job as a hospital porter when he was in the sixth form at school because he was thinking about going in for medicine himself then and wanted to see— He killed him! Oh God, he killed him, and it's been killing me trying not to know it. He's been going to pieces ever since, and s-saying it's all my fault – and it's obvious why. My husband's a murderer!'

The last words were delivered on a despairing wail and Tina Levitt put her head down on the table and began to sob in earnest. Ron Henderson looked at Jane, his mouth a startled O, but his eyes sharp with speculation. As they stared at each other Jane was remembering, with sudden clarity, the needling words she had overheard Gavin Levitt saying to his wife at the interment: 'I see *he's* not here . . .'

With an abrupt sharp recall, Jane remembered, too, the way Gavin Levitt had almost stumbled into her as he turned away from the grave and the sight of the body in it. And the sick, shattered look on his face.

Maybe what Tina Levitt was telling them was actually

true. A completely different answer from all the assumptions they had been making.

Jane put a gentle hand on the sobbing woman's shoulder and leaned down to speak through the tangle of blonde hair, smoothing it away from the tear-streaked face with her other hand. 'Mrs Levitt? Tina? It's all right, and you were quite right to come to us. But could you tell us, please, who is the man you think your husband killed? What's his name?'

'You w-wouldn't know him. He's Richard Musthill's partner. Neville Pemberton.'

Jane, with her sympathetic fingers abruptly stilled, stared at her.

Neville Pemberton, the torso in the grave?

Dear heaven, was that where he had been all this time?

Chapter 21

'We took Mrs Levitt along to the morgue and she identified the appendix scar and the mole on the knee,' Doug Phelps told Jane. 'If we hadn't had that distraction about Pemberton having been seen, we might have sussed it from the house. Particularly with the kind of suits and shirts he went in for, and the fact he had his shoes made for him by some fancy bootmaker – I noticed that when we were doing the search, but there was no reason for it to click then. Anyway, we fetched a pair of shoes and tried them on the corpse, and they were an exact fit. Just like Cinderella!' His face showed his satisfaction. 'The guv's off arresting Gavin Levitt now. He said to thank you for that info about Levitt's reaction when the body was found, and he'll probably come back to you on that.'

'Fine. I'm here if I'm needed.' Chris Hollings had been out when the whole thing had blown up, so it had been Doug Phelps to whom Jane had handed Tina over. From then on it had automatically been CID's baby, a call going out to fetch the DI back in, everyone leaping into rapid action. Now, several hours later, it was nice of the DS to make a special trip up to Jane's office to bring her up to date on events.

'Not the line we were following at all, but this one fills in a lot of missing pieces,' Doug Phelps said cheerfully. 'We've always thought if we could only find out the victim's identity it would lead us to the murderer. Well, I must be off. Thanks for all your help.'

Some of that help had proved no more than distractions, Jane thought as he gave her a grin and went on his way.

The whole thing had been a crime of passion after all, not a gangland execution; not even the killing of an associate in dodgy business dealings but the much simpler matter of an enraged husband disposing of his wife's lover.

Neville Pemberton, the ladies' man. He had had other strings to his bow, too, to judge from that letter on his mat from someone called Sara. The clues had been there. Other things had simply got in the way.

An hour later, on her way home for the night, Jane ran into Kenny Barnes and found out how Gavin Levitt had taken his arrest.

'Did he come quietly?' she asked.

'No way.' Despite looking as cock-a-hoop as the rest of CID did at the solution of a case that had given them all so much trouble, Kenny pulled a face. 'He wasn't exactly steady on his feet even at this hour, but when he heard what we wanted he turned almost as hysterical as his missis. Denied the whole thing, said we must be mad. When he heard it was her that had shopped him, he went ape, said the silly cow had got everything wrong. You should have heard the names he called her. He's certainly got a temper on him. He turned green when he heard we knew it was Pemberton in the grave, though. And he admitted he'd met him the night before the funeral and that they ended up having a fist fight, and that it was in the churchyard, but he says Pemberton was alive when they parted. Swears he walked away. Not that anyone's believing him.'

'Your Mrs Emmett's story turns out to be true after all, doesn't it? Two men having a fight in the churchyard?'

'Yes, it all ties in. All we really need now is where he took Pemberton afterwards – or his body, if he was already dead by then. He didn't chop him up on the spot, so he has to have taken him somewhere. But no doubt we'll manage to sweat that out of him. They're getting him a duty brief, he doesn't seem to have one of his own, but in the meantime he's on lots of black coffee to make sure he's sober enough to be properly questioned and without a chance of his claiming afterwards that he was too drunk to know what he was saying. I'd say the guv will get a confession out of him by morning.'

That prediction at least proved untrue. When Jane arrived in the morning she heard on the grapevine that Gavin Levitt was still protesting his innocence and had lost his temper and sacked the duty lawyer, too. He was now saying pugnaciously that he didn't need one, since he wasn't guilty of anything. That seemed extraordinarily unwise, unless he was hoping to swing some story about not having been allowed legal representation, to get out of things that way. The man must be crazy if he thought he could avoid a murder charge on those grounds, though. Motive and opportunity had been established, and everything else seemed to tie up.

Well, not quite everything. Who had cleaned out the

Jersey bank account? Not Neville, since it had been cleared after his death. And where had the money in the account come from? If not from Musthills, from where? Jane had found that nagging her last night. Pointlessly, probably, since the DI would be asking himself those questions too, with far more likelihood than Jane of finding answers. But what exactly had Neville Pemberton been up to, apart from laying somebody else's wife? Was he involved in bribing council officials? If he and Tina were lovers, he had undoubtedly been privy to useful information about council business.

Oh well, it was all in CID's hands now. What had she put off yesterday, with everything else that had been going on? Damn, those youth club visits . . .

She would leave out the visit to the Tissingham cult, at least for today, just in case the DI should decide to invite her to sit in on the questioning of Gavin Levitt. He probably wouldn't, and she had no right to expect it, but you never knew.

Jane took herself out for a quick tour round as per CI Lowell's instructions. After lunch, she found a message from Chris Hollings asking her to call at the CID room if she had time and made her way down there with a swift lightening of heart. At least she would know what was going on.

The DI was fairly crackling with suppressed energy, despite looking as if he might have been up most of the night. He looked up from his desk and gave her one of his brisk, friendly grins.

'Hi. I'm letting Gavin Levitt stew for a bit, but I thought you might like to listen to one of the interview tapes from his morning. We've managed to nail something which should interest you. Not an admission of murder unfortunately, but he's come out with something else. Something I'm sure a solicitor would have stopped him saying,' he added. 'The super's pulled in an independent witness to the fact that he insists he doesn't need a brief, and has been sitting in himself, too. But have a listen to this.'

'You say he's still denying murder?' Jane asked as he reached for the portable tape recorder in front of him on the desk.

'Fervently. He insists Pemberton was alive when they parted. And protests that he wouldn't know how to cut up a body. But, on the other hand, he runs a small medical supply firm, and what he sells includes detailed anatomy charts, so we could assume he has the knowledge. His wife certainly seems to think so. Though where he did it is another question. Anyway, that aside, for now. I'll run this through from earlier for you, since it leads in.'

Gavin Levitt's voice broke out hoarse but clear as Chris pressed the switch. 'Yes, I've told you, we had a fight, but I didn't kill him! And yes, he did fall into the grave. He landed on the tarpaulin and took it in with him. I don't know who put it back again. I've already told you all this! It was just a scuffle, I even gave Neville a hand to pull him out again. I did take another swing at him but I missed.'

'So you admit there was a struggle in the churchyard. And that Mr Pemberton fell into the grave,' the DI's disembodied voice said with flat patience. 'But you say you helped him out and then continued fighting.' Hardly surprisingly, disbelief came clearly through the words as he went on, 'But then you say you stopped, and shook hands and parted?'

'I didn't say that. I mean, yes, we did stop fighting, but I didn't say anything about shaking hands. Anyway I've explained why we stopped. We suddenly saw someone, over by the hedge, watching us. I've told you all this.'

'Tell us again.'

'Neville shouted "What do you want?" but whoever it was had already realised we'd seen him – or her, I don't know, it was dark – and ran off. I couldn't really see. It was just a white face looking our way. It certainly wasn't there to start with. Anyway, the fact that someone else had been there brought us to our senses. Neville said something about "Serve you right if whoever that was heard what you were shouting".' The voice sounded deeply uneasy for a moment, but then went on doggedly, 'Then he said he couldn't give me any more time because he'd got an appointment. And he went. He walked away!'

'Whose idea was it that you should meet in the churchyard?'

'I've told you, his! Some sort of stupid idea of a joke as far as I could see. He said he had to be in Tissingham anyway and a graveyard was a nice quiet spot for a private conversation. But he was alive when we parted.'

'So you keep telling us. You admit you were angry enough to fight him but you expect us to believe you simply stopped and let him walk away?'

'Yes. Yes!'

'Don't you actually mean that he was unconscious after the fall? Knocked out? Perhaps even seriously hurt? So that you carried him to his car—'

'No! I've told you, he walked away!'

'Tell us again what you were fighting about,' the DI's voice said persistently, the drip of water on stone. Chris leaned forward to point a finger, indicating that this was the part he wanted to draw to Jane's attention.

'Wasn't the fact that he was having an affair with my wife enough?' Gavin Levitt's voice inquired defensively. Then, with a clear flare of resentment, 'Silly little cow, the connection could have put both of us right in the firing line if—'

'In the firing line?' the DI asked into the sudden pause.

'Damn you, all right! I was – I was supplying Neville with information. Council information. And he had to choose Tina to have an affair with!' the voice broke out angrily. 'He knew the risk I was taking. Of all the stupid things to do, to choose her.'

'What information were you giving him?' That was the super's voice, quiet and polite but coming in quickly so as to give Gavin Levitt no time to think out his answer.

'Information on tender bids. What they were so he could undercut. But that's not murder.' Gavin Levitt's voice held a whine. Jane could imagine how much he had been sweating. 'It was just business. I'd – I'd run into a cashflow problem, bloody recession, and Neville said he could help. In exchange he wanted to land a particular contract and suggested I found out what the other bids were. So I did, that's all.'

'And he paid you?'

'Well, yes, that was the agreement. It only came up because we'd been chatting about how the council did things.

And he made some joke about someone putting in a tender with an extra top sheet, a blank one, and someone could fill in the figures afterwards. It was over a drink at a club and it was just a kind of game at first, working out how it could be done, how you could actually cheat the system after the bids were in. As long as someone could get at them during the week before they were actually opened. After the deadline but before the tender-opening ceremony.' He was babbling now, the words coming out of him in a rush, clearly too caught up in his explanation to think whether his audience understood the complexities of council tendering. Jane did. 'We had a kind of jokey conversation about how that would be the only feasible time. Then he rang me up later and said he'd bail me out the debt I'd been talking about if I'd actually do it. So I did. I knew where the Tender Box key was kept and I managed to get hold of it and make a copy. We did it the way we'd worked out, and over the phone he told me what figures to put in after I'd looked at the others. Look,' Gavin's voice said with desperate persuasion, 'I'm telling you all this because it shows I had no reason to kill him. He was paying me, and I needed the money, so I wouldn't want to get rid of him, would I?'

'Did you do it more than once?' the super's voice asked, sounding no more than mildly interested.

'Yes. Well, after it had worked the first time, he said— But that's not the point, the fact is we were helping each other out!'

'Dishonestly.' That was the DI's voice again, harsh, playing bad cop to the super's good cop. 'Perhaps it was a matter of thieves falling out. Perhaps you told him it was too risky if he was sleeping with your wife. Too close a connection if anyone started looking into a leak of information. Or perhaps he said he wasn't interested any more because he'd rather have your wife. So, since you were angry anyway, and he wasn't planning to pay you any more—'

'No! You've got it wrong.' Gavin Levitt sounded as if he must be twisting and turning in his seat. 'I'd already told him we'd better stop after Richard died, in case his heirs started taking too much interest in the company. But he said that I wasn't to worry, things would be all right. I hadn't much wanted to go on with it anyway, but he said I had to, there were things in his records which he could make sure someone would notice.' The desperate voice seemed unaware that by suggesting he was being blackmailed, he was giving himself an even better motive for murder. 'Then I found out about Tina. Yes, I was angry. And yes, I took a swing at him. He was so bloody smug about mucking me about. But I *didn't kill him!*'

Chris's hand came out and clicked off the switch. He looked at Jane with an eyebrow raised. 'After that we're back with his protestations that Pemberton was alive when they parted,' he said. 'But I thought you'd like to know we'd got him for your corruption case. A clear admission. You needn't explain to me exactly what he meant about the tender bids,' he added hastily. 'The super seemed to know what he was talking about, even if I didn't entirely follow. You did?'

'Yes.' So that was how they had worked it – close to the theory Jane had suggested in her report, but making more sense, with the theft perpetrated after the deadline. The only way, in fact, that it could be done, and she should have thought of it. She had been right at least in her choice of a councillor as the most feasible culprit. 'Clever,' she said, half to herself, but drily.

'The corruption thing gives us a useful second motive. Something to hold him on while we sweat the rest out of him.' Chris was wearing the cheerful look of a man hopeful of a result. 'I'm presuming he's admitting to the fight because he knows somebody saw them, and he doesn't know that we don't have that witness.'

'Except for what Mrs Emmett heard.'

'Yes, there's that. We may even find this other person will come forward, with a bit of publicity. It would be interesting to know what he or she heard the two men saying, though what would be really useful would be if the witness said only one man was on his feet at that stage.'

'Levitt might crack and admit at least to manslaughter, and then the cutting up afterwards out of panic.'

'I'm hoping we'll get him at least that far. And we might also manage to trap him with the Jersey bank account. I haven't raised that so far – saving it.' Chris sucked his lips and Jane could see him considering the angles. 'My thinking on that is that Pemberton could have had the bank book in his pocket, plus some code to show how to get at it, and Levitt found it when emptying the suit pockets.'

Jane might have known he would come up with an answer to that one. 'Forge a signature and make a very fat profit?' she inquired.

'Wouldn't even need a signature as long as he had the code. It was a wire transfer to clear the account. We had to push to get even that – it's the kind of bank that's thoroughly leery about giving any information at all. They only loosened up to say how the account was cleared after we informed them that the NP of NP Associates was in fact dead. But they still won't give a destination for the money. I suppose that's too much to ask. I'd say Levitt found a home for it, though, wouldn't you?'

Possibly. His continuing protestation that he was innocent and therefore didn't need a lawyer seemed stupidly arrogant, however. And mystifying. Surely he would want the best advice the law could give. Jane frowned thoughtfully, but the DI was going on.

'By the way, Levitt's claiming he looked shocked when the body was found – your witness observation – because it was "like landing up in a nightmare", and he "suddenly thought Neville might have gone back for something and fallen into the grave again with a heart attack". Not a very believable story. And when I had someone look through the witness statements we took after the funeral, it turns out we haven't got the Levitts' presence listed. So I reckon he sloped off before we arrived and took his wife away with him. Hardly an innocent reaction.'

'No. What has he said about why he didn't go home until an awful lot later? Mrs Levitt said it was around two in the morning when he rolled in, didn't she?'

'He says he went off by himself to think,' Chris said drily. 'That's what he's stuck to so far. And I have to say that he didn't come back bloodstained, as far as she knows. Her description is "mud-stained". But it's always possible that he put on some sort of overalls and ditched them afterwards. And from what his wife says about his behaviour ever since, I think we can probably break his story. And we certainly will,' he added, 'once we find out where he took the body to dismember it and what he did with the missing pieces. I've already put in to get the divers into that flooded gravel pit where the car was found.'

He had everything well in hand. Jane was grateful that he had brought her in to tell her about it. He need not have done, with the super already in possession of the facts about the corruption scam. She was opening her mouth to voice her gratitude when his phone gave a raucous buzz. He reached to answer it.

'Yes, hold on a minute, I'll be right back to you.' He looked up at Jane with a smile. 'Sorry, I need to deal with this, and that was all I had for you, okay?'

'Sure, thanks, I'll take off. I appreciate being filled in on it all.'

He made a pleasant gesture, and she left him. Friendly grins acknowledged her as she crossed the CID room, reminding her of all the time she had spent working in and from it. Except that her desk was no longer her desk, things looked much the same.

Chris was really quite matey nowadays, she thought as she made her way back to her own area. She had worked for him in reasonable amicability while she was his sergeant but she had thought he probably welcomed her departure. Maybe she had been over-sensitive. They had both known she wanted his job.

She and Adrian really must, she decided with a touch of guilt, offer a return dinner invitation soon. Though it would be best to wait until Chris had finished grilling Gavin Levitt and the murder case was thoroughly put to bed. And as long as Adrian wasn't in the middle of deciding he had made a wrong choice and would really prefer to be with his good old friend Felicity.

Jane tried to tell herself that just because it had happened to Matty, it didn't have to happen to her. Did it?

She tore her mind away from that.

Chapter 22

'All I said was that I can't help being distracted when a murder case I've been involved in still has loose ends. And with no confession even after days of questioning it's impossible to get the whole thing tied up. So just because I forgot to do the shopping, there's no need to jump down my throat!'

'And all *I* said was that it wasn't your murder case so you bloody well ought to forget it!'

'Oh sure. Throw it at me that I'm just an administrator nowadays. I don't know why I bothered to change my job just so that we could have a life when we don't seem to have one.'

'You didn't change it *just* for that reason, so don't pile it onto me. Oh yes, I have noticed the way you say to other people that the new job was something you didn't ideally want, as if I'd somehow martyred you. Which I didn't,' Adrian said grittily, glaring at her. 'And if we don't have a life, that's hardly surprising considering you've barely spoken to me for a week.'

The row seemed to have blown up very suddenly and out of nowhere. And just when they were actually both home for the weekend. 'That's not true, I have spoken to you,' Jane retorted, glaring in her turn, 'on the rare occasions you're bloody here.'

'I can't help it if—'

'No, of course you can't, it's all me, isn't it? Oh, go off and visit bloody Felicity, I'm sure she's done the shopping! And for both of you, most likely. I'm sure she'll find time to cook you some of her expert and excellent meals, in spite of being on call this weekend.'

'She isn't on call, I am. And wait a minute, what *is* all this? No, don't you dare flounce off after throwing something like that at me!' He came round the table as Jane moved, barring her way. 'What's all that about her shopping for both of us? I don't live there!'

'You could have fooled me. And since your old college girlfriend is still so perfect after all these years, what the hell are you doing here? With thoroughly imperfect me? And incidentally, I do *not* flounce!'

'Yes, you do, you just did. And you've got the whole thing—'

'Sussed? Well, why not? I'm supposed to be a detective, or I *was*, and it scarcely takes much in the way of observation. You don't even like me to drop in at the practice any more. You like your women kept apart, presumably. Well, since you find this one so unlivable with, and you've managed to import the other one back into your life so conveniently— There's no need to raise your eyebrows like that, I'm not completely stupid!'

'Oh yes you are. Completely and utterly. You're an idiot.' Damn him, he was suddenly laughing. 'No, come here.' He captured her wrists in an extremely strong grip. 'I didn't know you were jealous. Well, thank Christ for that! And yes, you are unlivable with, but I knew that before I moved in on you so determinedly, didn't I? I love you, you stupid woman! And as for Fliss . . . No, don't wriggle like that, I'm sure as hell not going to let you escape. Fliss has been a pain in the neck!'

'Really? Nobody would have ever guessed.'

'I was hardly going to tell you, was I? When—'

'You mean she's after you?'

'No! Nothing of the sort, thank God. That would be plain embarrassing. As well as unlikely, we were never each other's type. She was *not* my old college girlfriend!' He gave Jane's wrists a shake, and a broad grin lit his face. 'You really were jealous!'

'You can stop looking so pleased about it. You obviously knew each other very well. And— What did you say?'

'I said, you're a lousy detective. In your private life,' he added hastily. 'I didn't know her all that well, we were just in the same class in the same year. So we did a lot of the same things. All right?'

'If you say so.'

'And what I was trying to point out before was, I was hardly going to grumble to you that I wouldn't have taken her on as partner if I'd known she was going to be so bloody emotional. I'd have got a real feminist comeback off you for that, wouldn't I? I know she's been going through a bad time and I don't want to be unsympathetic, but I wish I'd remembered that as well as being a good vet she was always apt to be in some emotional state or other and crying on various people's shoulders. Not mine,' he added quickly, leaning forward to force Jane to look him straight in the eye. 'Not mine, or,' he added ruefully, 'I might have remembered and been a bit more prepared for it.'

'But she has been crying on your shoulder now?'

'A bit. But no longer – I hope. The reason she's got this weekend off when it ought to be mine is because her man's coming down. He wants her after all, apparently. It sounds like a dead messy relationship to me altogether, but let's just hope this is the end of all the storms.'

'She's not leaving, is she? Oh hell, Adrian, not after all your—'

'No, it seems he's prepared to come and live down here. He's a writer or something so he can live anywhere. Oh damn!' Suddenly he was looking quite comically put out. 'Don't say I'm going to have to go on keeping you two apart.'

'Why?' Jane asked suspiciously, beginning to bristle again. And just when she had begun to relax into an almost miraculous lightening of heart. 'Why did you have to keep us apart?'

'Because, my love, Fliss had this fixed idea that you look just like the girl he ran off with in the first place. So every time she saw you she'd go into another state. Not that he wasn't already married. You have to take that one on board first of all. He's been toing and froing between Fliss and his wife for the last six years, never quite making up his mind to leave the one for the other. Then all at once he took off from both of them with a third female he'd just met and decided he'd fallen instantly in love with. But he has now apparently tired of her and wants to settle for Fliss. I imagine his wife has got sick of the whole thing and doesn't want him back anyway.' Adrian raised an eyebrow, looked at Jane, and added, 'Sounds an untrustworthy type altogether to me. And I think I will keep you away from him, for my own reasons.'

'Now you really are being stupid.'

'Oh, I don't know. Though if you were really as jealous of Fliss as you sounded—'

'If you'd talked about it I would have known, wouldn't I? And anyway, if I'd been singing someone's praises as loudly as you were hers, you'd have—'

'Yes, well, I'm prone to it, aren't I? Jealousy, I mean.' He pulled her abruptly right into his arms with a possessiveness she minded not at all.

'Sometimes. And never with cause. You – you really do mean I've just been imagining things?'

'Yes.' He gave her a deep and breathstopping kiss.

'So that isn't why you've been dead snappy lately? No, all right, I do believe you.'

'You'd better. I'm a one-woman man, me.' He kissed her again, lightly. 'You know, quite apart from anything else, I didn't want to admit I might have made a mistake in taking her on. I'd convinced myself she was the answer to everything. She is a good vet, I wasn't wrong about that. I'd just reckoned without having to do all the extra nursemaiding because she kept on remembering how miserable she was. All that emotion – no, don't kick me on the shins, I didn't say it was because she was a woman.'

'I wouldn't dream of it in the circumstances. I won't tell you you ought to be more sympathetic about other people's broken hearts, either. Poor old you, a stormy life at work when you've already got one at home.'

'Not always. I'd rather have you stormy than doing a good imitation of a frozen tundra. Particularly . . . Do you suppose we could rely on nobody needing my veterinary services this afternoon? Because I have a really good idea of how I'd like to spend it.' The expression in his eyes and the way his hands were moving were immensely promising.

They had a lot of making up to do. Jane leaned against him with a sense of relief, and pleasure, and gave him a wholly loving grin.

'That sounds like the best idea in the world to me,' she said.

Monday morning saw her sailing into work feeling, she thought with amusement, so undeniably cheerful that she probably looked like Rebecca of Sunnybrook Farm. There was a lot to be said for a blessedly uninterrupted weekend. She could offer pious thanks to fate that no farmer had come up with a sick cow, sheep, goat, or anything else four-legged requiring attention. Life, and love, were both very good. Enough to make anyone feel smoothed-out all over.

She gave the duty sergeant a sunny smile as she signed in and offered another one to Kenny Barnes when she met him in the corridor a moment later.

'Morning, ma'am. You look as if you've lost a tanner and found a shilling.'

'Do I? Must be the nice hot weather.' She decided she had better pull herself together and gave him more serious consideration. 'Your expression doesn't look as if anyone's managed to get a confession out of Gavin Levitt yet. Still no joy?'

'No, ma'am, he's still holding out. He's started taking things a bit more seriously since he got remanded in custody, and he's got himself another brief now. If we could just find out where he did the cutting up.' Kenny let out a sigh. 'I'm beginning to lose count of the searches we've made. Oh, that Jag from the gravel pit definitely was Pemberton's, I don't know if you'd heard that. And there were bloodstains on the leather of one of the seats, in spite of the water.'

'You've got the method of transportation, then.'

'Nothing to prove it was Levitt who used it, though, and he still swears blind he last saw Pemberton alive. He won't admit to knowing anything about the money either. The guv's beginning to wonder about Mrs Levitt on that one. Whether she decided to shop her husband as a cover for the fact that she's got the loot.'

'Any sign of where the money actually came from? Where Pemberton got it?'

'No, except it definitely didn't come from Musthills. The general feeling is that we may never know. He could have won it on the horses or at cards for all we can tell.'

Anna Musthill and Heather Benbridge would have to find some way of running Musthills without either of the partners now. Perhaps that would please them – if they could get the firm over the corruption scandal which would inevitably become public before long.

Anna had been told that Neville's body was in the grave, also that she had been right that he was responsible for bribing a councillor: facts which she had accepted with a degree of triumph. Hopefully she was taking less pleasure in the knowledge that a charge of wasting police time was still being seriously considered, and she had been advised not to leave the country in the meantime. Perhaps she would stay on in any case and try to run Musthills herself – though if both the sisters chose to involve themselves in it, Jane could imagine the firm might well find itself in a state of constant war.

She gave Kenny a sympathetic grin. 'Cheer up, it's not all bad. At least you're a lot further on than you were a week ago. A definite ID for the torso and a promising suspect in custody.'

'Yeah, and the guv certainly isn't planning on letting him wriggle out of it. Not even with this new and rather efficient brief riding herd on whatever he says. I wish we could find the head and the hands, but the divers haven't had any success on that so far.'

They both moved aside as someone else came along the corridor; then, since it was apparently someone in search of Kenny, Jane gave him another smile and walked on. So Gavin Levitt had started to take things seriously enough to get himself another lawyer after all. Why had he not seen the danger he was in before? That protestations of innocence were in no way enough?

Adrian was probably right, Jane thought, being in a mood to think Adrian was right about most things just at the moment. She should stop letting her mind nag on over the murder. Not that she had raised the subject again. If only she had not got this feeling, like a prickle up the back of her neck, that there was something she knew, or had seen, which would tie up a loose end. Something that would complete the pattern.

Was it connected with the shadowy figure Gavin Levitt claimed he and Neville Pemberton had both seen, on the edge of the churchyard? That might of course be a fiction from Gavin Levitt; except that it did fit with the trainer print found under the hedge. A useful witness to either side, if he or she actually existed. But if a witness to murder, that person had certainly not come forward.

Could Gavin Levitt be telling the truth? It seemed unlikely, well against the odds. Surely there were far too many strikes against him. That claim that Neville Pemberton had had some other late-night appointment in Tissingham – it seemed an irrational thing to insist, yet Gavin was insisting on it. She remembered the desperation in his voice. 'He said he had to be in Tissingham anyway.' And then, 'He said he couldn't give me any more time because he'd got an appointment.' If that was true, an appointment with whom?

The Benbridges? Another meeting with Heather, that late at night, to persuade her to sell?

Heather, who had seemed so blankly disbelieving of her sister's claim to have seen Neville. Disconcerted by it. Opening her mouth to begin, 'Oh, but—' Heather, who right from the beginning had made no bones about not wanting the police to investigate Neville's doings at Musthills.

No, surely not. Heather Benbridge might have a theatrical turn of temper, but murder and dismemberment? How, and where? Scarcely at her tidy home, among her children. If Neville really did have another appointment in Tissingham, it was far more likely to have been a romantic one. Some other love affair.

Some other jealous husband?

It was no use, speculation merely led to more speculation, and nothing Jane tried seemed to provide the answer she was seeking.

She discovered that she had reached her office without having had the least idea of where she was going. Talk about walking around in a dream, and she had probably cut all sorts of people dead on her way upstairs. She picked up the post which had been left on her desk. The top one was a folded message with 'Personal' typed neatly on the side of it, and she flicked it open. It was a brief missive.

'Dr Ingle rang to say, if you are free for lunch today she could meet you at twelve thirty. If she doesn't hear to the contrary she will see you at the usual place.'

It was signed by one of the communications constables and was timed 7.30 a.m. Matty must have been having one of her early starts. Jane checked her diary and saw that she would not have to cancel. Good. It was about time the two of them got together again. She rather wanted to raise the subject of Steve's visit, too, just to make sure there was no misunderstanding.

She arrived at the Sea Rose at lunchtime to find Matty waiting for her, a darkly graceful figure sitting with her head propped on one hand as she studied a newspaper. She looked up with the flash of a white grin as Jane came up to her.

'Hi. Sorry it was short notice, but I hoped you'd be able to make it.'

'This week doesn't look as if it's going to be prone to

emergencies. I've had a few since last time I saw you. You know we've identified the torso at last?'

'Yes, I was there when they brought someone in to do it. Knowing who it is seems to have got the whole thing solved for you. I've just read something in this paper about it.' Matty rustled through a few pages of newsprint. 'Oh yes, here it is, though it's only a paragraph. It doesn't say much, only who the corpse is and that he's a prominent local businessman. But also that somebody unnamed is in custody and "helping the police with their inquiries", with charges expected soon. I expect you've already seen it,' Matty added amiably, handing it over.

'No, there wasn't anything in any of the nationals I've seen. They must have been too busy with the latest royal scandal, let alone who's invading whom at the moment. Friday's local was on to the fact that we'd got an identification at last, but they hadn't picked up that we'd got a suspect in custody . . . Oh, this is Saturday's paper!'

'I didn't have time to read it so I'm catching up,' Matty said tranquilly, giving Jane a grin. 'Sounds as if you had a busy weekend too.' She looked up as the waitress arrived. After they'd ordered, she sat back with an appearance of contentment. 'So, corpses aside, how's life with you? How's Adrian?'

'Absolutely fine. Look,' Jane said quickly, 'I'd better tell you, Steve came to see us—'

'I know. He told me. I've just been up there for the weekend.' Matty gave a half-smile, her face calm. 'I thought it was time I did.'

'And you made up?' She was looking far too cheerful for

that not to be true. 'Well, good, if that's what you want. After all, you and he—'

'No, that's the point. It was weird, I found I wasn't even upset any more. All the way there I was thinking, well maybe he's right, I've just been bloody-minded and unforgiving, we'll start again, it was just a slip but it doesn't have to be important. But when I got there I found I didn't want to start again. It's just – over.'

Jane blinked. Matty didn't seem at all unhappy. 'Are you sure?' she asked. 'He was after me to plead with you on his behalf.'

'If you're going to, I'm afraid it won't work. He thinks I'm a hard bitch – well, maybe I am. But the fact is, I – I don't think we were really in love with each other at all. I think we were just . . . intrigued with each other. He was different. And I was different, for him. It was all amazing, and great, and . . . Oh, I don't know. It's no use you looking mystified,' Matty said with cheerful exasperation, 'because that's just how it feels.'

Their salads arrived. Matty started eating hers with every evidence of appetite.

'You don't look miserable,' Jane said cautiously.

'That's because I'm not. Oh yes, I was. At the beginning it felt like the end of the world. But I guess I . . . just needed to be away and doing something different, to wake up and realise that Steve's a very sexy guy, and it was fun, but we didn't actually have more than bed in common. If this hadn't happened when it did, I think we might have ended up split anyway. Because once we'd finished finding out about each other, we'd probably have ended up boring each other to death.' The cheerful eyebrow she raised at Jane across a forkful of grated carrot looked entirely genuine.

'You seemed to be so happy together,' Jane protested.

'Well, we were. For a time. But it just – died.'

'For both of you?'

'Well, no, though I think he'll come to admit it in the end. If he's honest. And if he can run it by his macho sensibilities.' Matty made a shrugging movement with her shoulders. 'At the moment he still thinks I'm just being unforgiving, but it really isn't that. I kind of looked round and it was gone, you know?'

'Just like that?'

'Seems so.' Matty stretched, and pulled what was all at once a very sour face. 'You know what's really annoying? That my mama was right. I can't help remembering what she said to me privately when she left: "I realise what you see in him, Tiamat, but it won't last!" Oh God, I *hate* that!'

She looked so much like her mother even as she said it that Jane was abruptly aware of sides of Matty that she really didn't know; and she felt a brief, involuntary inclination to feel sorry for Steve. He had tangled with something tougher than he realised. The ability Matty had to decide quite coolly that something was not what she wanted after all and move on – it was, just for a moment, a strong reminder of her mother's dismissiveness. Then the feeling was gone as Matty let out a warm chuckle and reached across to tap Jane across the fingers with her fork.

'You're looking kind of shattered, honey. Don't. Steve's heart won't be broken for long, and mine certainly isn't. You were surprised when we got together, remember? So it's nothing that out of the way that we've split. Let's change the subject and I'll tell you something nice and cheerful. You know I said I'd found I like pathology, which is one good thing out of all this. Well, it looks as if I may stay here when my three months is up.'

'Really?'

'Yup. Ruth Ledyard's had her baby and she's decided she'd like to stick with motherhood for at least a year. She told me she's always had it in mind but she didn't want to let Dr Kremer know because she reckoned then he'd make a point of finding fault with every temporary replacement just to force her to come back. But since I get on with him . . .'

'You're going to stay?'

'It looks pretty definite. The old curmudgeon hates change, and I've said I want to stay. So it seems very likely that he'll agree.'

'That's terrific! Oh good,' Jane said with a grin, 'my own personal hotline on autopsy reports. Yes, I do know it's not supposed to be my business any more, but at least I'll always know what's going on.'

'You're coping with not being in CID okay? I know how you were about it. Do you remember,' Matty said with a suddenly reminiscent look on her face, 'what idealists we both were once? At university? When you were going to be a lawyer and change the world that way, and I was going to do the same through medicine. Oh God, weren't we *young*!'

Her look of mock-gloom made Jane laugh. 'Gee, thanks, and where did you park your zimmer frame?' she inquired. 'And I'm not sure I was ever starry-eyed enough to think I could cure all society's ills.'

'Oh yes you were. We both were. Maybe you still are, at that,' Matty said with a grin, and went on before Jane could open her mouth to say drily that she was not, no way, not after several years in the police. 'To prove my point, see if you can name one person who believes in a principle and lives by it!'

'Mother Teresa of Calcutta?'

'Various people are in two minds about that, but I suppose I'll allow you that one. But see if you can come up with one you've actually met.'

Senander. Jane turned her head to shake his image out of it. If Matty was in a mood for cynicism she would only shoot that one down. A guru? With a cult following? Much too easy a target. 'All right then,' she said flippantly, 'Adrian. He holds the principle that animals need curing, and does it.'

'That doesn't count, and it's love talking. Though I'm glad it is, for you.' Matty gave her an affectionate grin. She really was looking remarkably cheerful. 'Listen, if I'm going to be staying here, will you have time to help me look for a flat? Or a small house, at a pinch? I need to find something quite soon so I can get a man-with-a-van to clear my possessions out of London – before my ex decides to throw anything I've left behind out of the windows.'

So Steve had become 'my ex' without a flicker. Well, if that was the way Matty wanted it . . . Amazing that she could simply draw a line under the relationship, without bitterness, and move on.

You just never knew with people, Jane thought.

Chapter 23

You just never knew with people.

The thought came with a sense of sour bitterness this time as Jane stared down at the piece of paper in her hand. She ought to have been less easy to take in. But at least she had had the sense to ask Geoff Madox to make a further check. It was pure curiosity which had made her do so, but that was a bitter thought too.

She had had the idea that there was one place which might give them Senander Baba's real or original name, and that it would be interesting to know it before she called on the cult again. A memory of Senander's accent had made her phone down to the collator's office after her lunch with Matty and suggest it would be worth making an inquiry to Australia House on the name Senander Baba. Sergeant Madox had agreed and this morning she had barely sat down at her desk before he buzzed her.

'Ma'am? That inquiry you gave me yesterday to Australia House. They said they'd pass it on and I've just had a fax in answer from the Sydney police. It's on its way up to you, since I thought you'd want all the details straightaway.'

The details were in her hands now, a very prompt reply to their query.

'Senander Baba, alias Philip Abbot. Date of birth 12.1.57, Sydney, New South Wales. Most recent criminal record: five-year prison sentence for fraud and aggravated burglary. Previously served time for ABH, two years, and breach of probation, six months. Also a long record as a juvenile. Family known to us long-term: father (deceased) habitually in and out of jail; one brother believed to be involved in organised crime; another serving a life sentence for murder. No record here for Philip Abbot since his last discharge from jail eight years ago. Changed his name during his last prison sentence and on discharge founded a group called Spiritual Growth (since disbanded). No more known.'

Someone with a sense of humour had added a personal comment at the end of the message. It said, 'If you've got any of the Abbots over your side, we're not a penal colony any more, so don't send them back – please!'

Senander Baba was actually Philip Abbot, with a long criminal record which included both fraud and violence.

How had she been so gullible?

Eight years ago, he had been a fully paid up member of the criminal fraternity. He had no record since but he would probably claim, with that damned charm and charisma of his, that he was a reformed character, that nowadays his life was entirely virtuous.

It might even be true. It might seem real, to him, that he should be in charge of reforming the lives of lost juveniles. All the same, Jane thought grimly, that community needed a particularly sharp eye keeping on it from now on. If this information had been known, Martin might not have been so readily released into Senander's care. *Damn* the man, how could he have taken her in so badly? She should have made an in-depth check sooner, right from the start; she should have followed up that Australian accent much earlier. It was disillusioning to know what an easy mark he had found her, how simple it had been for him to make her believe in him.

Even now, there was a part of her which wanted to think he was genuine. He had said nothing that could not be true. It was at least theoretically possible that he had genuinely found a faith to reform him and change his life. All the same, Jane knew that she would tell Philip Abbot, alias Senander Baba, very levelly that the police were now aware of his record and would be keeping a very careful eye on him in the future.

She had thought of going out to Tissingham Manor today anyway; now she definitely would. This morning. Right now, in fact. There was nothing in her diary to stop her.

She parked her car outside the manor gates as she had done before, and set off up the drive with determined steps. Then, abruptly, they slowed. She had come this far on sheer anger, but now professional caution came back to take over. She would have to take this visit with care. And a degree of politeness. Cults had been known to be set off into violence by anything they considered to be police harassment. The man who used to be Philip Abbot had declared a belief in peace. Could she count on that? She remembered that martial arts class.

She could be making this visit simply to inquire about Martin and Elena, and it might be as well to stick to that, certainly at the start. It was a valid reason for her presence. She walked on and saw that the front door, surprisingly, was standing wide open.

It seemed the community had grown less watchful. Jane tried a tap on the knocker, but there was no response. She hesitated, then walked in. If she remembered it right, the passage ahead was the one she had been taken along, and would lead her to the room Senander – Philip Abbot – seemed to use as a study.

It did, but the room was empty. Its far door was open too, but when she peered in nobody was there either. Last time, she recalled, the place had felt just as deserted but the acolytes had all been out in the gardens. Or in the craft workshop. Perhaps she should leave, come back another time. She walked on, however, to find herself in the confusing network of corridors she remembered. Stairs up had led to dormitories, but she could hear no sound from above.

No, she had better go. This way might lead back to the front door.

It didn't. She crossed an empty room with its door wide open to try to orientate herself by what she could see from the windows. She seemed to be at the back of the house, because that was, surely, the sunken lawn she had seen from its other side. No class was taking place on it today. Jane retraced her steps and tried to guess which branch of the corridor might take her back in the direction of the front hall. The place was such a warren. She was beginning to feel intrusive. Even if she had been shown round before, the young members of the cult might be offended by her wandering about. Martin certainly would. Where the hell were they all, anyway? And their so-called guru?

She was just thinking ruefully that it would be unfortunate if she walked into a group rapt in silent meditation when she spotted a downward stair and made for it with gratitude. It was familiar; she recalled that it led down to the kitchen. And there was a way out to the garden from there.

She came out into the wide basement room with its big scrubbed table and its built-in dresser, and stopped, wondering what it was about it that was different. It was very tidy, but then it had been before. There were still some pieces of mismatched crockery on the dresser shelves, and a large old-fashioned kettle standing on one of the cookers.

What was missing was the one touch of brightness that had been there before, she realised suddenly. The cheap but cheerful modern mugs which had been hanging on those hooks along the front of the dresser.

Maybe they were using them. Or perhaps they had put them away in one of the cupboards. Maybe they had put the threadbare teatowels she remembered hanging up to dry away too. So why did she suddenly feel that it wasn't just that nobody was here now, but that nobody was here at all?

A sound behind her made her swing round. No, she was wrong. One person was here at least – Martin. He must have come in through the doorway from the scullery. He wore no robes, merely a T-shirt and scuffed jeans; and he had stopped dead to stare at her with those strange gold-flecked eyes, giving her a wary, brooding and deeply suspicious look. The one person with whom she couldn't communicate without somebody there to translate. Except Senander had said he could lip-read when he chose. Jane gave him a very friendly smile and said carefully, 'I've come to see Senander, but I can't find him. Where is everybody?'

She could swear he understood. He took a step closer to her, watching her face. Then he made a gesture which seemed to suggest the word 'Gone'.

'Gone? Away? Everyone?'

He nodded briefly.

'Senander too?' Jane asked.

That seemed to make him wary. He stood looking at her for a moment; then he stepped back with that light grace of his, and beckoned her to follow with a sharp gesture. But not to follow him out of the room, apparently. He took her to the blackboard on the wall and picked up a piece of chalk from the runnel beneath it. He looked at her again as if to make sure she was watching him. Then he began to write, in clear but small capital letters, starting at the top of the board and moving down line by line.

'I CUT THE MAN'S HEAD AND HANDS OFF. I KNOW HOW TO DO THAT. I BURNED THEM IN THE FURNACE. THEN I BURIED HIM IN THE GRAVE WHERE I SAW THE MEN FIGHTING. IT WAS A GOOD PLACE TO HIDE HIM.'

He stood back and watched Jane read it. Then he added, 'YES, I KILLED HIM. I KNEW WHAT I WAS DOING.' And he signed it at the bottom with that same neat signature Jane had seen him write on the tape recording: M. Jones.

She tried to take it in, cold with shock and a sense of danger. With a numb lack of thought she reached for the chalk and wrote 'WHY?' on one corner of the board.

He took the chalk back from her. 'I THOUGHT HE WAS AFTER ELENA.'

But why was he suddenly confessing? Because of what had appeared in the newspapers? Out of an unwillingness to let someone else take the blame? She had got that far, aware of the danger she must be in but barely able to grasp it, when somebody else came rapidly into the kitchen. Senander appeared in the same scullery doorway Martin had used. He stopped dead just as Martin had, his face surprised, his eyes lighting on Jane with a query in them. Senander, but an unfamiliar Senander: no robes today, just a white shirt and jeans as scuffed as Martin's. A tall, lean, muscular figure with only the shaven head to make him unlike anyone else.

His eyes went immediately from Jane to the board. She saw him take in what was written there. Before he could do more than let out a brief exclamation, there was a blur of movement beside Jane. A drawer in the end of the table was swept open, something was pulled from it – a large, very sharp, meat cleaver. She saw it as it flashed in front of her face. At the same time, Martin caught hold of her with a sweep of his other arm and held her in a tight and inescapably strong grip which twisted her wrist high up against her back and pulled her against him. She let out an involuntary yelp of pain, but no more, as the cleaver came threateningly against her throat.

'Martin, no!' There were just those two words before Senander's fingers flew into sign language. Jane felt Martin give a wild shake of his head behind her. There was a brief guttural sound from him which was almost like a snarl. Then she was being pulled backwards, the cleaver still against her throat. It was too dangerous to try dragging against him with her weight, or stumbling, or trying to catch him off balance to tumble him over her head. He was too much of an expert in movement for her to chance it, and far too strong. The grip holding her had trained muscles behind it. Martin knew exactly what he was doing.

From the way Senander held back, all the while desperately trying to sign, Jane knew the danger she was in was all too real. The boy was out of control. Or all control except his own. She felt herself pulled backwards again, across towards the far wall. And suddenly, apparently, through it as Martin wrenched open a door she had not seen, drew her backwards through the opening and slammed the door shut behind them. He turned her round and pushed her up a steep flight of stairs ahead of him. He still held her wrist in an iron grip. Out through another door; along a passage; up some more stairs. She couldn't even try to reason with him or use her trained negotiator's skills. He wouldn't hear her.

The maze of the house made it difficult to tell where he was taking her, except that it was upwards. Why not out of the house; out to where she had left her car? It made no sense. He dragged her on up another flight of stairs, his face a blank mask whenever she managed to get a sight of it. It seemed to be true that everyone else had left; they saw nobody, heard nobody. Jane did her best to convey by gesture and movement that she planned to be co-operative, particularly since the cleaver made a threatening movement if ever she tried to lag. Was that, she wondered bleakly, what he had used to chop up Neville Pemberton? Why had he written, 'I know how to do that'? What had Neville been doing at or near the manor so that he could be suspected of being after Elena?

She was pushed up a narrower flight of stairs somewhere at the top of the house and along a passage in what had probably once been servants' quarters. And then through a low boarded door, rapidly unbolted, out onto a flat gully between two sloping areas of roof.

In the sudden fresh air and sunshine, Jane was urged and threatened up one of the slopes, over the top to the other side, and down a steep rake of slate. Martin took care to steady her as she descended. He put her against the column of a brick chimney, and she clung to it gratefully, trying not to let her breath come in gasps. She was unsteadily aware of the smoothness of the slates and their steep slope. It was a long, and very straight, way down beyond the small battlements which put up square stone fingers just a foot down from her, where the roof ended. She could, in fact, see half across the valley in which the village lay if she looked out over the very topmost foliage of the nearer trees.

Jane remembered looking up at those battlements from below on her first visit to the house. They had seemed an amusing folly, somebody's decorative idea of a castle wall as part of the manor's weird amalgam of styles. There had been an area of heavy stone paving directly below, a long way down at ground level. That memory seemed to make it even more urgent to wrap her arms round the chimney, hoping it was as stoutly fixed as it felt. Martin seemed to feel no need for such support, standing out of her reach with graceful balance, his face blank with concentration, that classically beautiful profile so like a statue.

A scraping noise made her turn her head. Senander must have been following them. His shaven head appeared, the the rest of him, to sit astride the roof ridge, no closer. Martin had seen him too, and one threatening gesture towards Jane with the cleaver invited his guru's stillness. But he turned his head away the moment Senander tried to sign to him, shutting him out.

'He won't hurt you,' Senander said in Jane's direction. 'He may look as if he means to, but he won't.' His voice was gritty with strain, and the fact that he made no move suggested that he was unsure of the truth of his words. 'Martin! Oh damn it to hell, *look at me!* Martin!'

There was a sudden burst of shouting from below. It sounded alarmed. Somebody from the village must have seen them on the edge of the roof, Jane thought. And Senander on its crest. Words which sounded like 'Hold on, help's coming' floated up, but whatever plans Martin had, a simple rescue was not likely to be part of them.

The boy was standing quite still with an expression of silent, calm concentration. For a second everything about him seemed turned inwards. He laid the cleaver carefully down on the tiles. Then he stepped backwards with one neatly balanced movement onto the top of one of the battlements. The he took another swift backward step – into thin air.

Senander let out a despairing cry. Jane swallowed a sharply indrawn breath. The sound which came up from below, the distant, muted, terrible thump of something hitting the ground, had a horrible finality. At least a hundred feet; and onto stone. The human body was not designed to survive that.

Jane knew suddenly, with absolute clarity, that that was what Martin had meant to do all along. He could not have borne to be locked up. She had seen what he had been like in a cell. She had not been a hostage for his safety. Her presence under threat had been to stop Senander preventing his intention.

She wondered what would have happened to her if she had refused to co-operate. Was there anything she could have done? What could she have done to prevent the intended act of a boy who couldn't hear her and who had just confessed to murder?

Senander came swiftly past her, slipping and sliding down the slope to peer over the edge. There were voices again, floating up; and somewhere, though still distant, there was the wail of a police car's siren. Help arriving, but too late. In a moment, Jane might manage to stop clinging to her chimney. And the man she ought to think of as Philip Abbot might stop his intense stare downwards, move out of his frozen stillness, and help her back to safety. She knew the shock and grief he must be feeling. If there was one thing she could not deny, it was that he genuinely cared about Martin.

She saw a muscular twitch of his shoulders; she saw him move back from the edge. His face was suddenly as blank as the boy's had been. His hand came down to scoop up the cleaver Martin had dropped. His glance swept across Jane, but she was sure he didn't see her. There was a look in the grey eyes that made her blood run cold. A look of such total, murderous rage that it was like seeing a completely different man. She flinched instinctively, one hand going up to protect herself.

Unnecessarily. He went up the roof in a blur of movement, one long arm pulling himself up over the ridge. Then he was out of sight, vanished.

Jane stared after him feeling bewildered, and chilled to the bone in spite of the warm sunlight shining peacefully around her.

Dear God, what now? What more could happen?

Chapter 24

The expression Jane had seen in his eyes made it urgent for her to move fast. Never mind dizziness or the slipperiness of slate. She was up over the roof ridge herself with the agility of a monkey, sparing only a brief thankfulness for rubber soles. A rapid slide down into the gully, a stumbling run for the small door hanging open. Where the hell had Senander – Philip Abbot – gone? One thing was sure, it could only be down.

As Jane raced downwards herself, she heard the distinct thud of someone moving fast ahead of her. Down below now, beyond the next staircase. It sounded as if he was taking the steps two at a time.

She reached the ground floor and stopped, breathlessly, to listen. Which way in this maze of rooms and passages had he gone? Where was he making for?

And why had he looked as he did? As if there was something he had to do?

She could hear the police siren quite close outside now. If Senander was making for Martin's body, which would seem his logical destination . . . Oh hell's teeth, had he gone suddenly mad? Was he likely to attack the police who must be making for the same place right now, out of some idea that they were to blame? She caught her breath and tried to orientate herself on which passage or room would lead her through to the front door. Then somewhere not far ahead she caught the sound of a sudden muffled crashing. And then another. And a man's voice shouting.

She let herself be directed by the noise, made a guess, and whipped into a room. It was a lucky guess. The room had a door the other end and from beyond it she could hear sounds of mayhem even more clearly. Two men shouting. More crashes. She hurled the door ahead of her open and found she was unexpectedly back in the black-and-white tiled hall. From the other side of it, through an open doorway, a man's voice yelled clearly above what appeared to be sounds of destruction.

'For fuck's sake, you knew that yesterday when the boy confessed to you and you started sending the other kids away! Phil! What the hell— Phil!'

The open door was surely the one that led into the office of A1 Data Commerce.

Jane skidded across the hall. No, she had not been wrong. Under the brightness of strip lighting, computer gear was in the process of being packed up into boxes. Desks had drawers pulled out showing that someone was in the middle of clearing them. An automatic shredder was humming away and spilling white streamers onto the floor; a basket which had held them was overturned. Across the nearest desk there was a gouge as if someone had given it a heavy blow with something sharp; a computer screen half out of a box had been shattered and cut almost in half; a keyboard had been similarly gashed in two and was lying amidst a drift of papers on the floor. And as Jane came through the door, Senander wielded another violent blow across a desk with the cleaver, sending a lamp skittering to the floor where its bulb exploded with a loud bang.

Beyond him, backed into a corner, was the man Jane had seen just once before, coming briefly out of this same office. What had that name in the phone book been? D. Armistead. Well, if this was Mr Armistead, he was plainly terrified.

And with good reason. His one-time tenant was arcing very close to him with a sharp cleaver and causing maximum random damage with every swing.

But he knew Senander's real name. Jane had just heard him quite distinctly address the man in front of him as Phil.

Phil – Philip Abbot. And he was plainly in an ungovernable rage. He looked extremely dangerous. His next swing caused the man in front of him to duck, then sink to the floor in a protective crouch. Jane tried to find her voice. Breathlessly but with as much command as she could put into it she said the first words that came into her head.

'Police! Stop, you're under arrest!'

Senander turned his head and regarded her. His eyes were still blankly cold. 'Tell her!' he commanded, turning his head back to the man in front of him and making a threatening gesture with the cleaver.

'He's gone crazy!' the man pleaded in Jane's direction. There was an Australian twang in his voice, too. 'I don't know what's happened, but get him off me! Oh shit, Phil, stop this, for God's sake.'

'I said, tell her!'

'Tell her what? What am I supposed to say? Look, I don't know what he's on about. Something must have happened to him.'

'Martin Jones has just thrown himself off the roof,' Jane said coolly, hoping the flatness of her words would jerk Senander into some kind of normality. Though it might be exactly the wrong thing to say. She needed backup, but if she went for it, murder might be done here and now in this room. Philip Abbot did have a past record of violence. The man in the corner seemed to take some comfort from the fact that he was standing quite still just at the moment, not swinging the cleaver, merely hefting it in his hand. The crouching man peered round at Jane, his voice taking on a defensive petulance.

'It's not my fault if the boy jumped off the roof. He probably thought you'd come to arrest him again. Phil, for fuck's sake, no!'

The cleaver had moved. It came down with a crash on the table next to which the man was huddled. 'I said, tell her!' the voice grated inexorably.

'You can't do this to me! I'm your *brother*, for Christ's sake!'

Was he now? Another Abbot. Another of the family Sydney didn't want back.

Jane was aware that she suddenly did have backup. There was a movement behind her and a uniform edged into her line of sight. A voice murmured 'Ma'am?' uncertainly, but one glance at the tableau beyond her must have explained why she was standing frozen just inside the doorway. She heard a mutter, then somebody else clearly radioing urgently for assistance. Philip Abbot took not one whit of notice of all that, merely balanced the weapon in his hand threateningly, all his concentration on his brother. He grated, with an inflexible note in his voice, 'Yes, this is my brother David. He's been calling himself Armistead, but his real name's David Abbot. And he's going to tell you the truth, here and now. Or I'll leave off chopping up his furniture and chop him instead – where it really hurts. Yes, I do mean it! Now, tell her loud and clear what you did. Tell her how you used Martin!'

The sweat beading on David Abbot's brow showed he believed his brother meant business. His face held a terrified pallor. 'All right, Phil, all right! You don't have to . . . All right!' His voice took on a gabbling note as the cleaver swung suspiciously low in the direction of his groin. 'I was the one who killed Pemberton. I got Martin to help me dispose of the body. I did it by persuading him Phil and his bloody community might be in danger if anyone found out. Phil didn't know anything about it until yesterday when Martin told him. Bloody hell, isn't that *enough*? It's not my fault the boy's so unstable that he goes and jumps off— Aargh!'

The cry was in response to a swing which came very close to slicing into him. Jane had begun a very slight movement herself, with the intention of trying to disarm Philip Abbot, but she desisted quickly as he turned his head and the chopper made the beginning of another arc. 'No, we haven't finished yet,' Philip said, his voice so cold Jane almost shivered. 'David's got some more to tell you yet. Haven't you?'

'Like what? Jesus! As if it wasn't enough that you bloody blackmailed me into giving your brood houseroom. I'm not a flaming charity! So I was bloody entitled to— No, all right, all right! What more do you want me to say?'

'Tell her why you killed this man Pemberton.'

'He was working for me. And I found he'd been . . . It was my neck or his! He'd – he'd got something of mine. And he said he was getting out anyway, that he was going to take his profits with him, and that he'd put in an anonymous tip-off if I tried to stop him. Christ, Phil, that's enough, surely!'

'Not quite. Tell them,' he seemed to be aware that he had a larger audience than Jane now, 'tell them precisely what you've been doing here.'

'Are you trying to get me killed?' The words were a mutter, but Jane heard them. 'You know what—'

'You'll be singing treble if you don't finish this!'

'All right!' David Abbot yelled, 'All right, I'll tell them, don't . . .' He was shaking. And who could blame him? 'Money laundering,' he brought out almost inaudibly. Then, as the cleaver made a threatening gesture, he produced it more loudly, almost a shout, in the direction of the doorway. 'Money laundering!'

Money laundering. Moving money around by computer, taking hot cash in, transferring it into invented shell companies, sending it round the world by wire until it was untraceable and legitimate. A1 Data Commerce advertised itself as investment brokers but it was obviously a highly illegal kind of investment.

Senander's rage abruptly seemed to die. He let out a

deep sigh and blinked as if coming to himself. Or as if he was very tired. He threw the cleaver into a nearby cardboard box, quite casually, as if he had found it in his hand and no longer knew what he wanted to do with it. Then he turned his head and looked at Jane, past the two burly constables who were moving swiftly into the room in his direction.

There was a weary look on his face, and he made no resistance at all when he was restrained, handcuffs clipped into place. He simply looked at her and gave a small resigned shrug.

Though his mouth was closed, she could have sworn he said, 'How do you think I know so much about dysfunctional families?'

'You do seem to have a knack for getting yourself into things.' Chris Hollings's voice was quite friendly, in spite of the dryness of the remark, and he gave Jane a look which combined resignation and a certain degree of wry amusement. 'A flair for trouble.'

'It's not voluntary,' Jane protested mildly.

'I know. But go on, tell me. You thought of something which sent you haring off without thinking twice and which sent the whole pile of dominoes tumbling.'

'No, I didn't, actually. It was just chance.' But the clue she had been searching for in the back of her mind actually had been there, had she been able to think of it instead of just stumbling into the truth by mistake: The Trefoil disk in Musthills' safe, which Neville Pemberton could only have got from a computer expert. And a computer firm at Tissingham Manor. That was the link, the reason why Neville might have had a late-night appointment in Tissingham, why he chose the village for his meeting with Gavin Levitt. 'So Levitt's unlikely story turned out to be true,' she said, 'and he's off the hook – after all those hours you've spent on him!'

'It's not a total waste, we've still got him on the corruption charge. But David Abbot for the murder. I've had a session with him and he's confirmed that forced confession. Martin Jones was still wandering about the house that night, apparently, though all the others were safely tucked up in bed. He came across David Abbot moving the corpse and got incorporated into the disposal plans. Don't ask me how Abbot communicated with him but he apparently found a way. Maybe in writing. We've had that chalked confession of Martin's photographed, by the way. Even though parts of it were false, it's signed evidence that he did the dismemberment.' And that the head and hands were burned in the manor's furnace.

'Using the grave was apparently Martin's idea,' Chris went on. 'The fact that he was walking through the churchyard after visiting his grandmother probably explains why Mrs Emmett didn't mention hearing the fight the first time she was asked. She might have been worried that he was somehow involved. And presumably he reassured her on his next visit that he wasn't, so she felt able to tell us about it. Perhaps he hadn't realised that she would, though I suppose since it wasn't really relevant to the actual disposal he might not have thought it mattered anyway. And she couldn't exactly have chattered on to him in a general way, could she? By the way, I'm told Martin knew how to use a cleaver so expertly because he used to work in a meat-packing factory. His father's. Mr Jones senior runs several large companies in the wholesale meat trade.'

So that was why Martin had written 'I know how to do that'. Expertise with animal carcases transferred to a human body. David Abbot had found himself a useful henchman – and to ensure his co-operation and his silence had convinced Martin that the murder might threaten the man who had cared for him and the community which had given him a home.

Chris was speaking again. 'Martin's confession seems to have been a bid to protect the others. His suicide – well, that follows, I suppose.' He paused, then went on, 'Philip Abbot claims he knew nothing about the murder until the boy finally told him what had happened.'

'I did hear David Abbot confirm that. That his brother knew nothing about the murder until yesterday. It's in my report.'

'Yes, I know. Philip Abbot freely admits that he planned to cover it up, though. Apparently he immediately decided it was time to move out and started sending the other kids off in small groups, to what he will only describe as a "safe place" where he and Martin planned to join them. If you'd arrived much later, you'd have found the whole lot had done a flit.' The DI's eyes held a grimly satisfied look. 'David Abbot had also decided it was time to relocate since he was losing his convenient cover. Nothing like filling the house with an innocent-looking group in weird robes to distract attention.'

David Abbot had asserted that his brother had blackmailed

him into giving houseroom to his brood. That had been in Jane's report too. The cult had only arrived at the manor a few months ago, whereas A1 Data Commerce had been there much longer, but all the same it was a clear indication that Senander – Philip – had known about his brother's activities from the start. Had he been part of them? Probably.

'Philip Abbot seems to be taking the whole thing pretty calmly, now,' Chris said, looking thoughtful. 'In fact the way he's been since he was brought in makes it difficult to imagine him wielding a meat cleaver. Less so after reading that fax from Sydney, but he's a pretty cool character, all the same. He's given a free and polite admission to being an accessory to murder after the fact and conspiracy to conceal. He says quite openly that he intended to take Martin out of the country. He merely shrugs when he's asked about his brother's activities – seems to consider it totally unimportant. I caught a cynical gleam in his eye which made me wonder just how much he was actually involved in the money-laundering himself, particularly bearing his record in mind.' He gave Jane a look with a lift of his eyebrow. 'Getting that information from Sydney – are you going to say that was luck again?'

'Just following up the Australian accent.' Nobody had had the lack of tact to remind Jane that she had actually vouched for Senander Baba on an earlier occasion. She was coming in for nothing but approval but it had a bitter taste. She tried not to remember seeing a boy step off a roof. And then a man who avowed peace swinging a lethal chopper in murderous rage. Philip Abbot was probably guilty of everything which would be thrown at him – she supposed.

'How much is David Abbot talking?' she asked.

'Admitting murder, how and when and the means of disposal, but refusing to answer about anything else. They dumped the car in the gravel pit after using it to transport the body. The motive for the killing's clear enough, even if he won't elaborate on that. He said before that Pemberton worked for him. He must have been acting as a bagman. But he'd been skimming – taking part of the money he should have handed in and banking it for himself. All those overseas buying trips he made provided a good cover for collecting the illicit cash Abbot was laundering. And Pemberton looked thoroughly respectable, a pillar of the local community with a genuine reason for his travels, so it was unlikely he'd be searched at any borders. Most of his trips were to eastern Europe, so I've heard, and there's a lot of hot money there these days.' Chris paused, then went on, 'We've got that admission Abbot made that Pemberton threatened to spill the beans, anonymously and from a safe distance, if he wasn't allowed to keep his profits. Rash of him,' the DI added drily, 'on his own in the middle of the night, with a man he'd been robbing blind.'

'Have you managed to get any idea how big the operation was?'

'Not really. Abbot seems to have been running things on his own at this end, but I'd say somebody must have set him up in business. He's not about to tell us who though. Or anything else about his operations. Whoever's behind him obviously frightens him a hell of a lot more than the police do.'

'He did say it was "my neck or his" when he was talking about the murder.'

'Quite. He'd have been held responsible for the missing money. And he probably feels it'd still be his neck if he talks now. So he's decided to take the rap for the murder and live out whatever sentence he gets rather than risk being found dead in his jail cell one fine morning.' Chris sounded practical, if regretful. 'Hopefully there's something in what he's left at the manor which will give us a clue, but he'd got far enough with his shredding to look as if there won't be much. All the programmes on the computers were shut down too.'

'It may not be relevant, but when we went into Musthills I did hear that Neville Pemberton had introduced some sort of investment into the company during the last year. Something called . . . What was it? Lennox Holdings.'

'Thanks, that might be useful. It might be part of Abbot's laundering operation, a move to legitimise some of the hot cash in a respectable company. The Jersey account, on the other hand, looks like the illicit share Pemberton was salting away for his own use. I'm pretty sure its disappearance was Abbot claiming it back. I suggested it to him but all I had in response was a tightly closed mouth.'

A greedy character, Neville Pemberton. And crooked in more than one direction. How had he and David Abbot got together? Jane wondered. Perhaps it had simply been a question of like finding like.

Chris stretched, looking like a man well pleased by the day's results, and gave Jane a smile which suggested they should both be satisfied. There would certainly be credit to be had for catching up with this piece of international villainy. 'A fair can of worms to turn up on our patch,' he said. 'A money-laundering operation going on right under our feet. Pemberton probably wasn't the only person slipping in and out of the manor unnoticed on night-time visits. You don't have to go through the village to reach it if you approach it from the other side, so— What? Something's occurred to you?'

'I was thinking of old Mr Baines in the cottage opposite the manor gates,' Jane said. 'You'll find a report in Rachel Welsh's house-to-house record, and he said something similar to me – about having seen comings and goings at the manor at night. It sounded like the confused ramblings of an old man, but maybe it wasn't.' Perhaps his desire to take Rachel upstairs to his bedroom had not been elderly lust or mental confusion, but a wish to show her the place from which he'd observed the activity.

'I'll check that with Rachel,' Chris said. 'Since we were concentrating on happenings the other end of the village, I'm not surprised we let it go by. A lot easier to know what's important with hindsight.' He gave her a grin, flexing his shoulders, and let his general satisfaction show again. 'The murder's the only part that will concern us; the rest's going to be down to the SFO. I can't say I'll be sorry to hand it over. We've got enough ordinary crime to deal with, and the other stuff's going to take a lot of long, slow and complicated unravelling. The financial mob's welcome to the Abbots and all their nefarious dealings.'

The murder tied up, the burden of the rest taken off his hands, CID able to move on. A pleasing result, from anyone's point of view. Jane stirred a little, and put a question.

'Are you going to be interviewing the Abbot brothers any more today?'

'No. We've got the confession, which is all we really need. We'll have them in court in the morning, then they can be transferred to the prison and wait for the Yard's experts there. Why, is there something you wanted asked?'

'Not that, no. I just wondered if you'd mind if I spoke to Philip Abbot. On the grounds of my proper job,' Jane added quickly. 'It seems to me that somebody ought to tell him what's happening about Martin Jones's body. I . . . I thought maybe I owed it to him to let him know that Mrs Emmett has been informed and intends to see to the burial.'

'Yes, sure. He does seem to have felt something for the boy, I'll grant him that, all things considered.' Things which included terrifying his brother into an admission of guilt. 'I've got no objection if you feel you ought to see him yourself.'

'Thanks.'

As she made her way towards the cells, Jane knew there was no real need for her to see Philip Abbot herself. She simply wanted to see him. If for nothing else, to remind herself that he was Philip Abbot, one-time crook, probably still a villain. She wanted to remember him that way, not as Senander Baba.

Chapter 25

The custody sergeant was dubious about letting her visit the prisoner in cell number five. 'I'd better send somebody with you, ma'am. He's been quiet enough since he was brought in, but according to the reports I've had he was thoroughly violent at one stage.'

'I know, but he didn't show any violence towards me personally. Or to anyone else except his brother. You can come and stand outside the door if it worries you but I can't see there's anything he'd have to gain by not behaving himself.'

'Well all right then, ma'am, if you say so.'

He checked through the flap before he unlocked the door, then stood within sight as Jane entered, and remained there on watch.

Philip Abbot was sitting peacefully on the cell bench. Sitting with all the tranquillity that was Senander Baba's. Jane saw the grey eyes take in the sergeant's lurking presence. He remained where he was, with no attempt to get up, and gave Jane a quiet, calm, slightly quizzical smile.

'Inspector?'

'I came to tell you—' She broke off, the official tone

suddenly difficult. 'I thought you'd like to know that I went to see Mrs Emmett, Martin's grandmother, to break the news to her. Though I – I only told her that he'd died after a fall.' She had co-opted the vicar's wife, too, to stay with the old lady in case of need. Mrs Emmett had drawn her tiny figure up after a very brief moment and shown acceptance, along with courage, and a sharpness which made it clear why Michael Mather had referred to her as a 'sparky old bird'. She had said, 'Well, he's gone then, poor lad. Don't fuss over me, there's no need. He was a good boy, whatever those parents of his may have said about him. And they needn't think I'll put up with any pretences from them either, when they didn't care about him when he was alive – and just because he couldn't hear.'

'Thank you for telling me,' Philip Abbot said quietly.

'Mrs Emmett intends to see to his burial. She – she was clearly fond of him.'

'Yes.' Philip looked up at Jane with a flash of pain in his eyes. It was quickly gone. 'I'm glad to know that his grandmother will bury him. Thank you, Inspector Jane Perry. By the way, why did you call at the manor today?'

She could have said it was just a visit to check on Elena's safety and Martin's good behaviour. Instead she gave him the truth. 'I'd just had word from Australia on your – history. So I came to warn you that we'd be keeping an eye on you in the future. There was nothing else. If Martin really did think I might have come to arrest him, I'm sorry.'

'He told me the truth after what was in Saturday's paper. He'd bought one to take to his grandmother. I knew something had been distressing him.' The man sitting so still on the bench spoke quietly, his mind abruptly absorbed in memory. As he looked up she saw a grim edge to his mouth. 'So then I told David we'd be leaving. And that he would be wise to do so too, but a long way away from me unless he wanted— Still, at that point I was only interested in seeing my kids were safe. Which they are, I'm glad to say, or should be. I've sent them to someone else doing the same work.' A rueful twist appeared on his lips. 'You're right, I used David. Well, he had a house and we urgently needed a roof, having lost our last one. But I should have known better, shouldn't I?'

Jane gave him no answer. She saw a look of amusement come into the grey eyes.

'Ah, I see,' he said. 'Once word had reached you about the Abbots . . . A condition for which there's no cure.'

'I didn't say that.'

'No, but you were thinking it. You're wrong, you know. People can change. I did.'

'In prison, I gather. At least that's where I'm told you changed your name.'

'And my life.' He lifted an eyebrow, his eyes quizzical, and actually gave her a grin. Damn the man with his charm and charisma! 'You look as if you think I picked up my faith like an infection. I don't know, maybe it's a fair description. But it is real.' He offered her a considering gaze, then a sudden charming smile. 'How's your shoulder these days? It looks better.'

'It's fine, thank you. It doesn't hurt. But that doesn't mean I believe—'

'It's all right, you don't have to believe in it for it to

work. It just does, that's all. It seems to be a side product of prayer and meditation. You know, everything I told you was true.'

'Was it?' She had to try to pull herself out of the fact that the damned charisma was working. Even here. Even with the custody sergeant still lurking within earshot. 'Your brother's activities don't seem to have been exactly truthful.'

'I'm not responsible for my brother.' He frowned briefly. 'But then again I am, aren't I? On principle. I should, all the same, have kept out of his way.' There was something bleak in that, and she guessed he was thinking of Martin again. 'As I said, I should have known better. It was a bad slip into old ways. Ah well. Next time I'll remember to be more careful.'

'Next time?'

'Well they'll have to let me out eventually, won't they?' He seemed remarkably light-hearted about it. 'And then I shall start again, I expect. Since it seems to be what I'm intended to do.'

'Start another cult?'

'I don't like that word. I meant another rescue mission for the young.' The set of his mouth suggested he really did mean it. That he intended to go on being Senander Baba for the lost and homeless, or such of them that he could find, when he came out of jail this time. Because that was surely where he would go. He had clearly known what his brother was doing, whether or not he had been part of it.

But, oh damn, it was far too easy to believe him, to believe that he had not actually been involved in anything but finding a roof for his flock. That he had been unwise, not criminal.

But he was the same man she had seen in a violent, murderous rage, committing mayhem, threatening bodily harm. She should remember that.

'Yes, I know, and I'm sorry if I frightened you.' His words almost made her jump with their grave apology; he was reading her mind again, in that maddening way of his. 'It was another slip, and a bad one for a follower of peace. I shall have to do a lot of self-examination over it. But I'd like it if you could believe that I do live exactly the way I told you I did. I share what I have. I offer what I can. I take only what's given. It's a simple enough creed, isn't it?'

He was looking at her with what seemed to be total sincerity. It was a pity that a lurking amusement came back into his eyes and she had to suspect mockery. 'Never mind,' he said, as if comforting her. 'I suppose I can't expect to convert the police.'

'I shouldn't try. What happens to you next is up to the courts.' Jane drew a steadying breath, and stared at him as inflexibly as she was able. 'I hope . . .' She hesitated, then, 'If you've really gone straight for the past eight years I'm sure it will count for you.'

'Oh, I shouldn't think so. After all I'm an Abbot, aren't I? So who'd believe me?' If there was a touch of cynicism in his eyes, it vanished as he gave her his extraordinarily tranquil smile. 'Well, a cell's no hardship to a life of meditation, don't worry.'

She would have told him that she had no intention of worrying but the custody sergeant's voice came from behind her. 'Ma'am?' He was clearly growing restive. He probably had a dozen other things to do.

'I've finished here,' Jane told him, and began to turn away from Philip Abbot's lifted eyebrow, his air of amused but relaxed peacefulness. 'Goodbye, Mr Abbot.'

'Goodbye, Inspector.'

The cell door was shut and locked behind her. Was it the same cell in which he had sat with Martin? No, that had been on the other side.

'Thanks, sergeant. I'm sorry to take up your time,' Jane said briskly.

'That's all right, ma'am. He's an odd one, isn't he? Still, from what I hear of his record, I suppose he's used to being banged up. He's been pretending to be some sort of guru this time, didn't somebody say?'

It had been Sergeant Morris on custody duty when Senander had come in in all his robes, not this one, though word had probably gone round about that previous visit.

'Mm,' Jane said, letting him take the noncommittal sound for agreement. 'Right, I've done all I had to do here, so I'll be off. Thanks again.'

She walked away. Pretending to be – or real? Why was it so exasperatingly difficult to tell? She ought to be able to, with all her years of experience in the force. Was Philip Abbot just a clever conman, keeping up his act, exceptionally adept at the role he had adopted for cover?

He was very good at it, if it was false. He had certainly had her believing in him before. But who could believe in him now?

With half of herself, Jane wanted to.

All the different cases with all their ramifications were over as far as she was concerned. And she had her own life to lead.

So, forget it.

More Crime Fiction from Headline

DEFEND AND BETRAY

The master storyteller of Victorian society

Anne Perry

After a brilliant military career, bravely serving crown and country in India, esteemed General Thaddeus Carlyon finally meets death, not in the frenzy of battle, but at an elegant London dinner party.

In a bizarre incident that shocks aristocratic London, General Carlyon is killed in what first appears to be a freak accident. But the General's beautiful wife, Alexandra, readily confesses that she murdered him – a story she clings to even under threat of the gallows.

Investigator William Monk, nurse Hester Latterly and brilliant Oliver Rathbone, counsel for the defence, work feverishly to break down the wall of silence raised by the accused and her husband's proud family; and with the trial only days away they search desperately for an answer to the dark and appalling mystery, in order to save a woman's life.

FICTION / CRIME 0 7472 4870 2